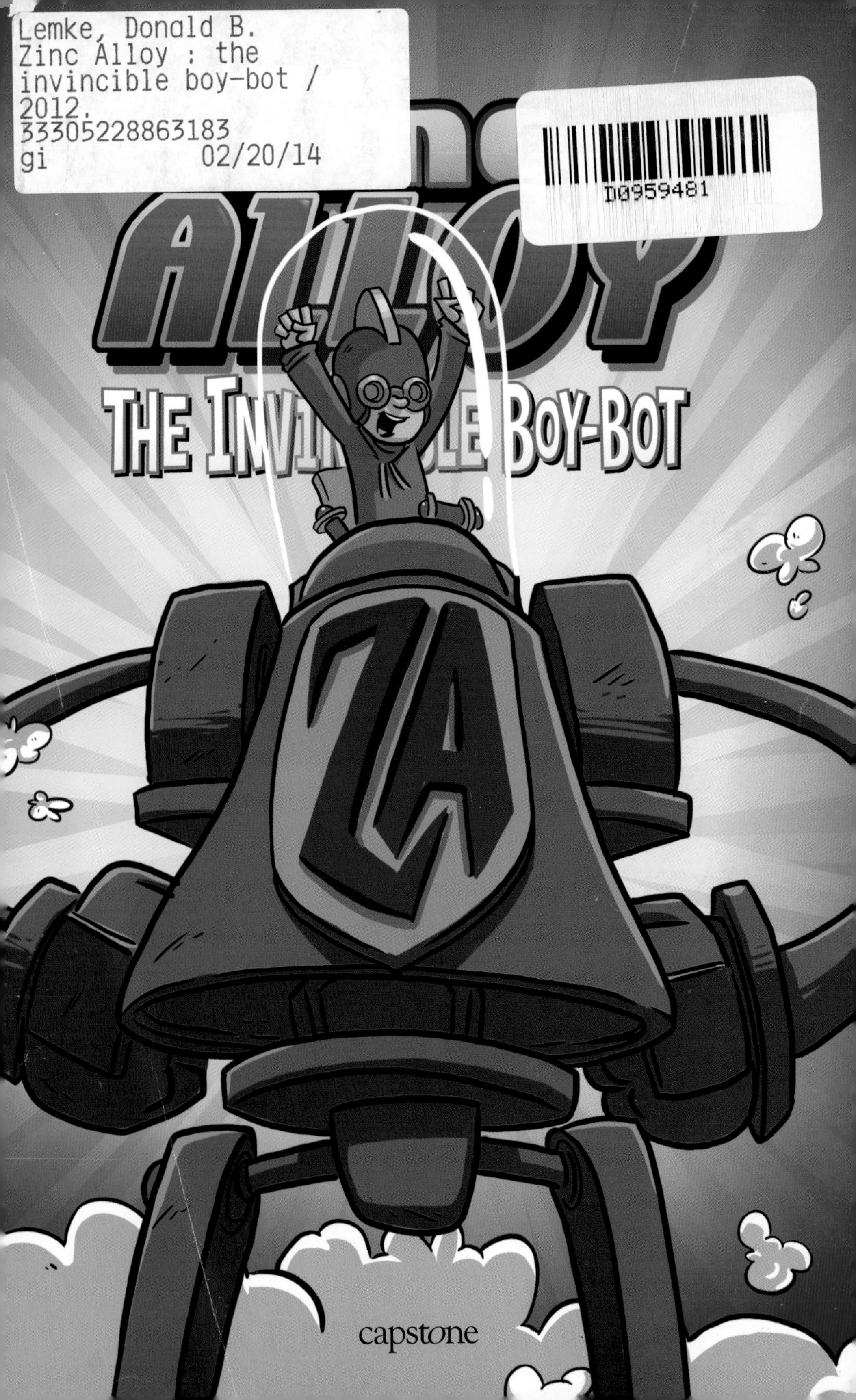
BOY-BOT
ZA
capstone

Zinc ALLOY
THE INVINCIBLE BOY-BOT

WRITTEN BY
DONALD LEMKE

ILLUSTRATED BY
DOUGLAS HOLGATE

ASHLEY C. ANDERSEN ZANTOP .... PUBLISHER

MICHAEL DAHL .... EDITORIAL DIRECTOR

SEAN TULIEN .... EDITOR

HEATHER KINDSETH .... CREATIVE DIRECTOR

BOB LENTZ .... ART DIRECTOR

BRANN GARVEY .... SENIOR DESIGNER

capstone

1710 ROE CREST DRIVE, NORTH MANKATO, MINNESOTA 56003
WWW.CAPSTONEYOUNGREADERS.COM

CATALOGING-IN-PUBLICATION DATA IS AVAILABLE
ON THE LIBRARY OF CONGRESS WEBSITE.
ISBN: 978-1-4342-4597-7

PRINTED IN CHINA
0412 / CA21200582
042012   006679

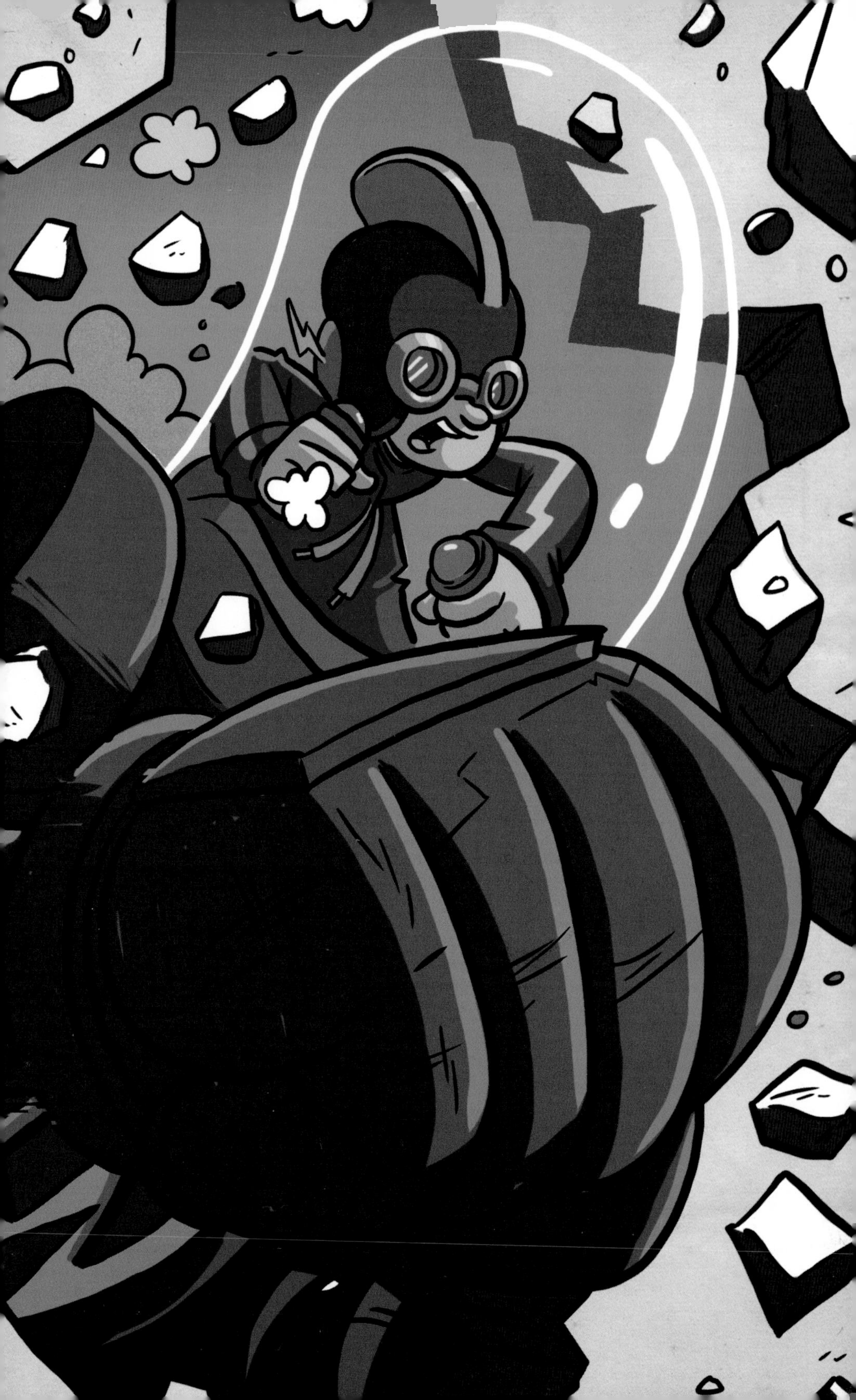

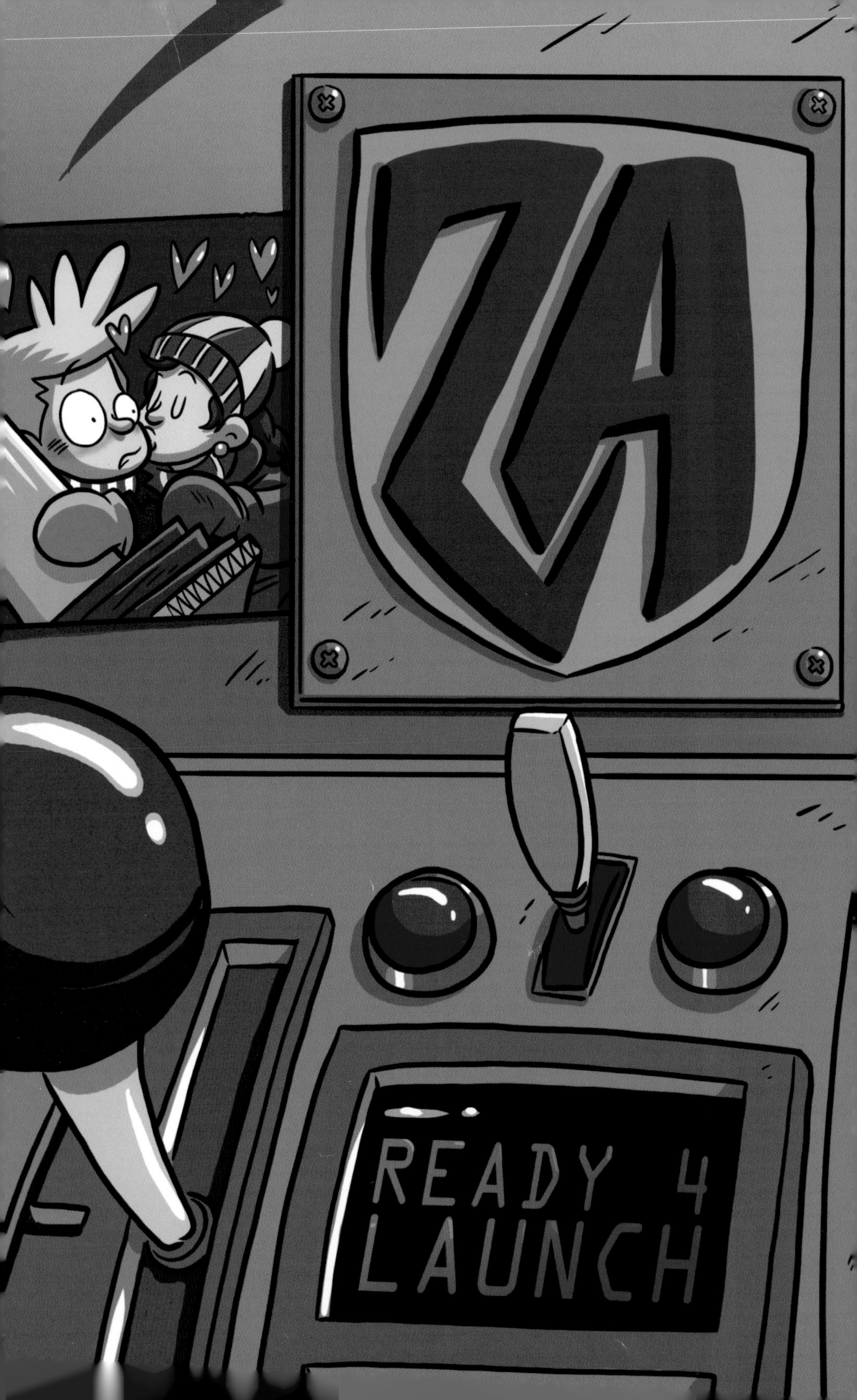

ZA
READY 4 LAUNCH

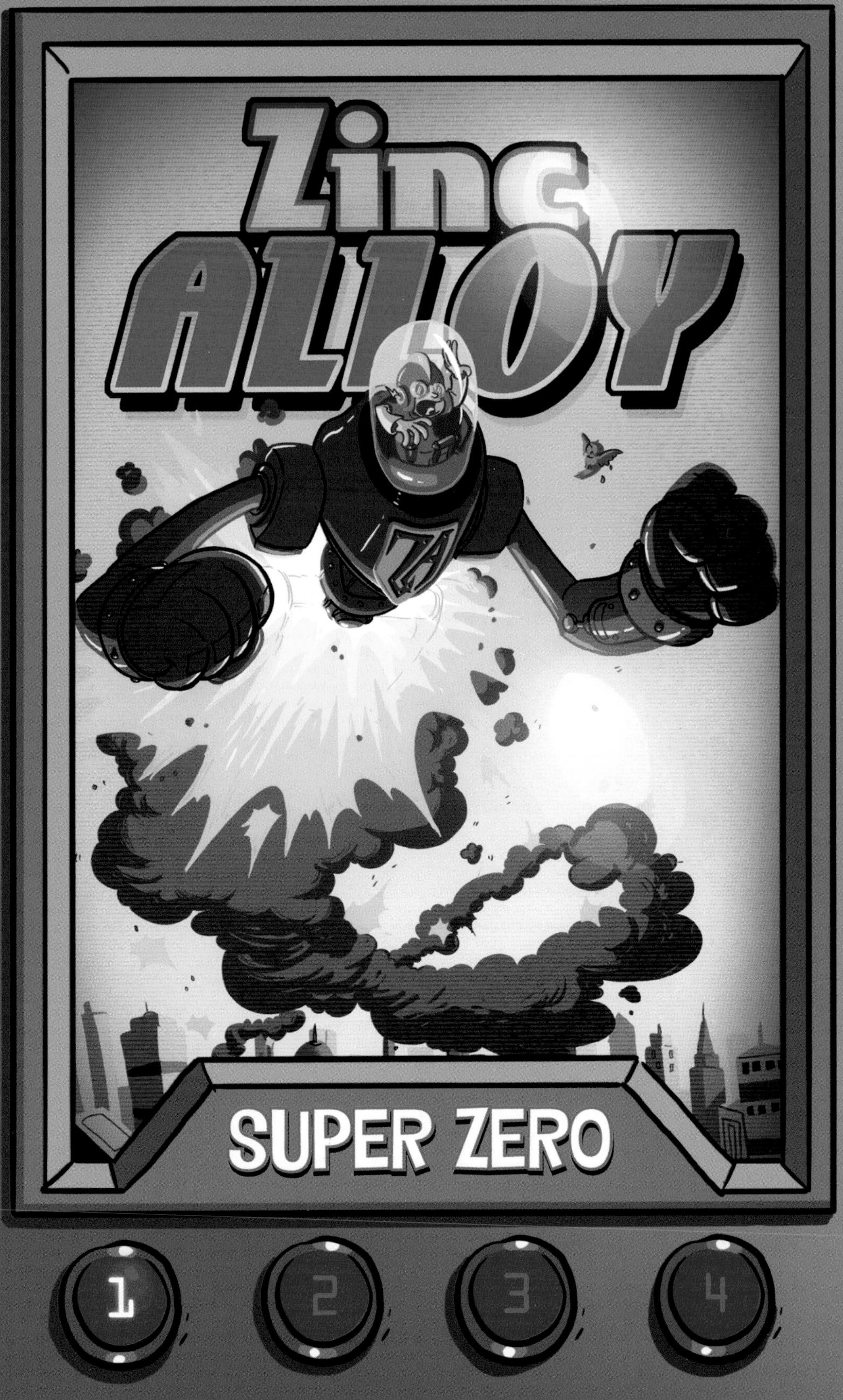
Zinc
ALLOY
SUPER ZERO
1
2
3
4

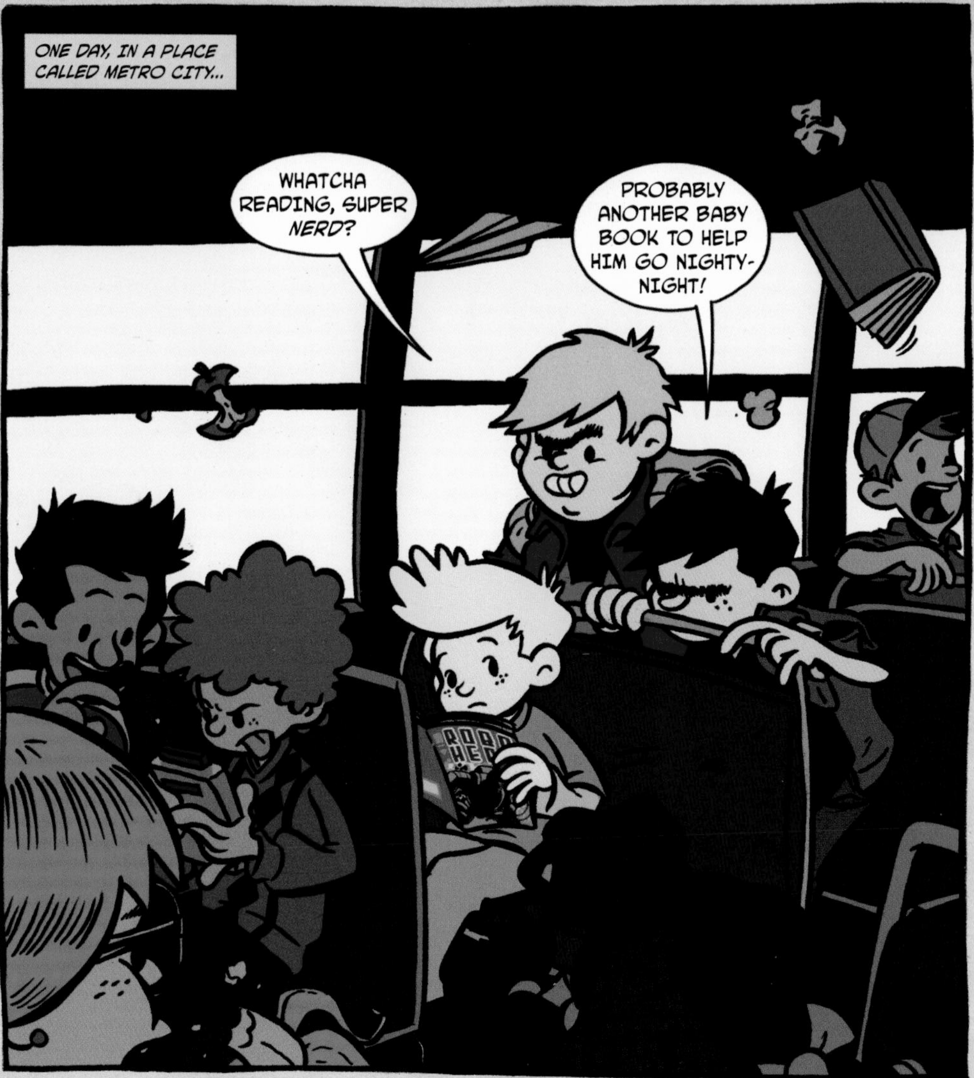
ONE DAY, IN A PLACE CALLED METRO CITY...
WHATCHA READING, SUPER NERD?
PROBABLY ANOTHER BABY BOOK TO HELP HIM GO NIGHTY-NIGHT!

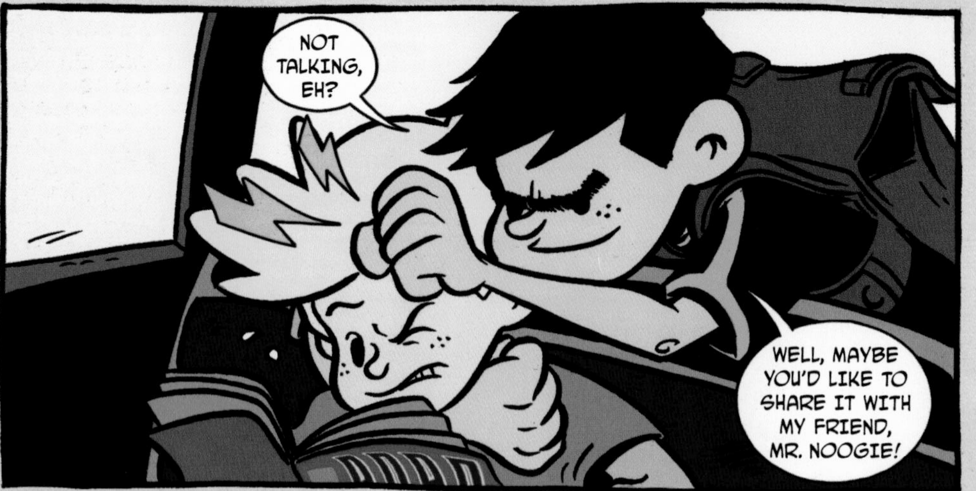
NOT TALKING, EH?
WELL, MAYBE YOU'D LIKE TO SHARE IT WITH MY FRIEND, MR. NOOGIE!

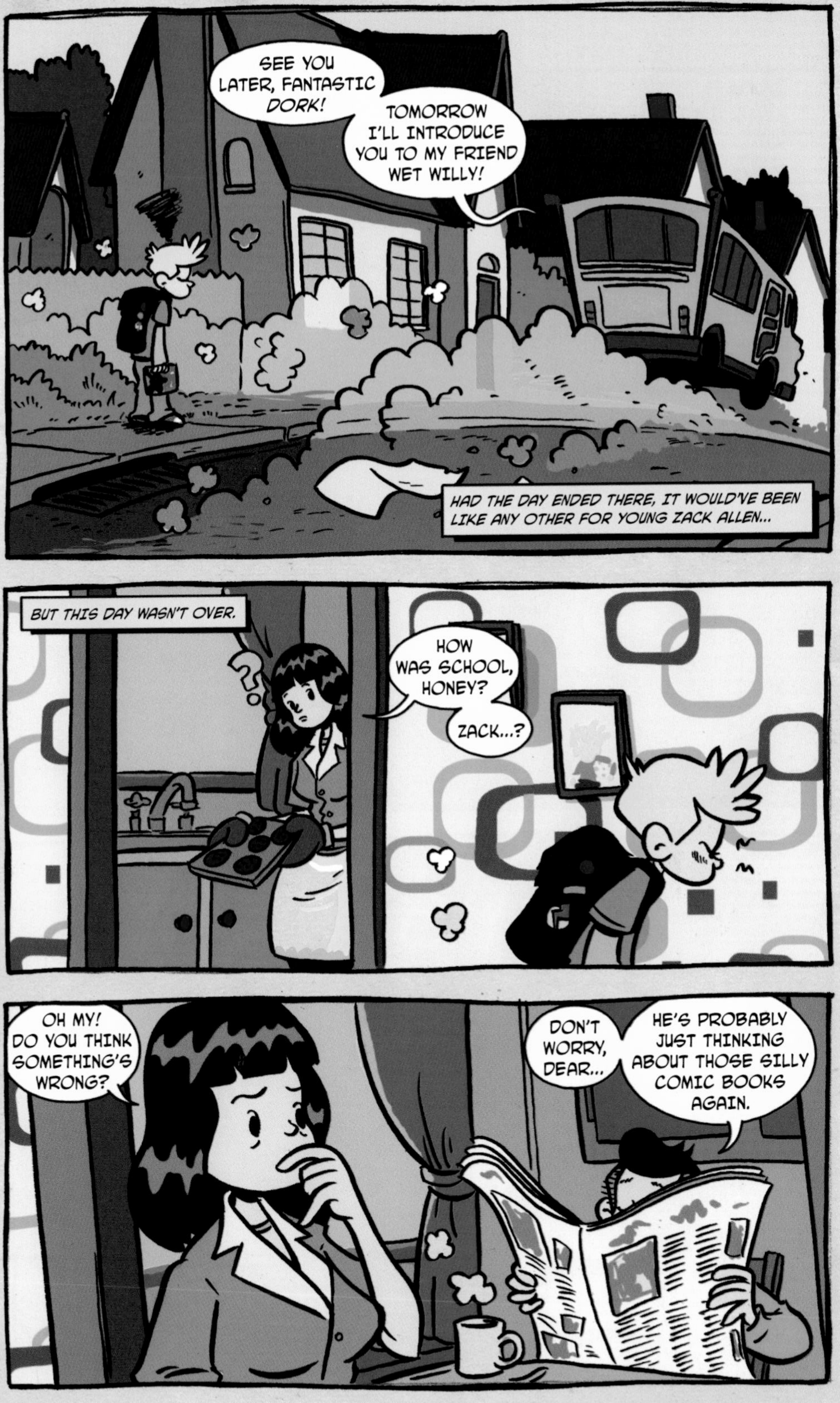
SEE YOU LATER, FANTASTIC DORK!
TOMORROW I'LL INTRODUCE YOU TO MY FRIEND WET WILLY!
HAD THE DAY ENDED THERE, IT WOULD'VE BEEN LIKE ANY OTHER FOR YOUNG ZACK ALLEN...
BUT THIS DAY WASN'T OVER.
HOW WAS SCHOOL, HONEY?
ZACK...?
OH MY! DO YOU THINK SOMETHING'S WRONG?
DON'T WORRY, DEAR...
HE'S PROBABLY JUST THINKING ABOUT THOSE SILLY COMIC BOOKS AGAIN.

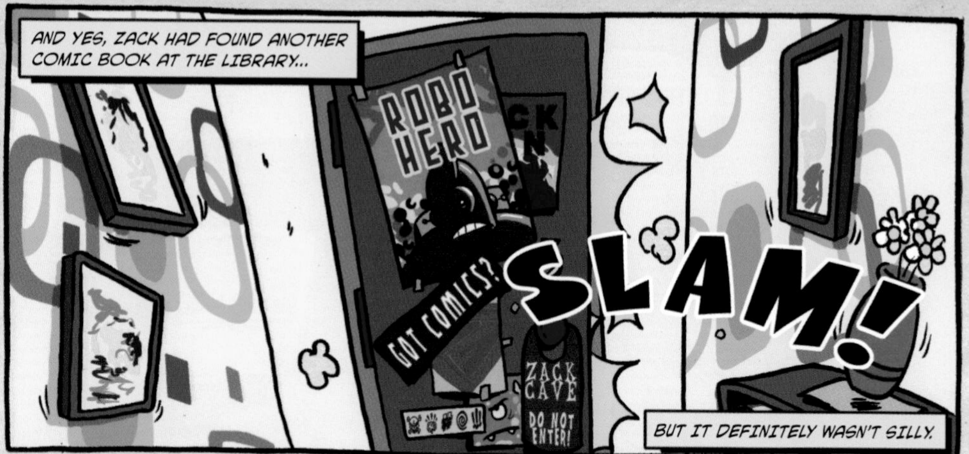
AND YES, ZACK HAD FOUND ANOTHER COMIC BOOK AT THE LIBRARY...
ROBO HERO
GOT COMICS?
ZACK CAVE DO NOT ENTER!
SLAM!
BUT IT DEFINITELY WASN'T SILLY.

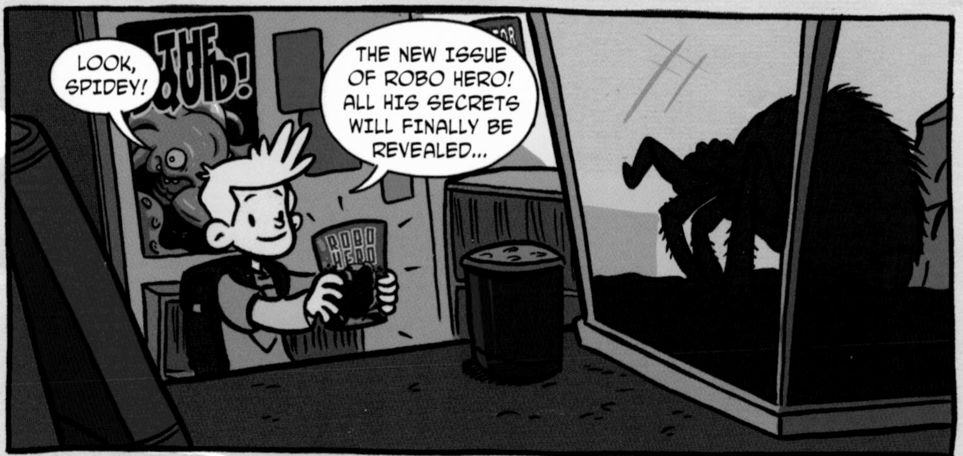
LOOK, SPIDEY!
THE NEW ISSUE OF ROBO HERO! ALL HIS SECRETS WILL FINALLY BE REVEALED...

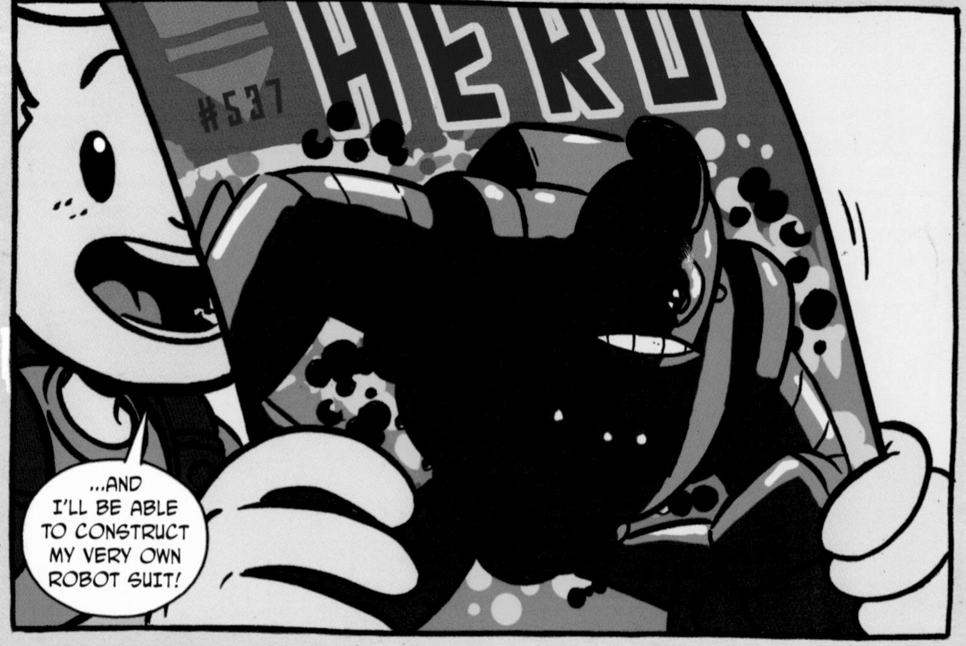
HERO
#537
...AND I'LL BE ABLE TO CONSTRUCT MY VERY OWN ROBOT SUIT!

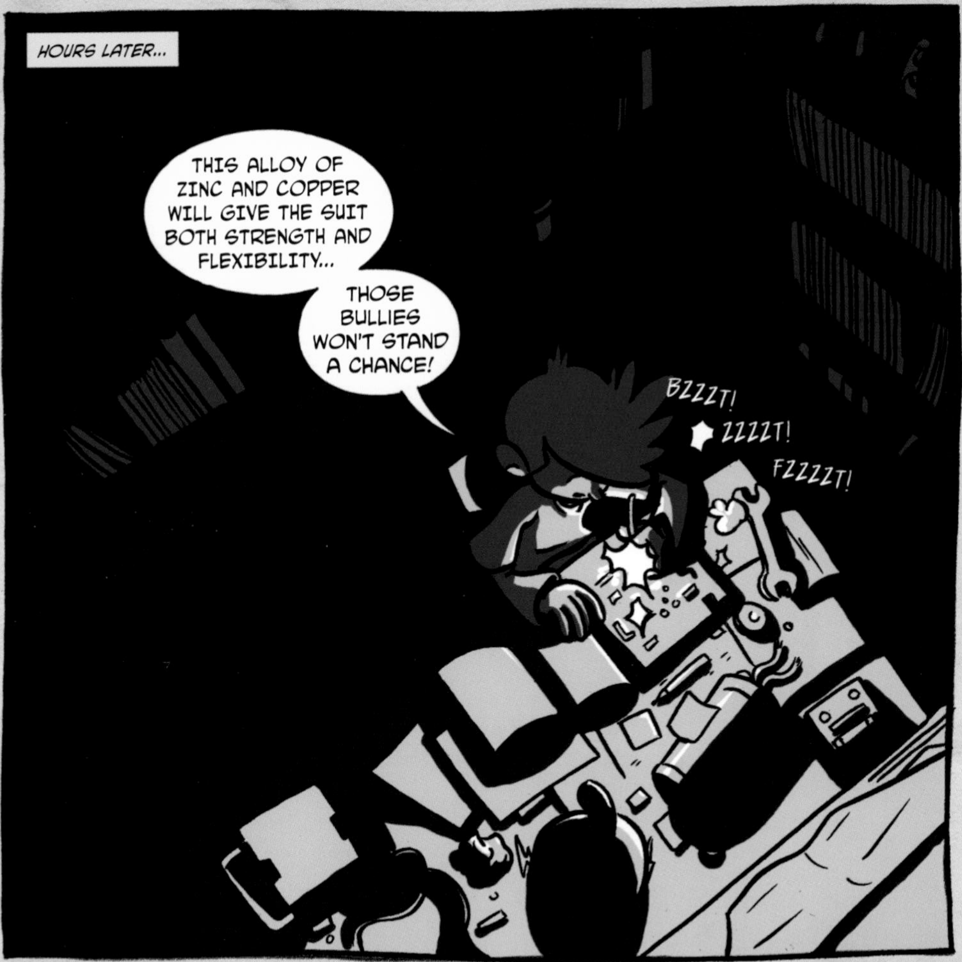
HOURS LATER...
THIS ALLOY OF ZINC AND COPPER WILL GIVE THE SUIT BOTH STRENGTH AND FLEXIBILITY...
THOSE BULLIES WON'T STAND A CHANCE!
BZZZT!
ZZZZT!
FZZZZT!

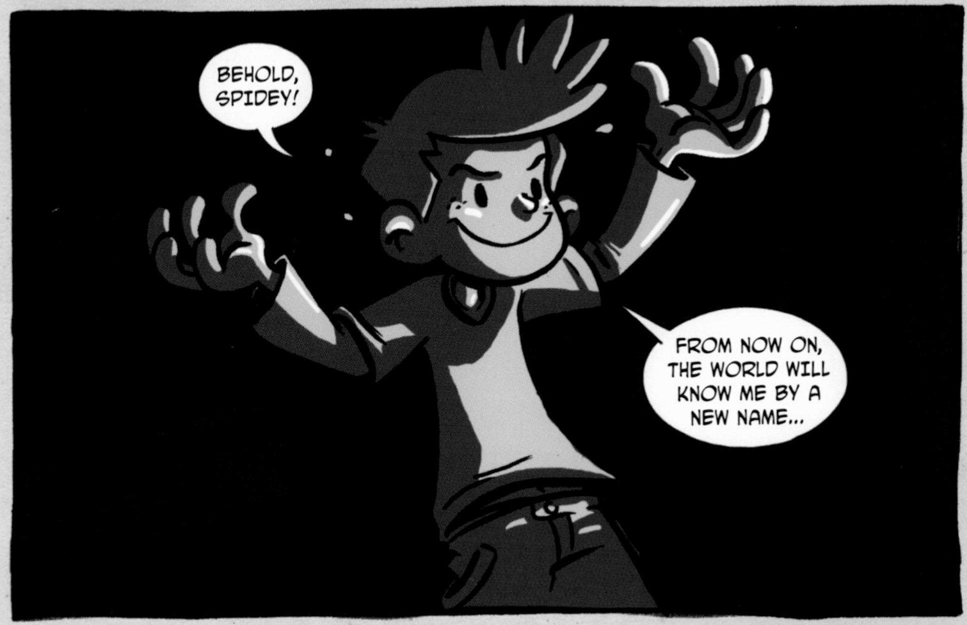
BEHOLD, SPIDEY!
FROM NOW ON, THE WORLD WILL KNOW ME BY A NEW NAME...

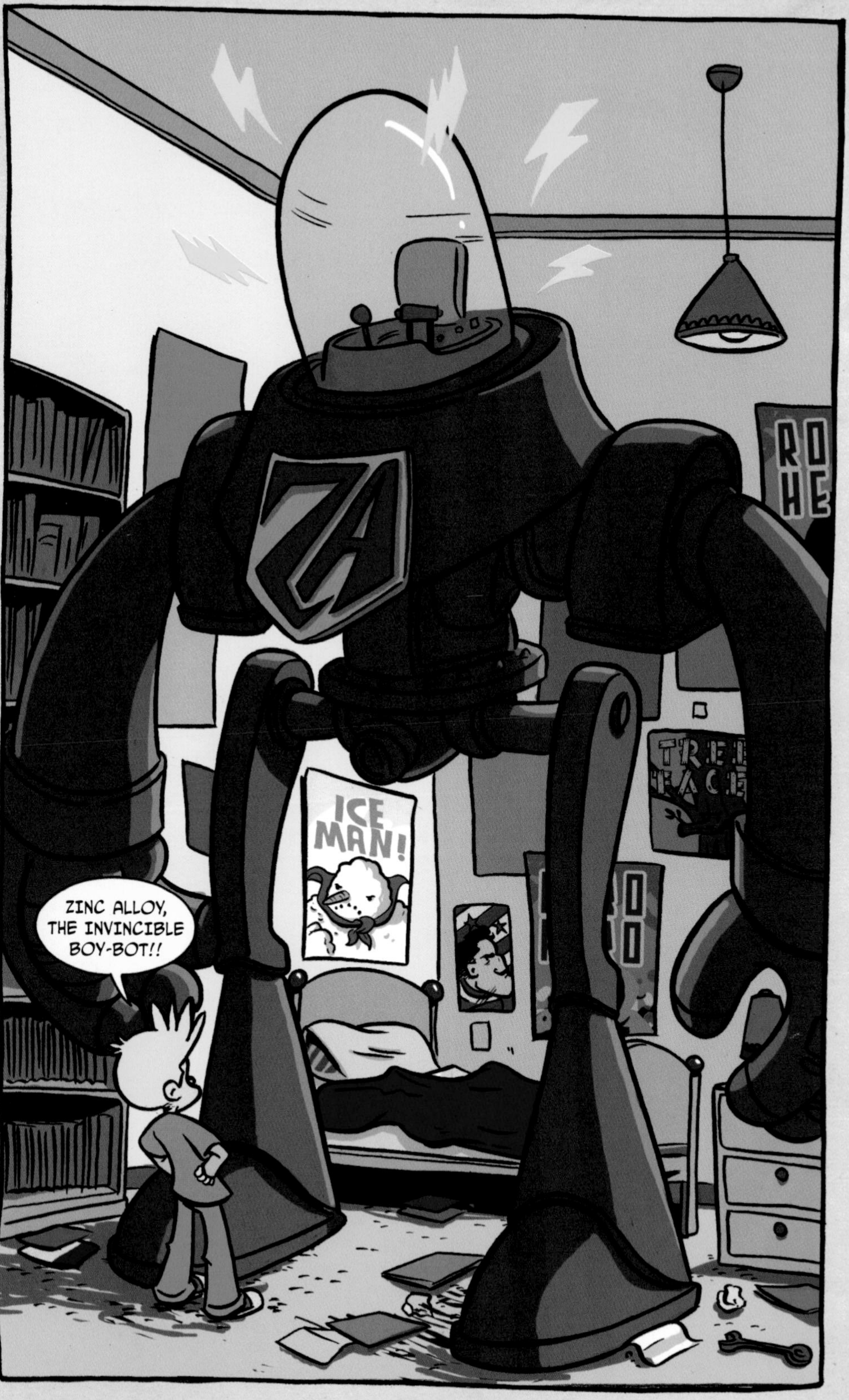
ICE MAN!
ZINC ALLOY, THE INVINCIBLE BOY-BOT!!

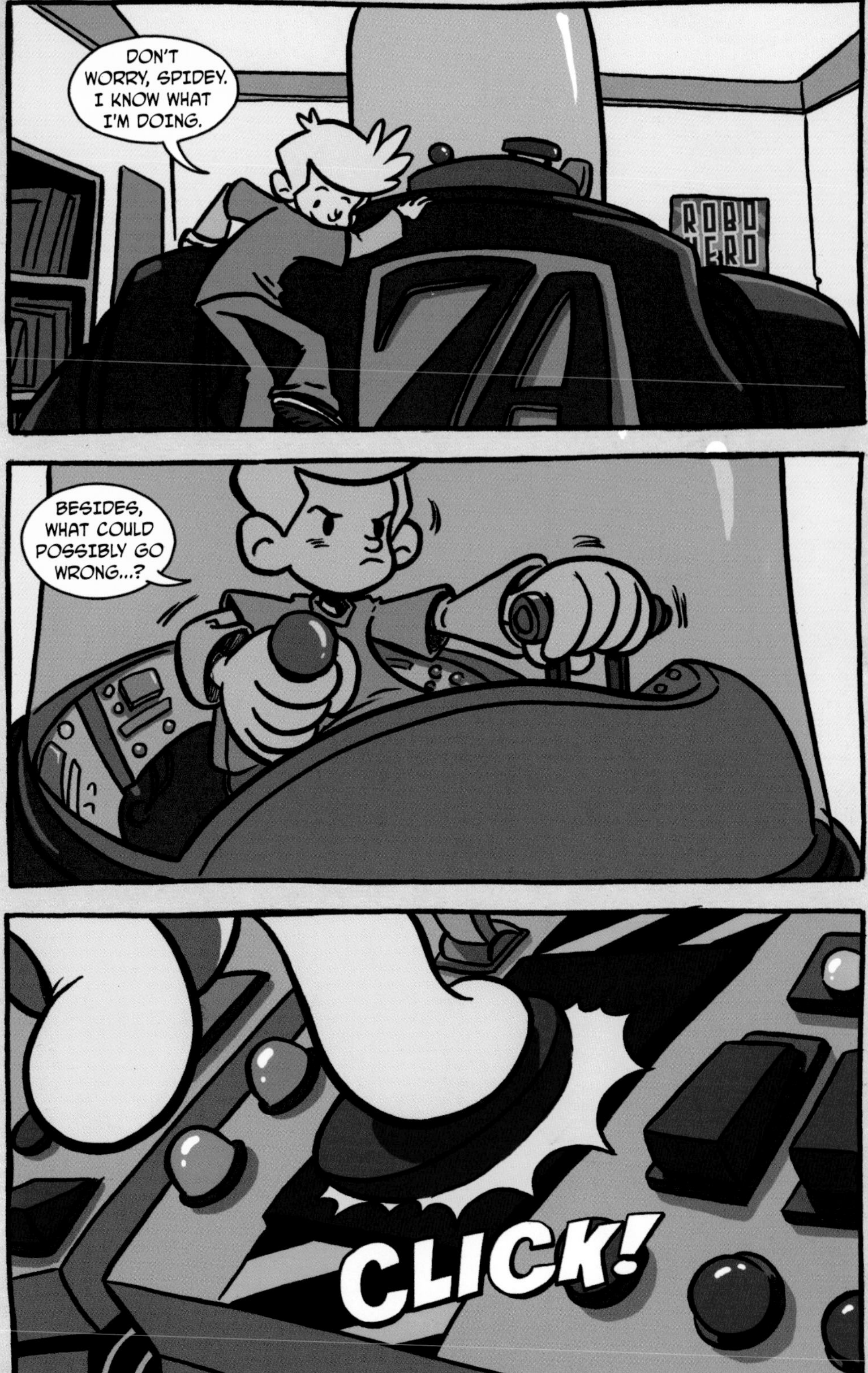
DON'T WORRY, SPIDEY. I KNOW WHAT I'M DOING.
BESIDES, WHAT COULD POSSIBLY GO WRONG...?
CLICK!

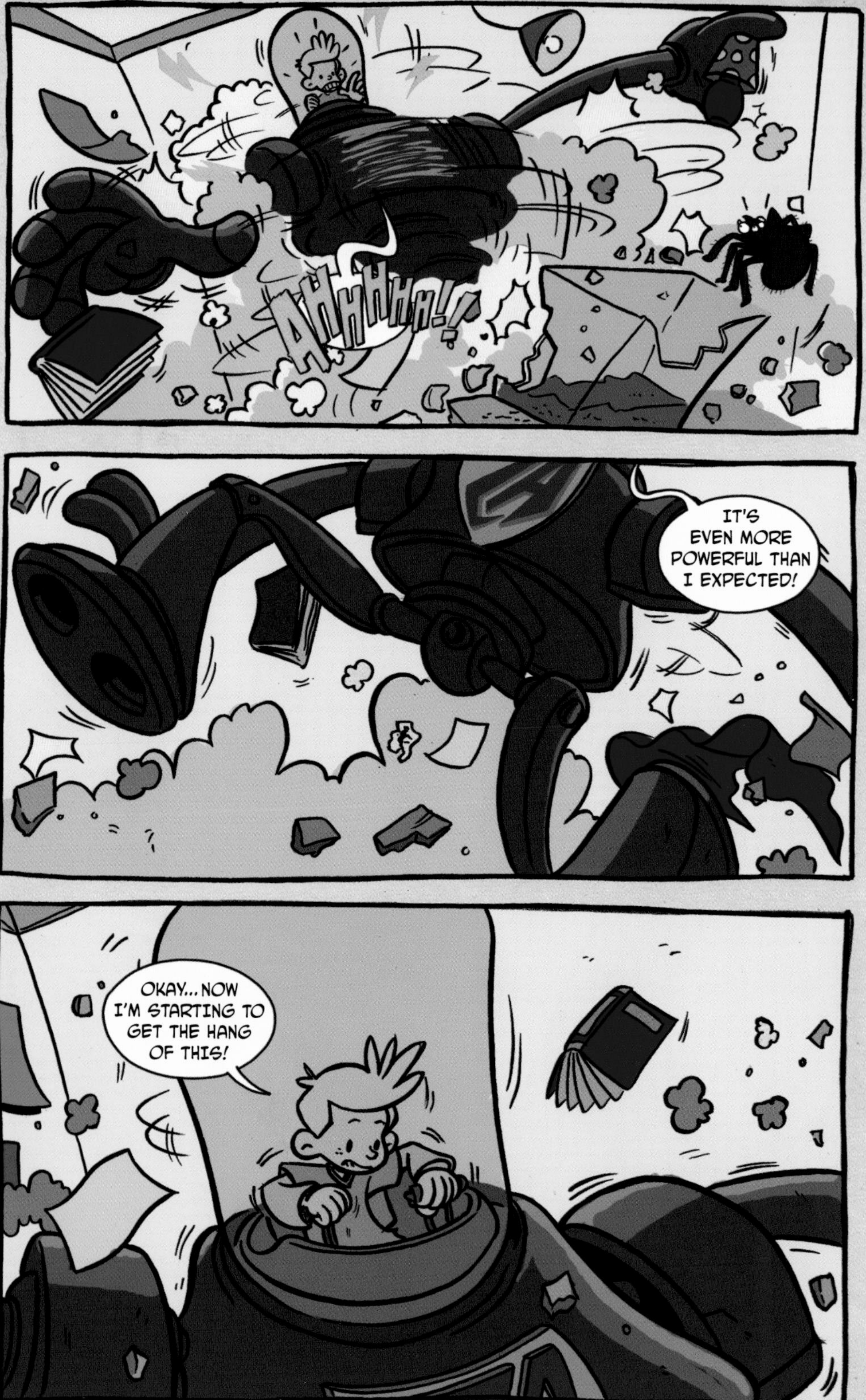
AHHHHHH!!
IT'S EVEN MORE POWERFUL THAN I EXPECTED!
OKAY... NOW I'M STARTING TO GET THE HANG OF THIS!

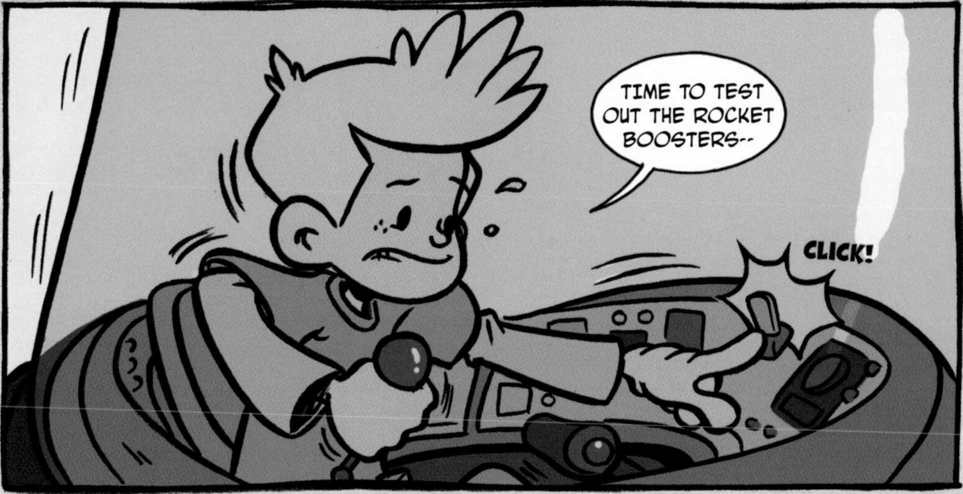
TIME TO TEST OUT THE ROCKET BOOSTERS--
CLICK!

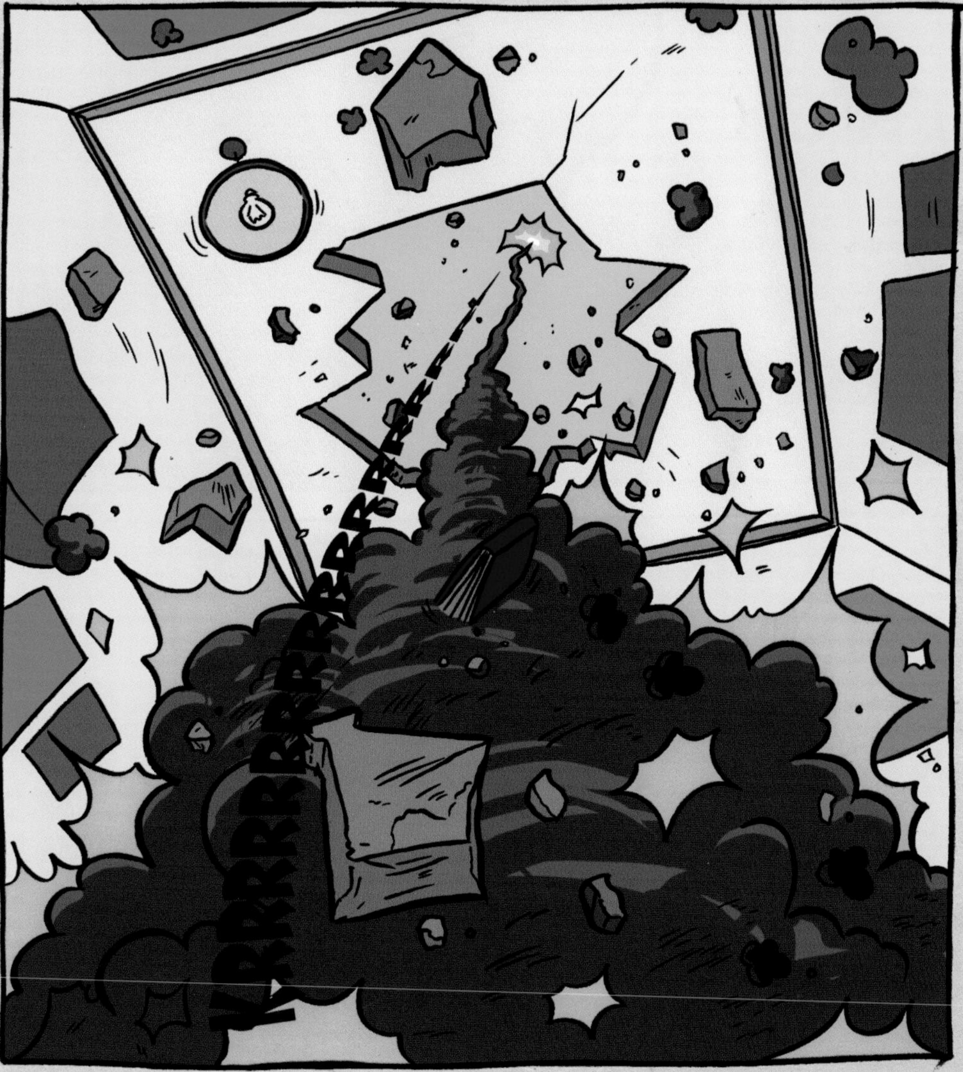
KRRRRRRRRRRRRRR

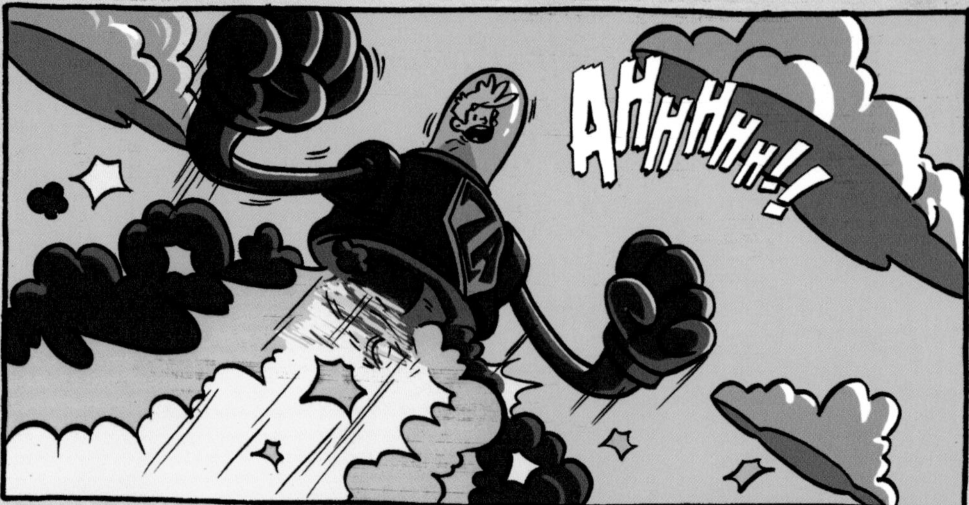
AHHHHH!!

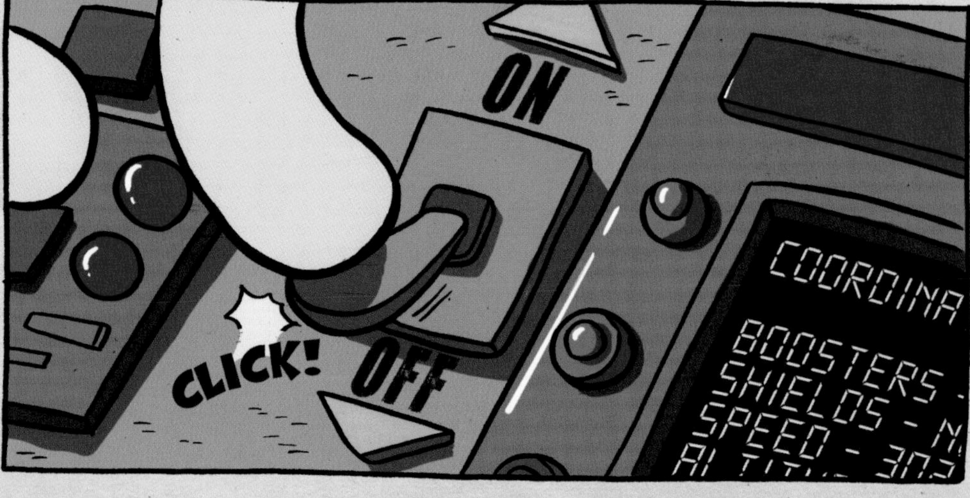
ON
COORDINA
BOOSTERS
SHIELDS
SPEED
CLICK!
OFF

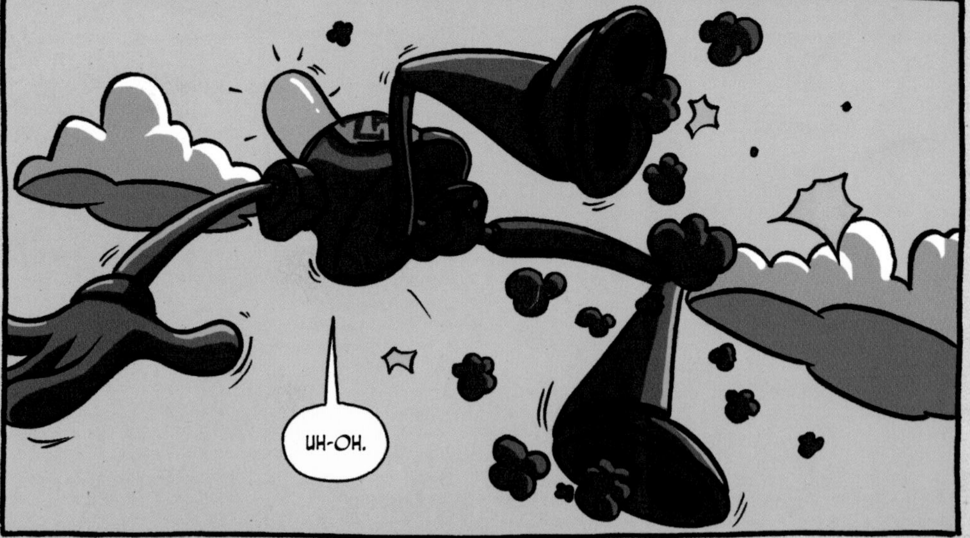
UH-OH.

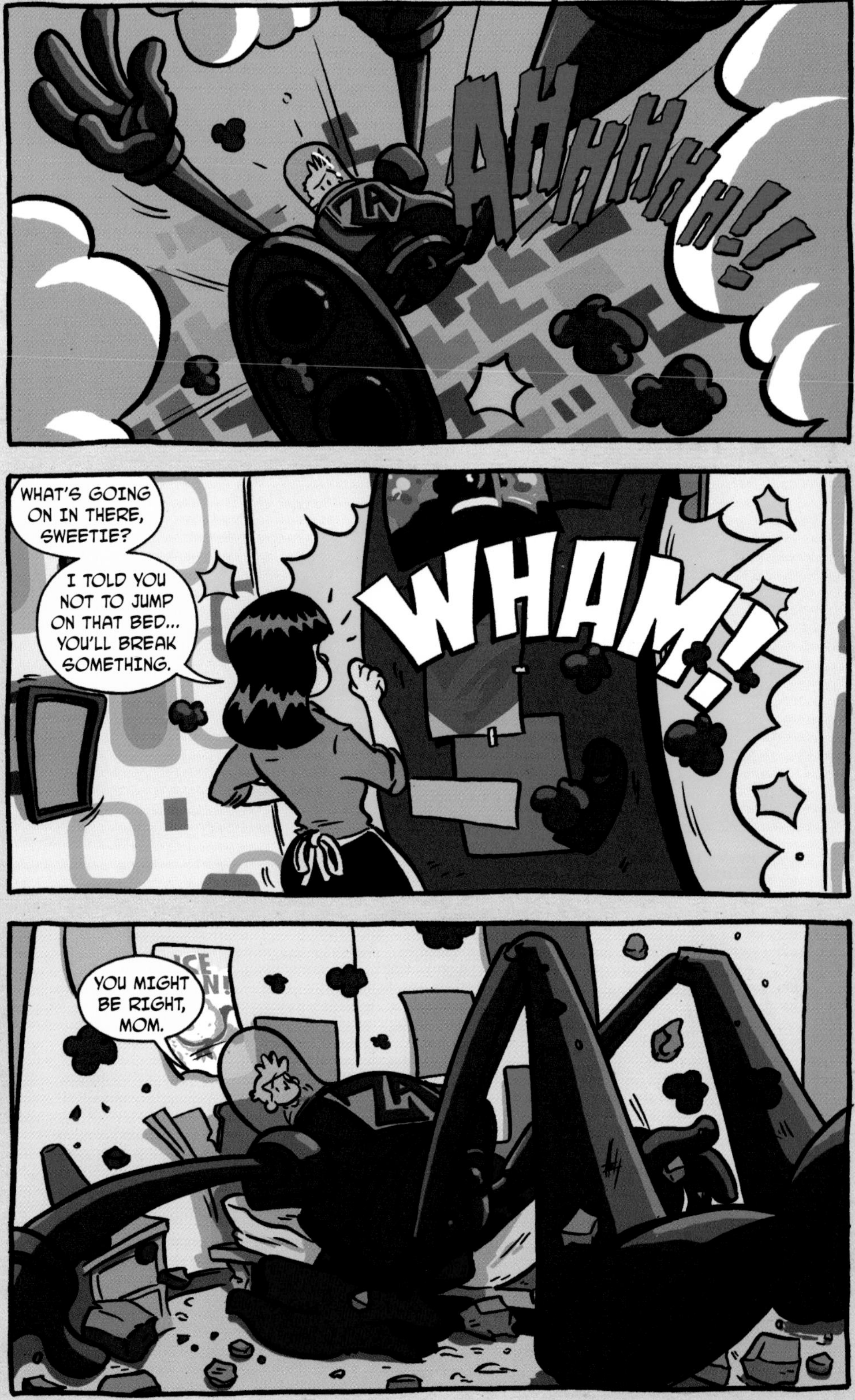
AHHHHHH!!!
WHAT'S GOING ON IN THERE, SWEETIE?
I TOLD YOU NOT TO JUMP ON THAT BED... YOU'LL BREAK SOMETHING.
WHAM!!
YOU MIGHT BE RIGHT, MOM.

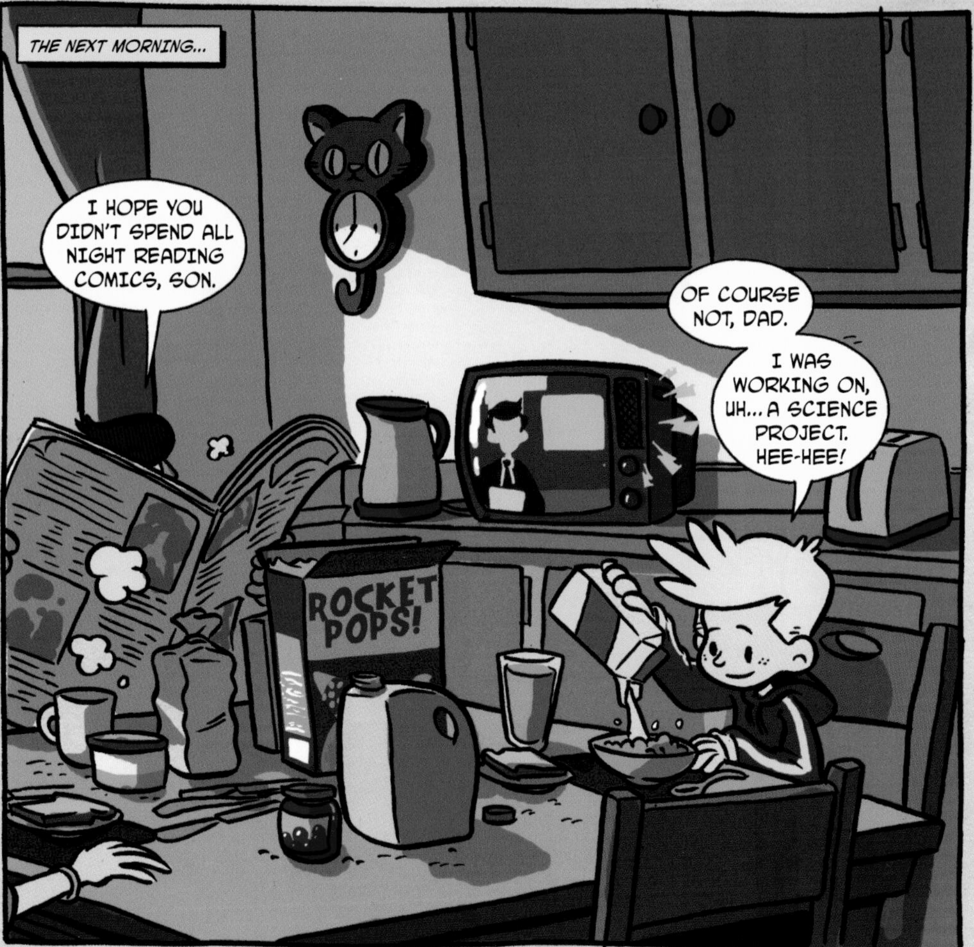
THE NEXT MORNING...
I HOPE YOU DIDN'T SPEND ALL NIGHT READING COMICS, SON.
OF COURSE NOT, DAD.
I WAS WORKING ON, UH... A SCIENCE PROJECT. HEE-HEE!
ROCKET POPS!

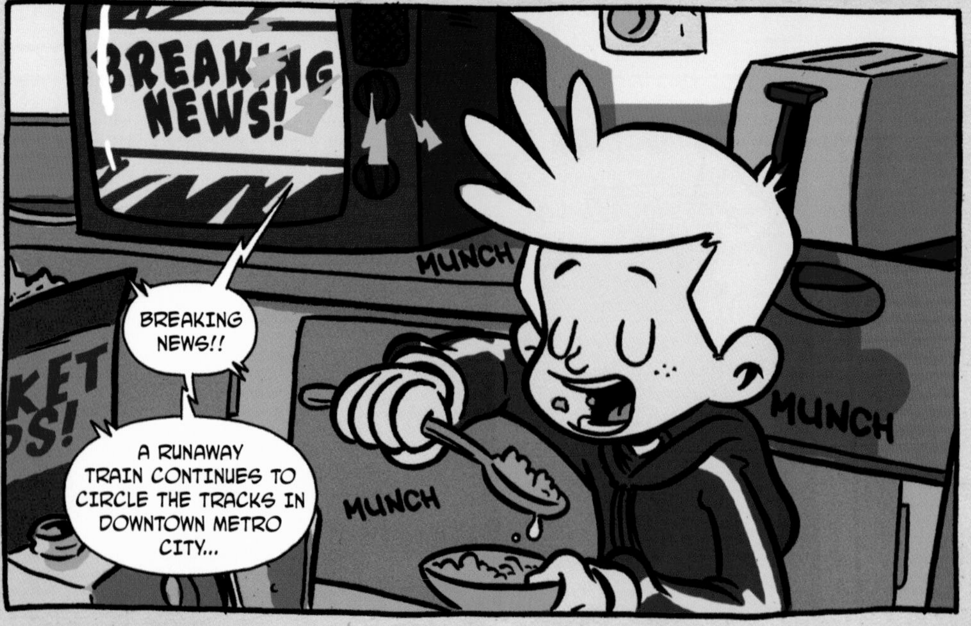
BREAKING NEWS!
MUNCH
BREAKING NEWS!!
MUNCH
A RUNAWAY TRAIN CONTINUES TO CIRCLE THE TRACKS IN DOWNTOWN METRO CITY...
MUNCH

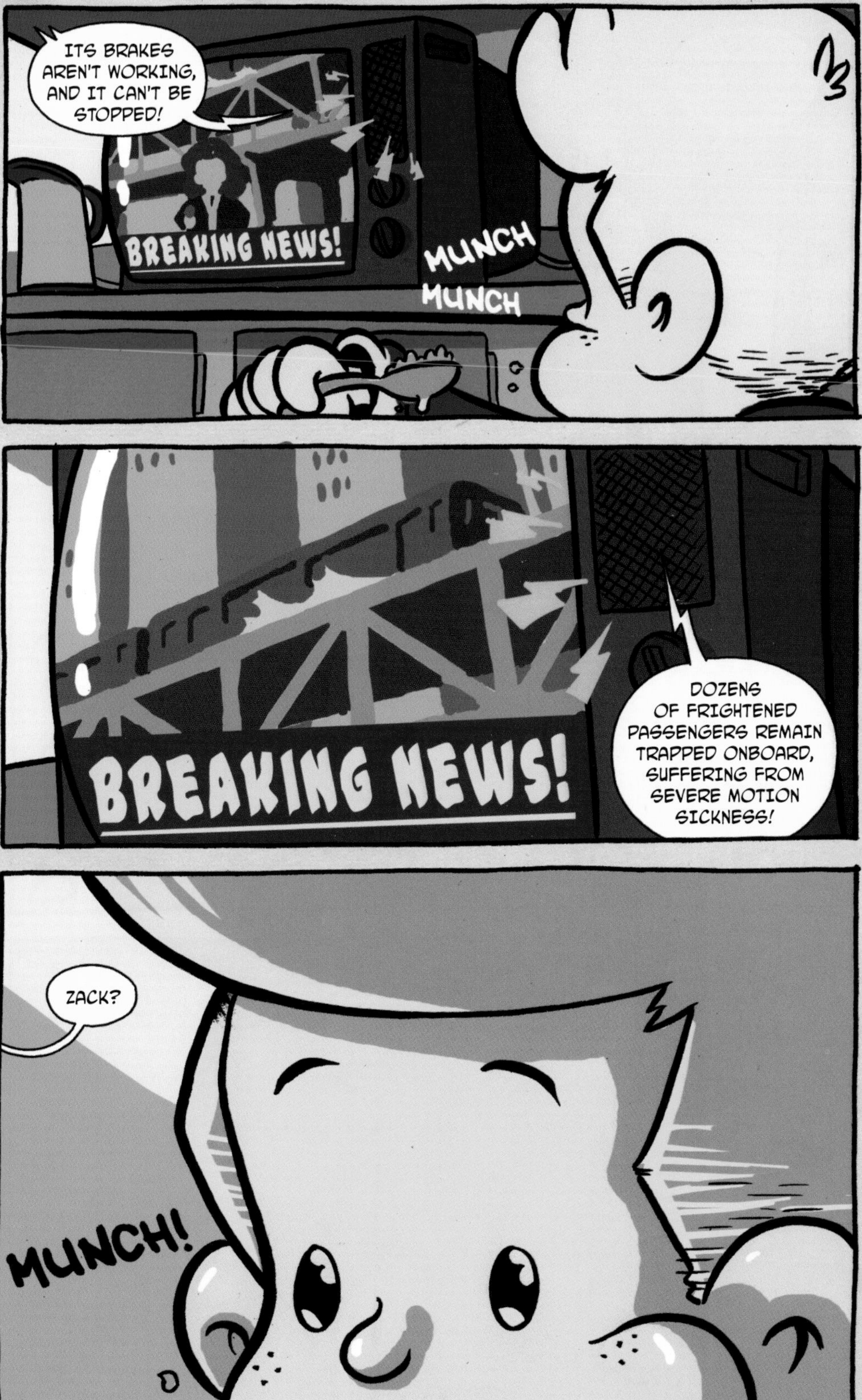
ITS BRAKES AREN'T WORKING, AND IT CAN'T BE STOPPED!
BREAKING NEWS!
MUNCH
MUNCH
BREAKING NEWS!
DOZENS OF FRIGHTENED PASSENGERS REMAIN TRAPPED ONBOARD, SUFFERING FROM SEVERE MOTION SICKNESS!
ZACK?
MUNCH!

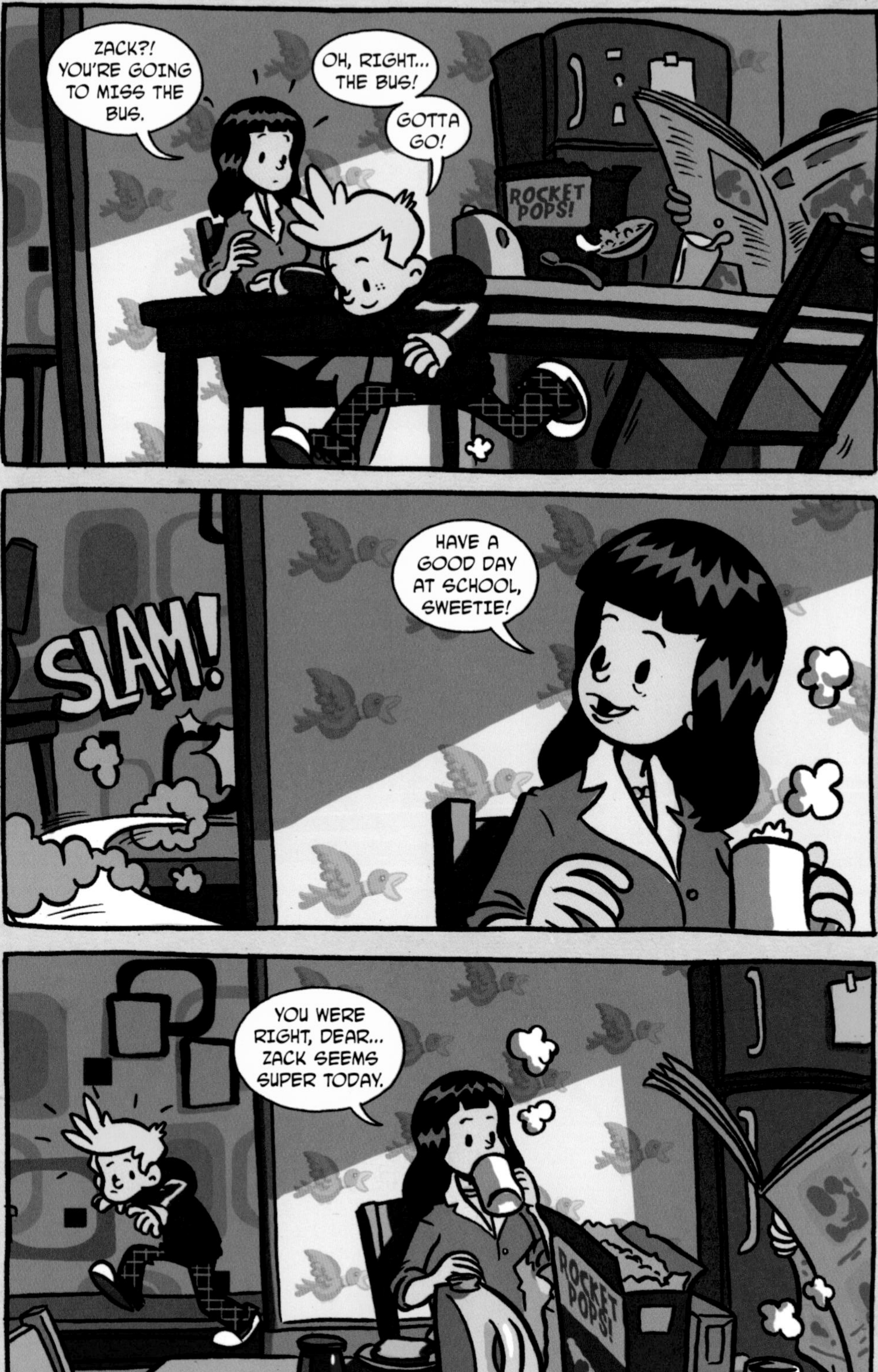
ZACK?! YOU'RE GOING TO MISS THE BUS.
OH, RIGHT... THE BUS!
GOTTA GO!
ROCKET POPS!
SLAM!
HAVE A GOOD DAY AT SCHOOL, SWEETIE!
YOU WERE RIGHT, DEAR... ZACK SEEMS SUPER TODAY.
ROCKET POPS!

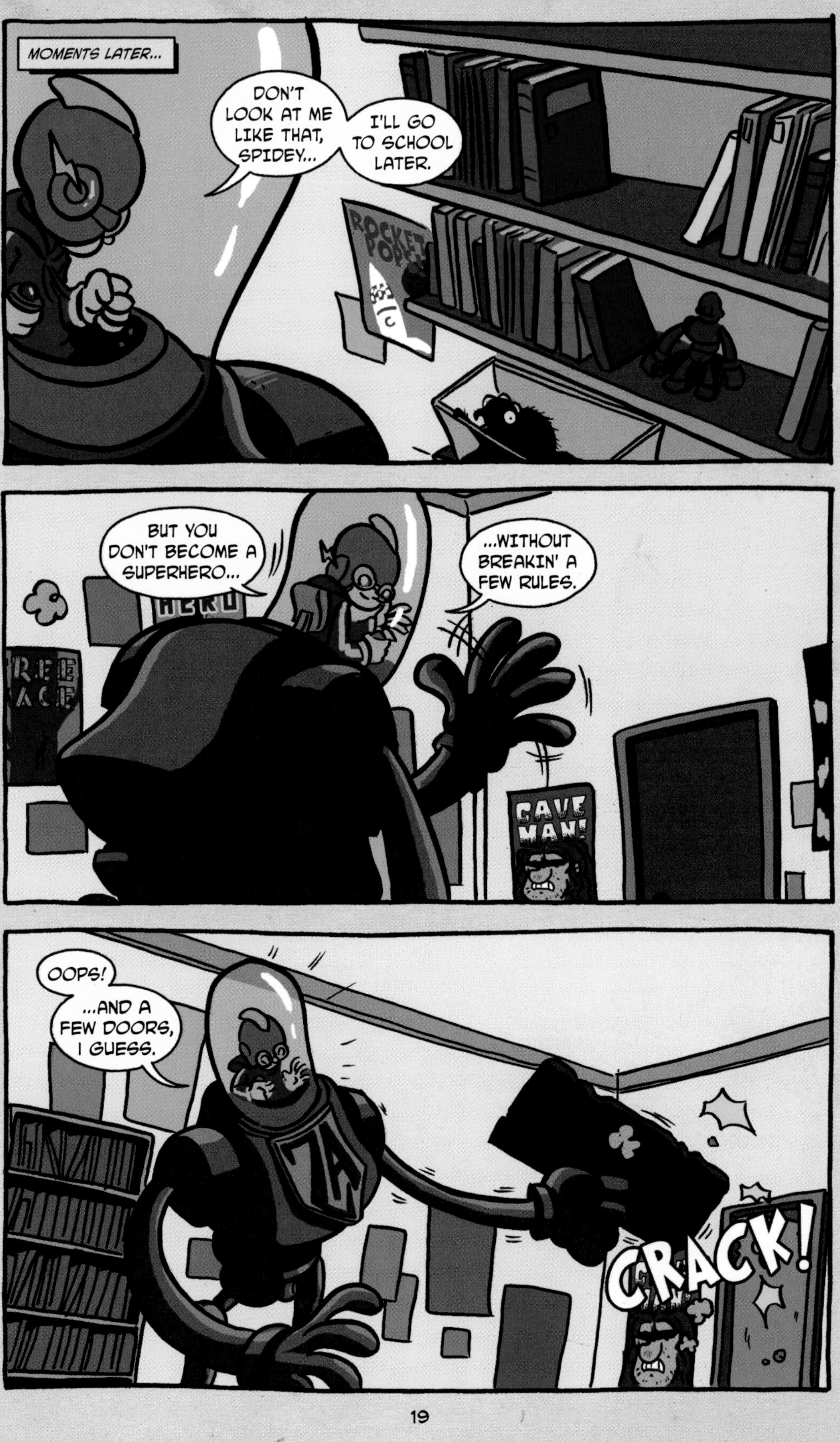
MOMENTS LATER...
DON'T LOOK AT ME LIKE THAT, SPIDEY...
I'LL GO TO SCHOOL LATER.
ROCKET POPS
BUT YOU DON'T BECOME A SUPERHERO...
...WITHOUT BREAKIN' A FEW RULES.
HERO
CAVE MAN!
OOPS!
...AND A FEW DOORS, I GUESS.
CRACK!

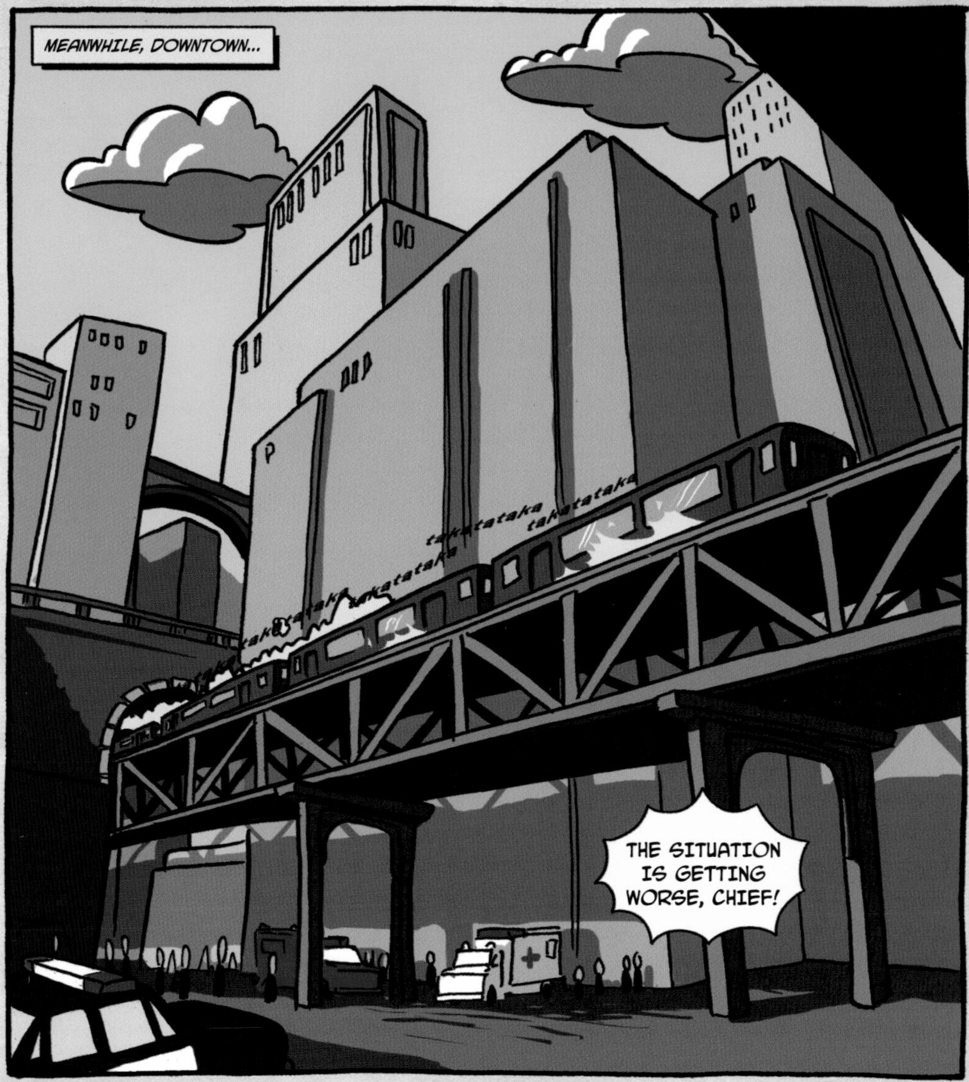
MEANWHILE, DOWNTOWN...
takatataka
takatataka
takatataka
takatataka
THE SITUATION IS GETTING WORSE, CHIEF!

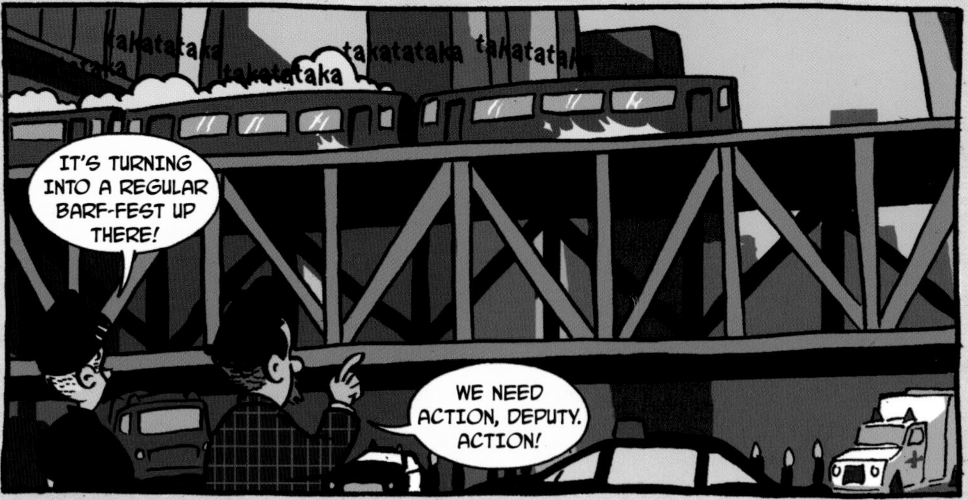
takatataka
takatataka
takatataka
IT'S TURNING INTO A REGULAR BARF-FEST UP THERE!
WE NEED ACTION, DEPUTY. ACTION!

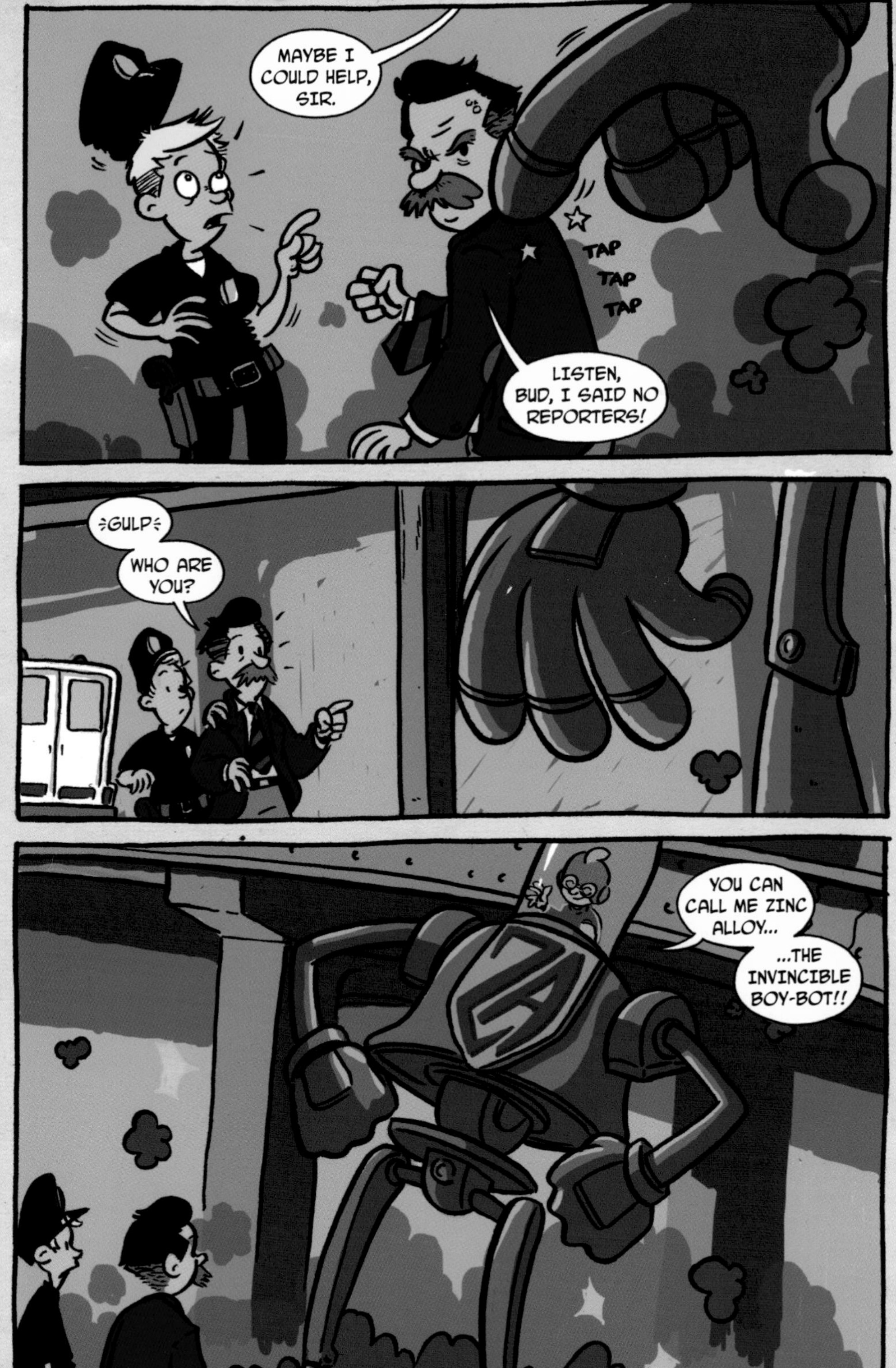
MAYBE I COULD HELP, SIR.
TAP TAP TAP
LISTEN, BUD, I SAID NO REPORTERS!
GULP
WHO ARE YOU?
YOU CAN CALL ME ZINC ALLOY...
...THE INVINCIBLE BOY-BOT!!

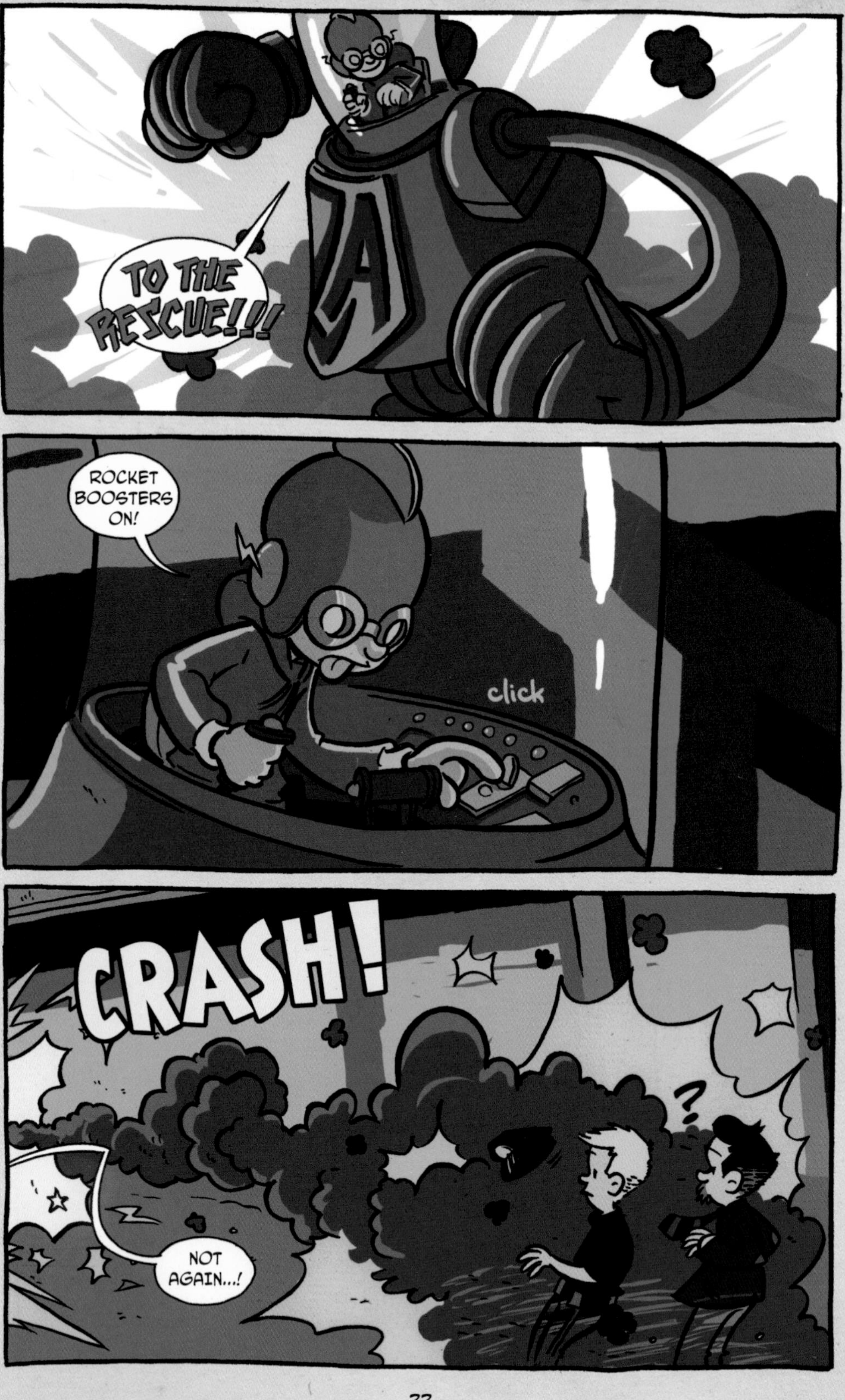
TO THE RESCUE!!!
ROCKET BOOSTERS ON!
click
CRASH!
?
NOT AGAIN...!

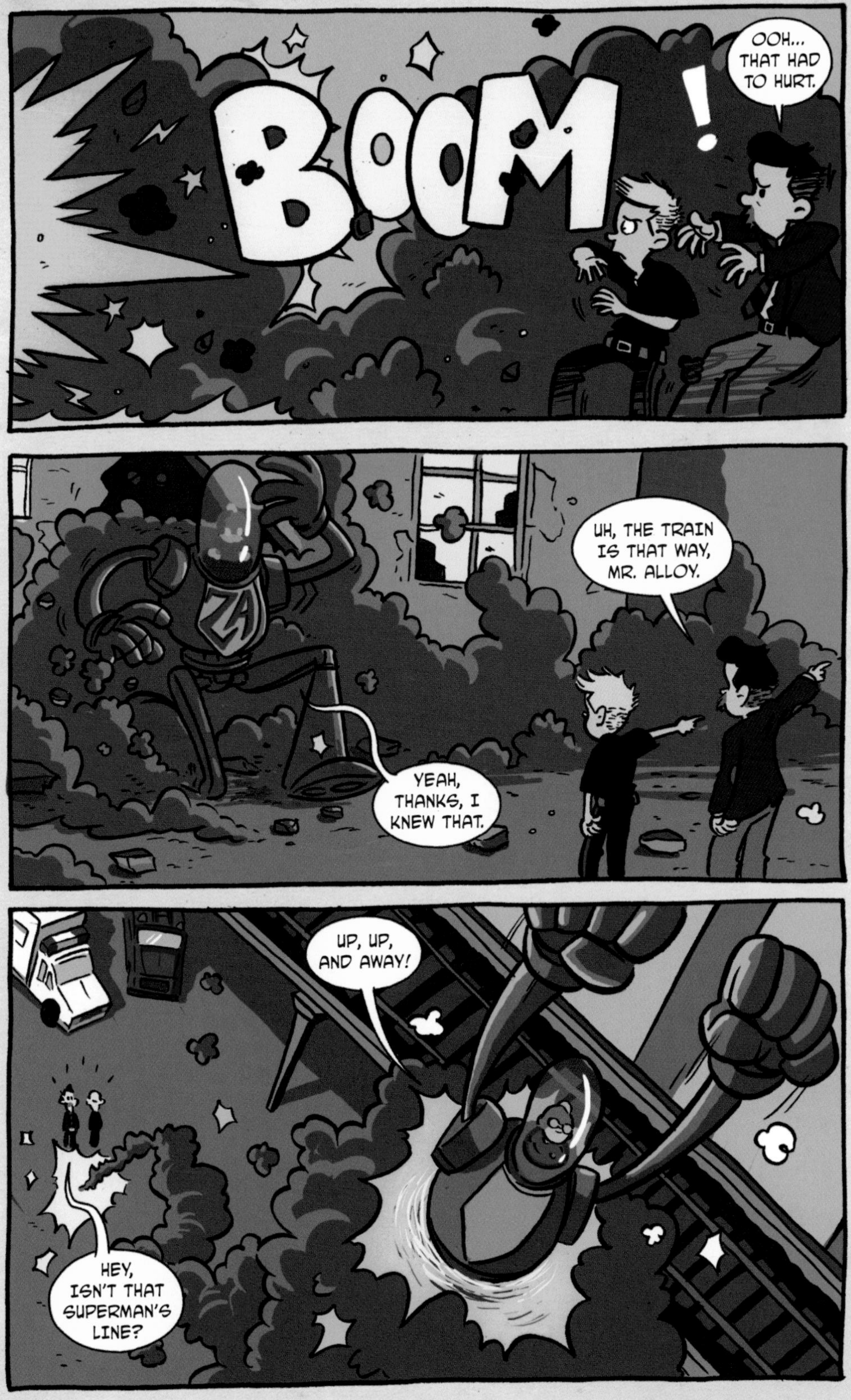
BOOM!
OOH... THAT HAD TO HURT.
UH, THE TRAIN IS THAT WAY, MR. ALLOY.
YEAH, THANKS, I KNEW THAT.
UP, UP, AND AWAY!
HEY, ISN'T THAT SUPERMAN'S LINE?

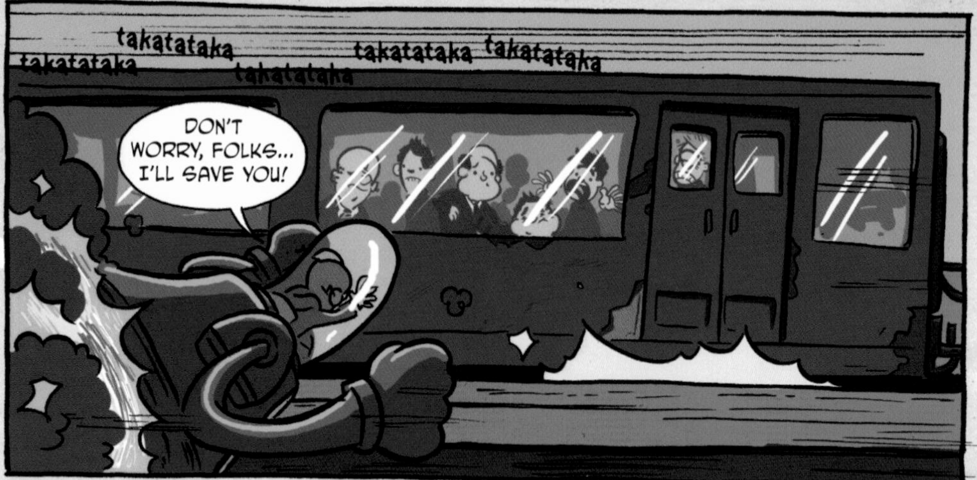
takatataka
takatataka
takatataka
takatataka
takatataka
DON'T WORRY, FOLKS... I'LL SAVE YOU!

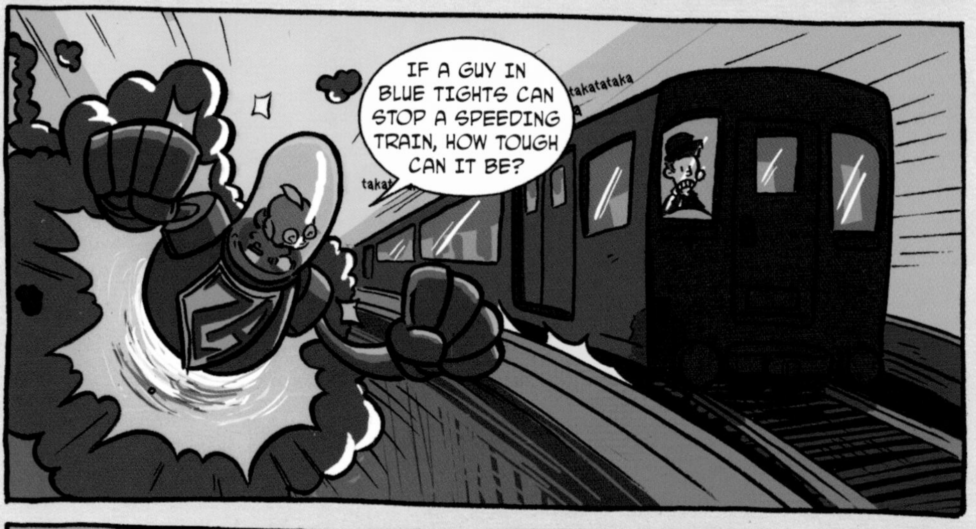
takatataka
IF A GUY IN BLUE TIGHTS CAN STOP A SPEEDING TRAIN, HOW TOUGH CAN IT BE?

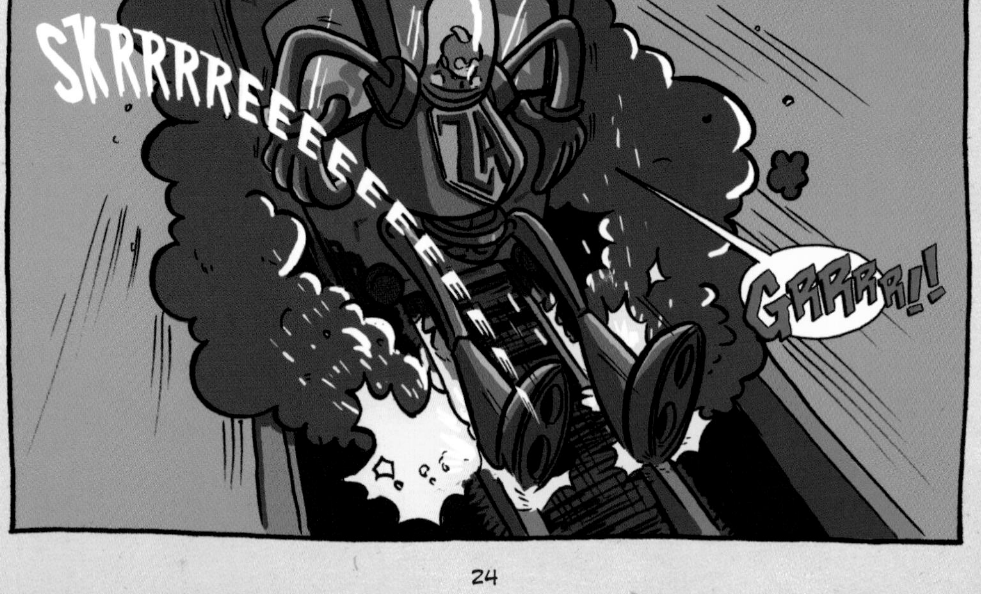
SKRRRRREEEEEEEEEE
GRRRR!!

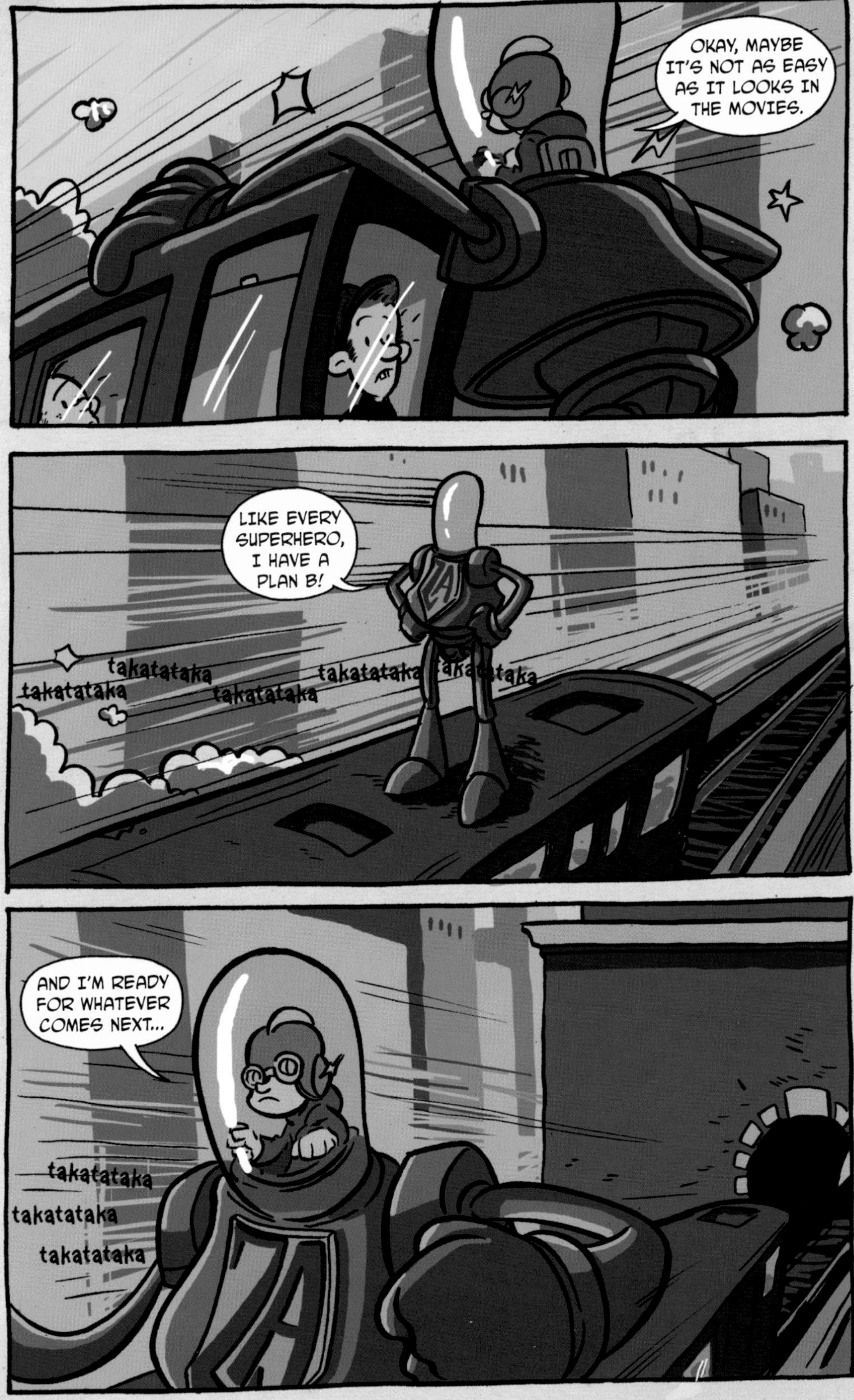
OKAY, MAYBE IT'S NOT AS EASY AS IT LOOKS IN THE MOVIES.
LIKE EVERY SUPERHERO, I HAVE A PLAN B!
takatataka
takatataka
takatataka
takatataka
takatataka
AND I'M READY FOR WHATEVER COMES NEXT...
takatataka
takatataka
takatataka

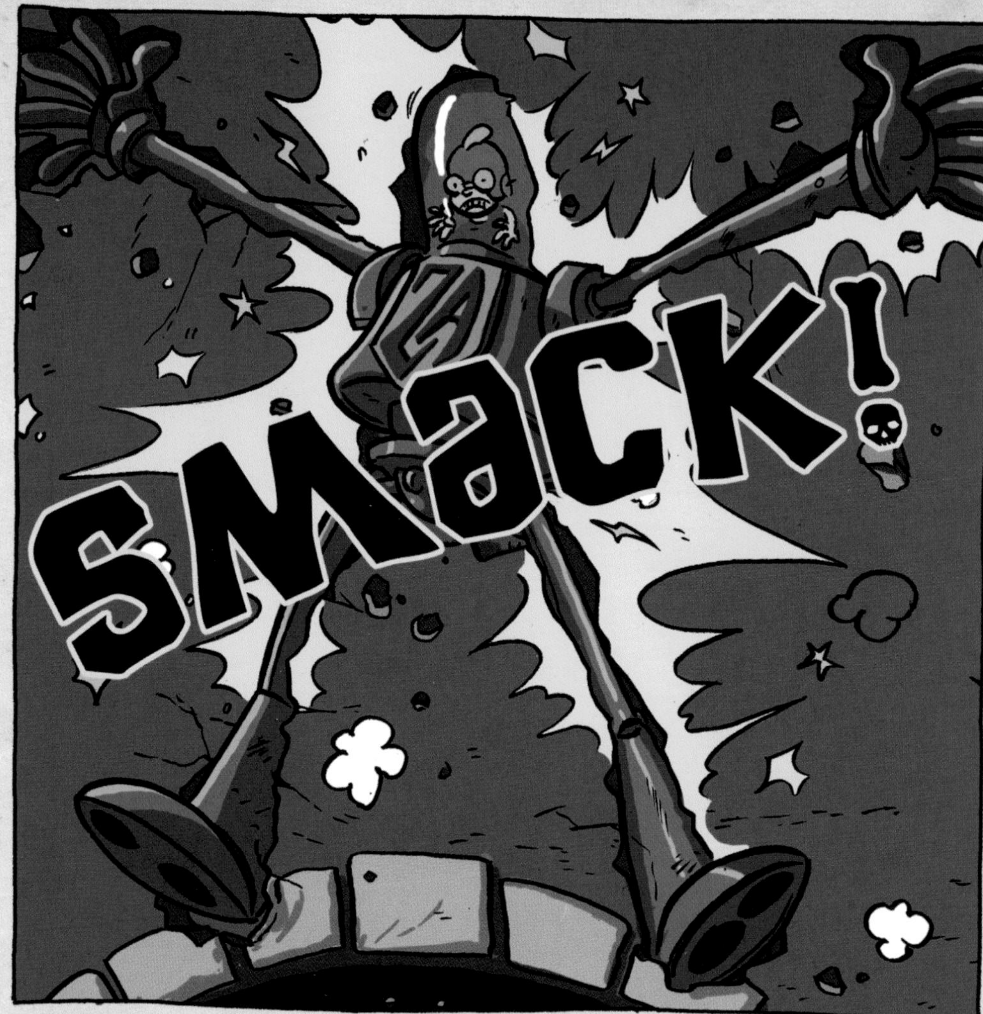
SMACK!

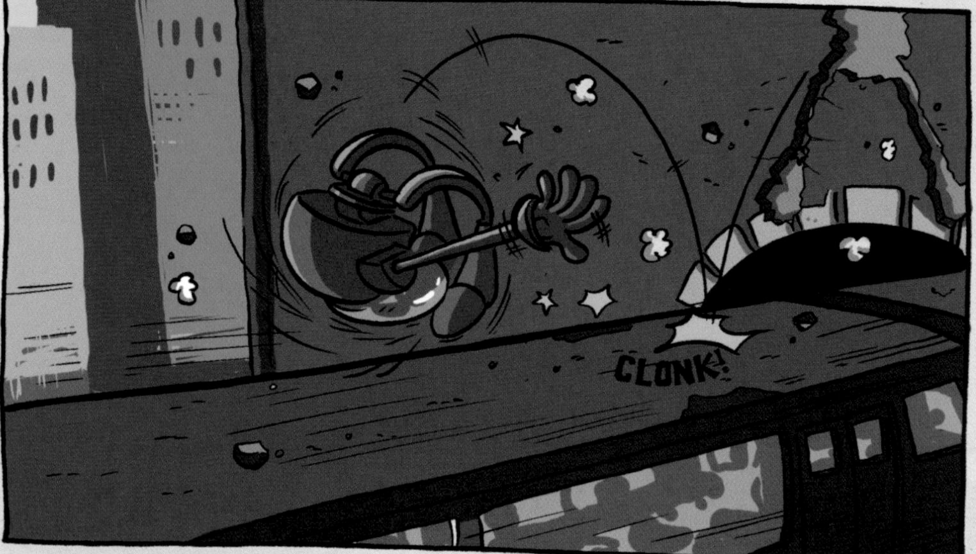
CLONK!

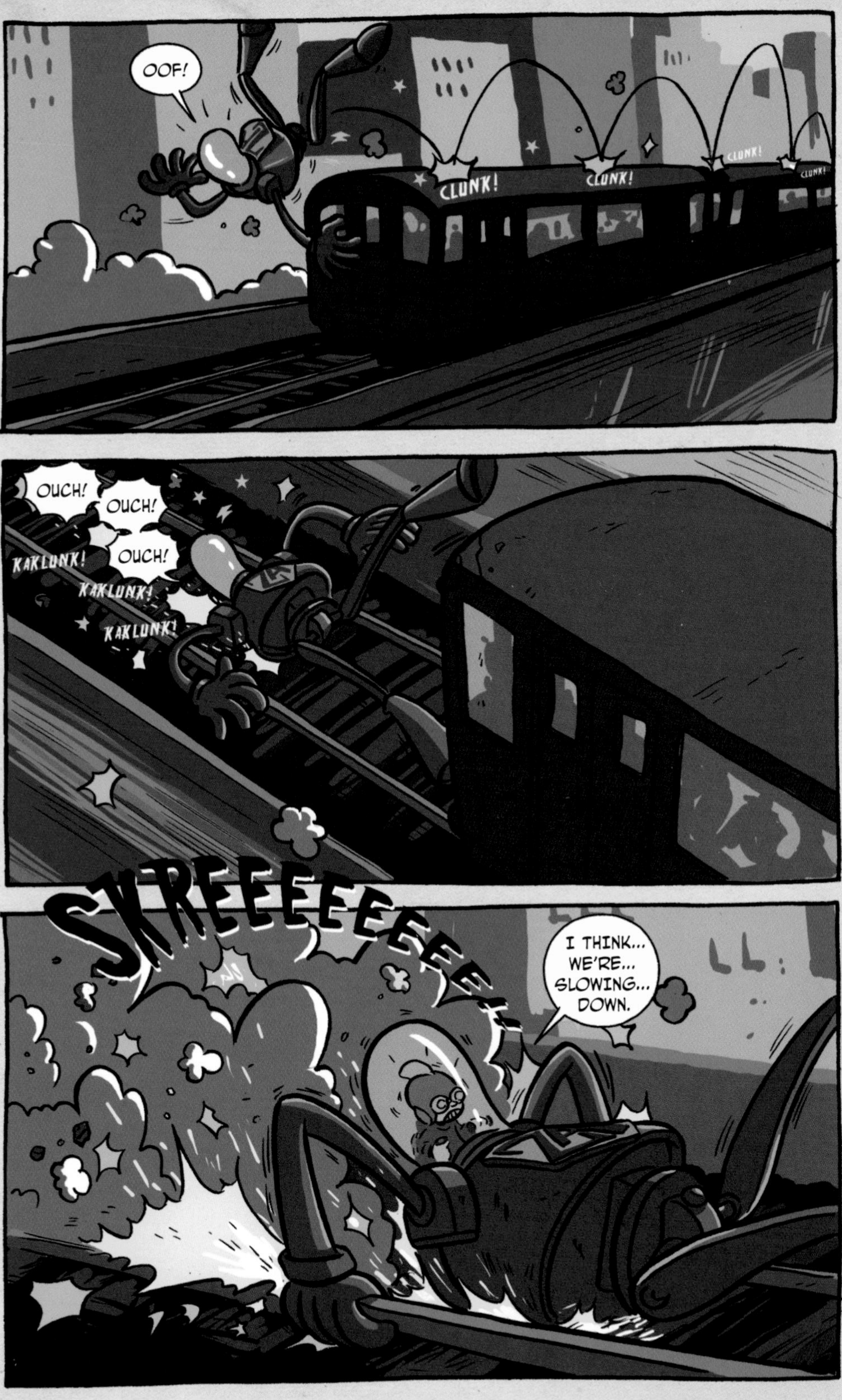
OOF!
CLUNK!
CLUNK!
CLUNK!
CLUNK!
OUCH!
OUCH!
OUCH!
KAKLUNK!
KAKLUNK!
KAKLUNK!
SKREEEEEEEEEE
I THINK... WE'RE... SLOWING... DOWN.

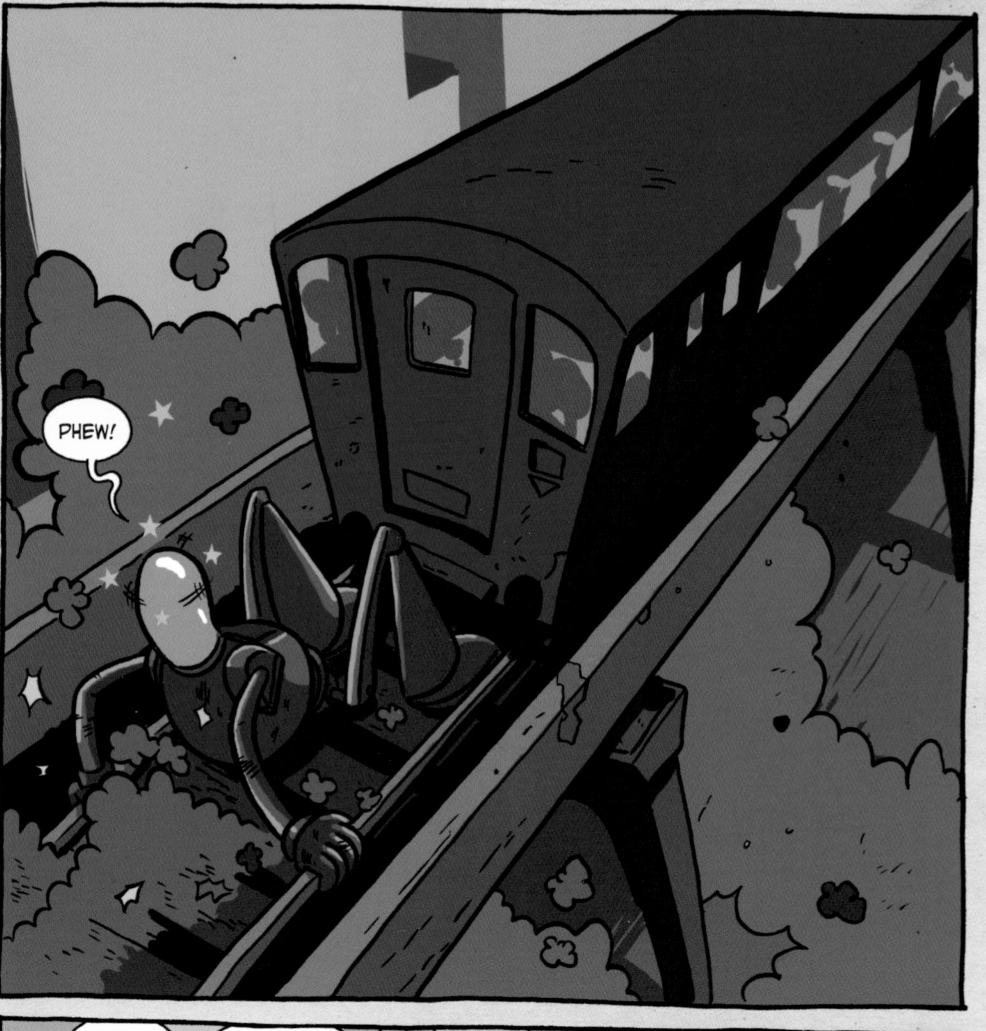
PHEW!

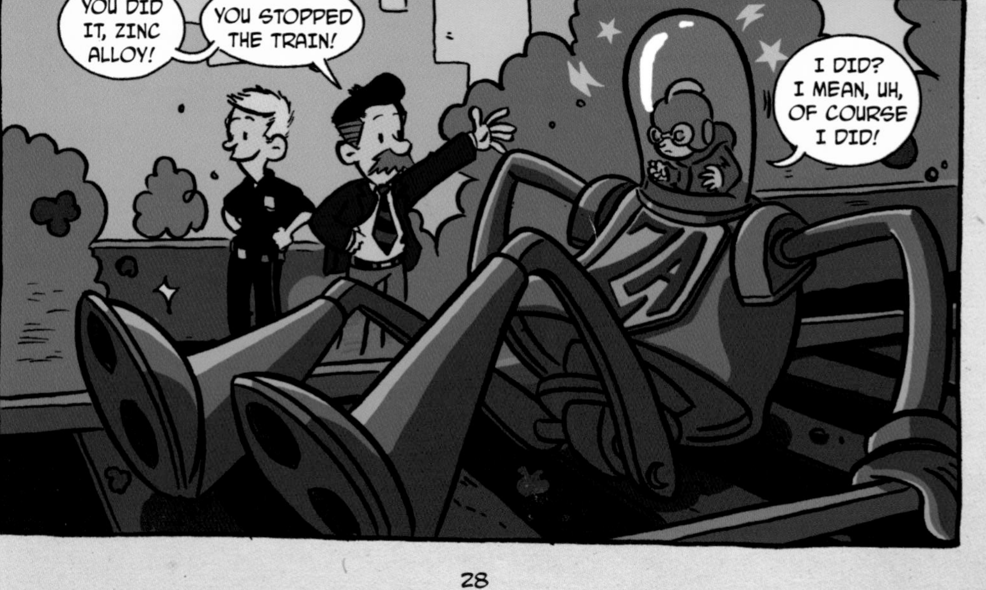
YOU DID IT, ZINC ALLOY!
YOU STOPPED THE TRAIN!
I DID? I MEAN, UH, OF COURSE I DID!

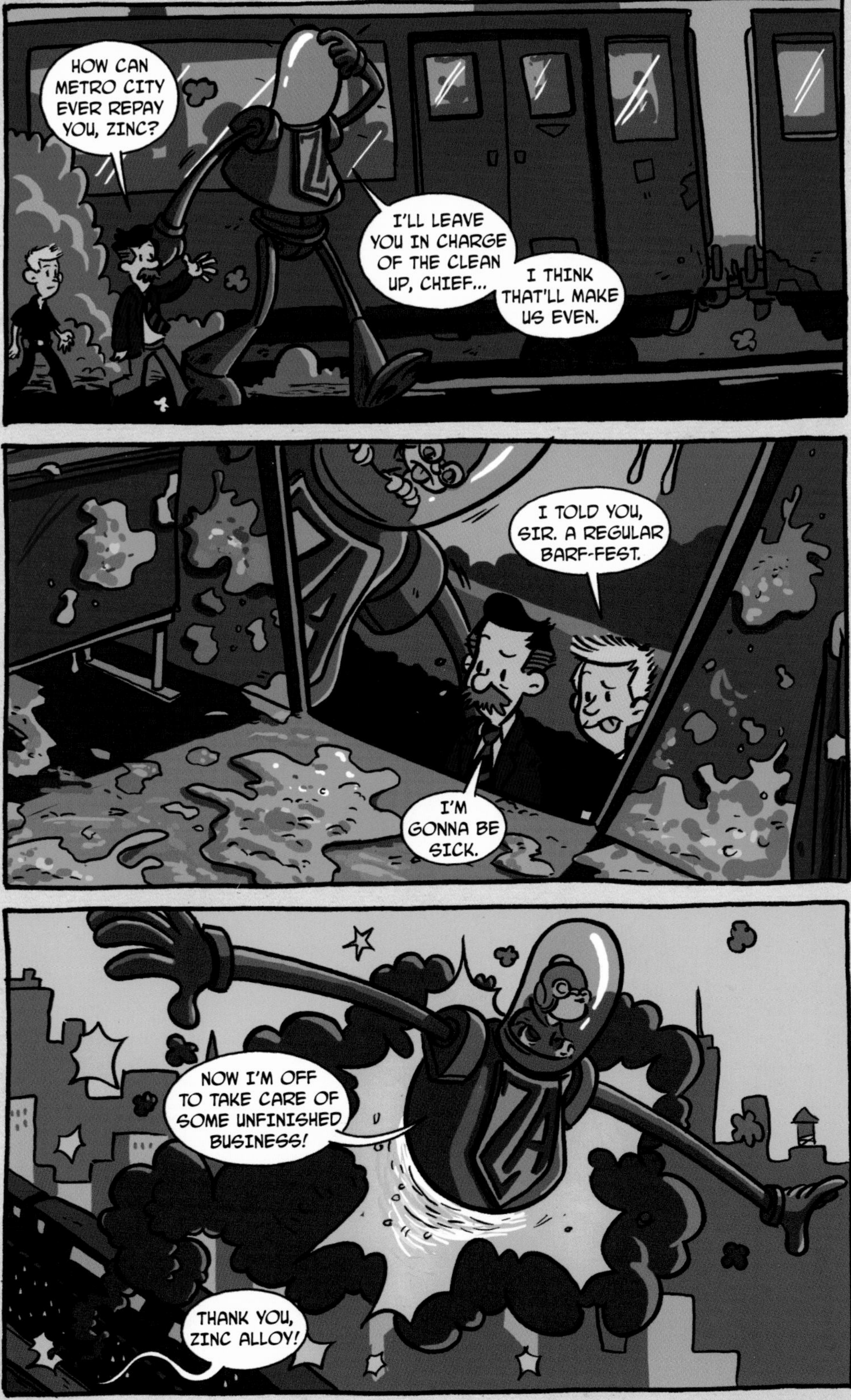
HOW CAN METRO CITY EVER REPAY YOU, ZINC?
I'LL LEAVE YOU IN CHARGE OF THE CLEAN UP, CHIEF...
I THINK THAT'LL MAKE US EVEN.
I TOLD YOU, SIR. A REGULAR BARF-FEST.
I'M GONNA BE SICK.
NOW I'M OFF TO TAKE CARE OF SOME UNFINISHED BUSINESS!
THANK YOU, ZINC ALLOY!

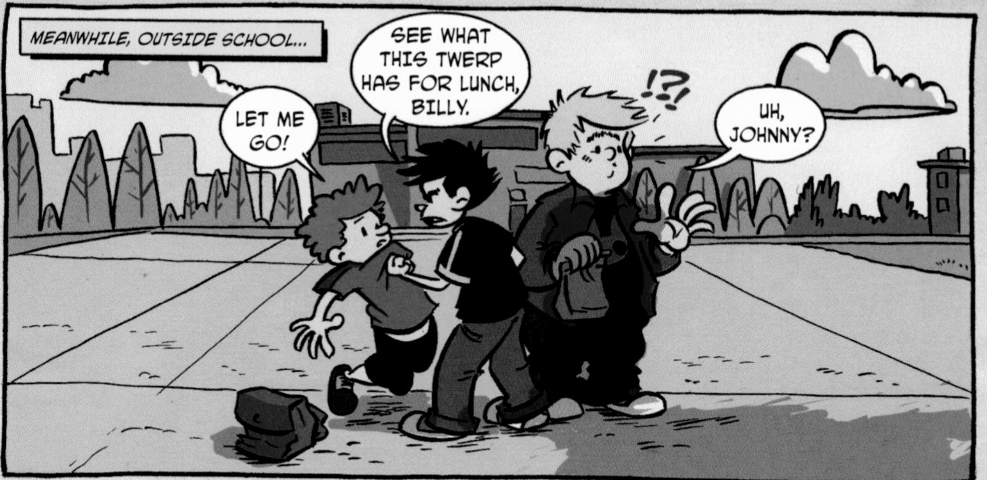
MEANWHILE, OUTSIDE SCHOOL...
LET ME GO!
SEE WHAT THIS TWERP HAS FOR LUNCH, BILLY.
!?!
UH, JOHNNY?

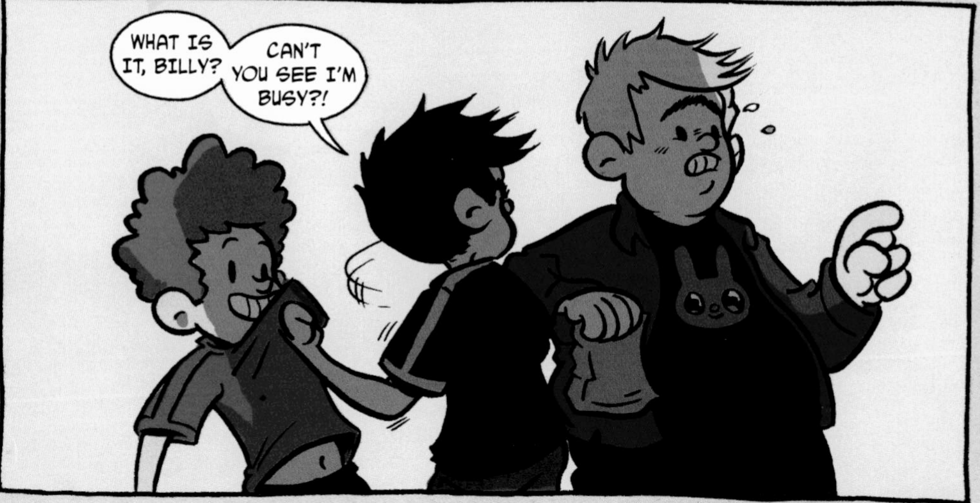
WHAT IS IT, BILLY?
CAN'T YOU SEE I'M BUSY?!

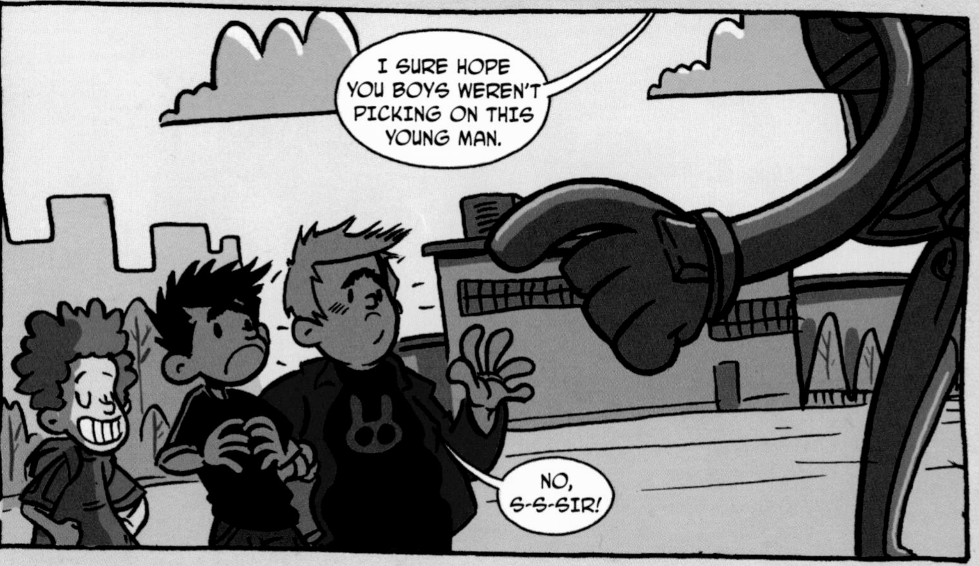
I SURE HOPE YOU BOYS WEREN'T PICKING ON THIS YOUNG MAN.
NO, S-S-SIR!

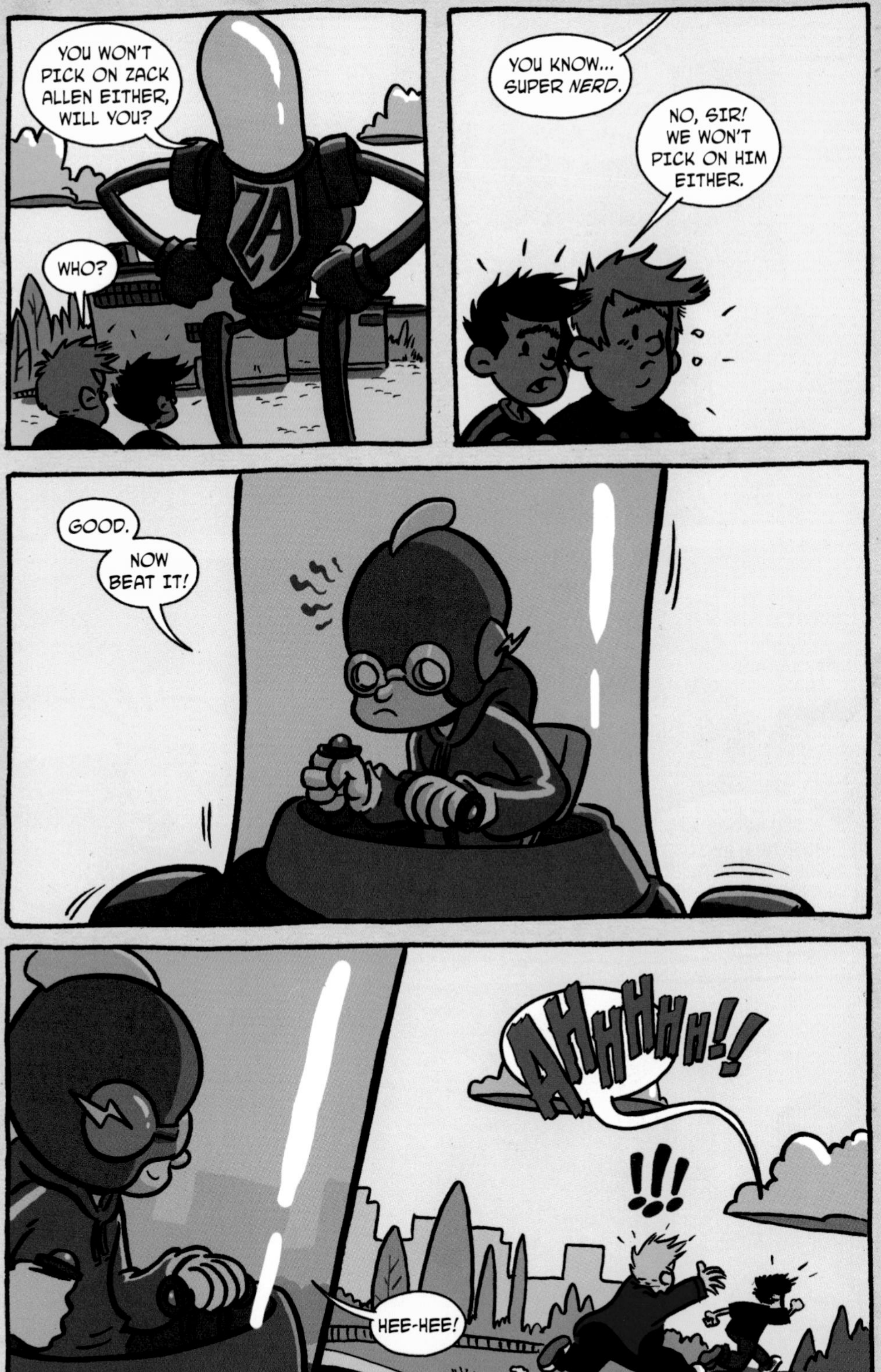
YOU WON'T PICK ON ZACK ALLEN EITHER, WILL YOU?
WHO?
YOU KNOW... SUPER NERD.
NO, SIR! WE WON'T PICK ON HIM EITHER.
GOOD.
NOW BEAT IT!
AHHHHHH!!
!!!
HEE-HEE!

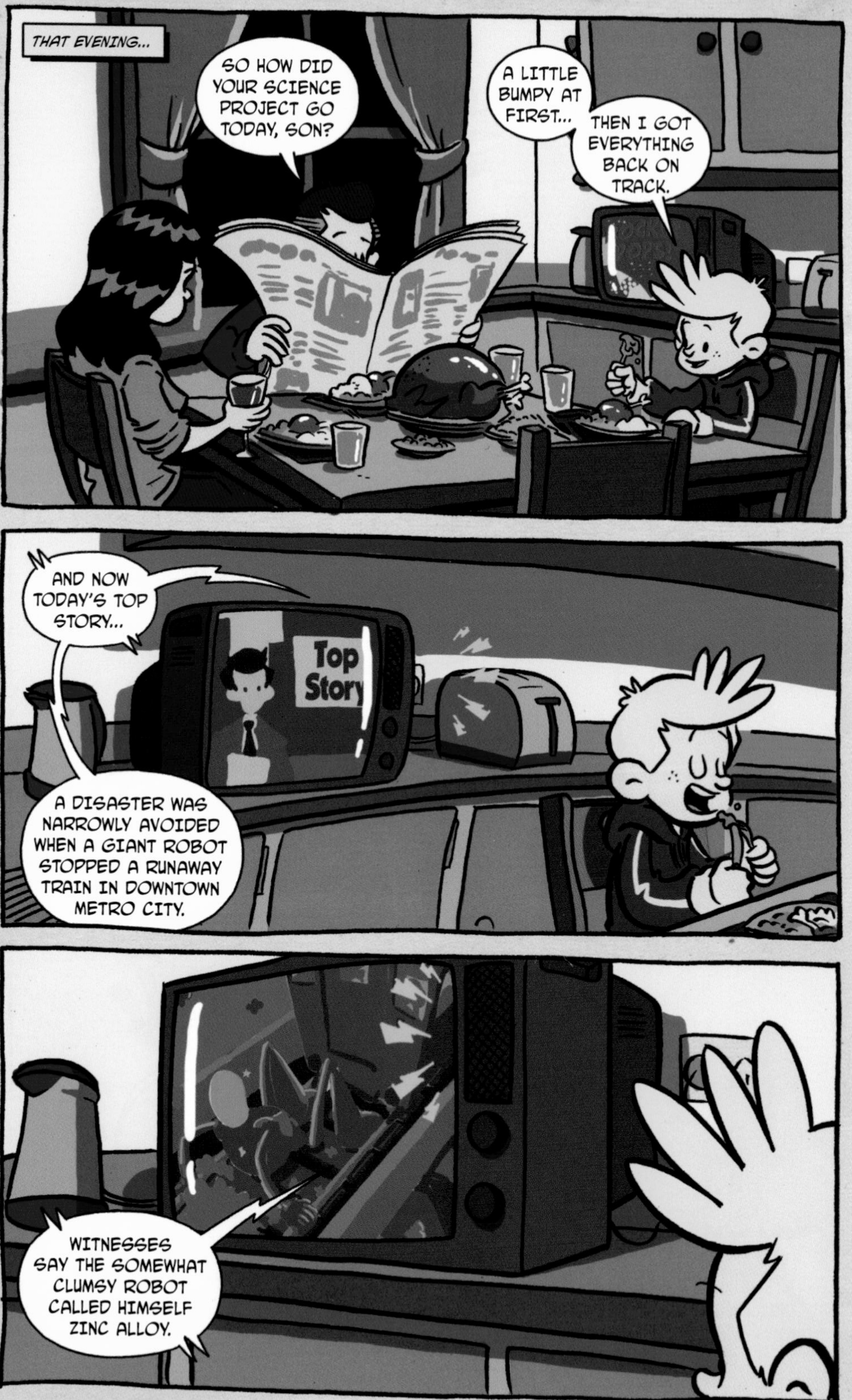
THAT EVENING...
SO HOW DID YOUR SCIENCE PROJECT GO TODAY, SON?
A LITTLE BUMPY AT FIRST...
THEN I GOT EVERYTHING BACK ON TRACK.
AND NOW TODAY'S TOP STORY...
Top Story
A DISASTER WAS NARROWLY AVOIDED WHEN A GIANT ROBOT STOPPED A RUNAWAY TRAIN IN DOWNTOWN METRO CITY.
WITNESSES SAY THE SOMEWHAT CLUMSY ROBOT CALLED HIMSELF ZINC ALLOY.

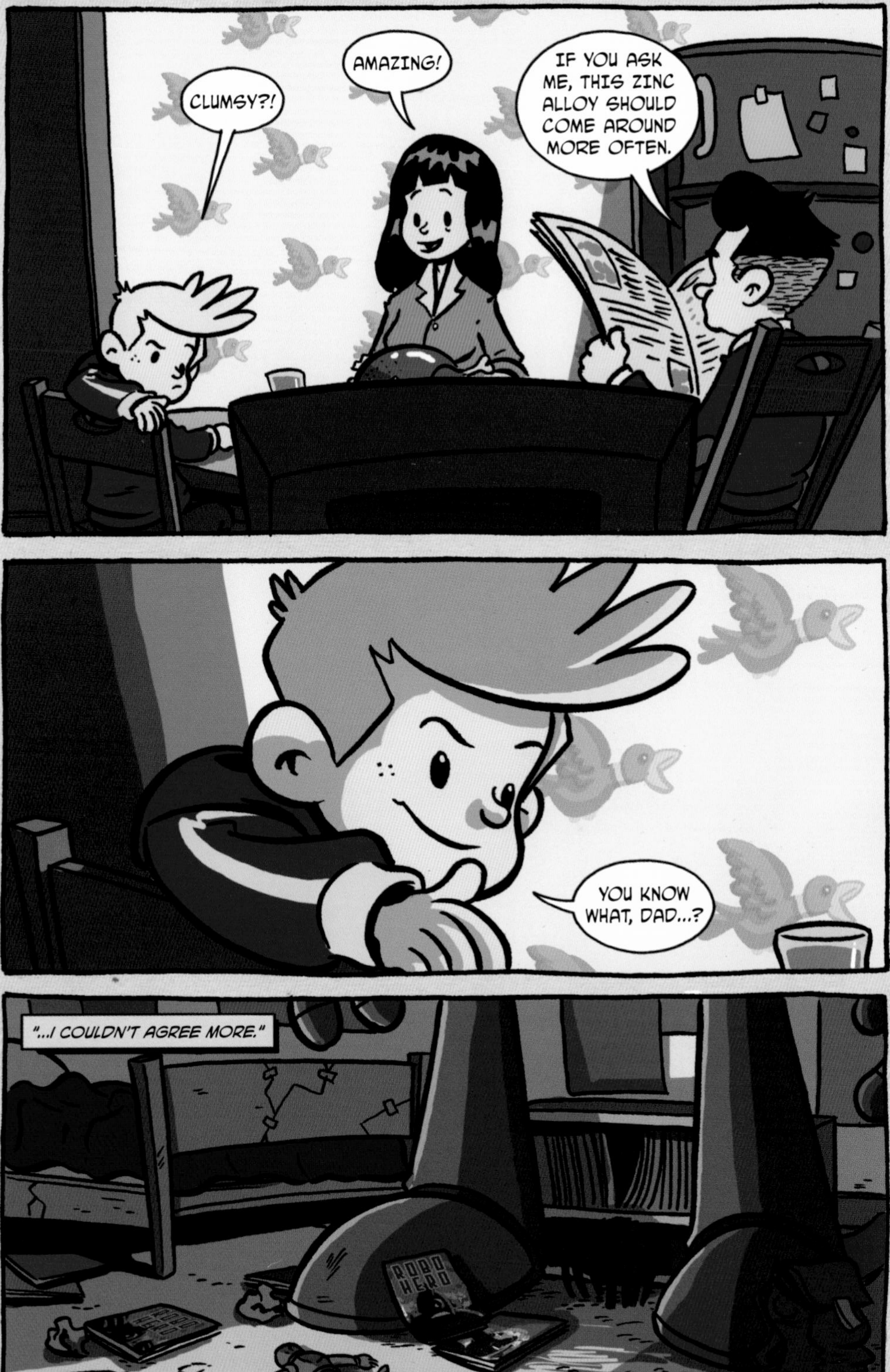
CLUMSY?!
AMAZING!
IF YOU ASK ME, THIS ZINC ALLOY SHOULD COME AROUND MORE OFTEN.
YOU KNOW WHAT, DAD...?
"...I COULDN'T AGREE MORE."

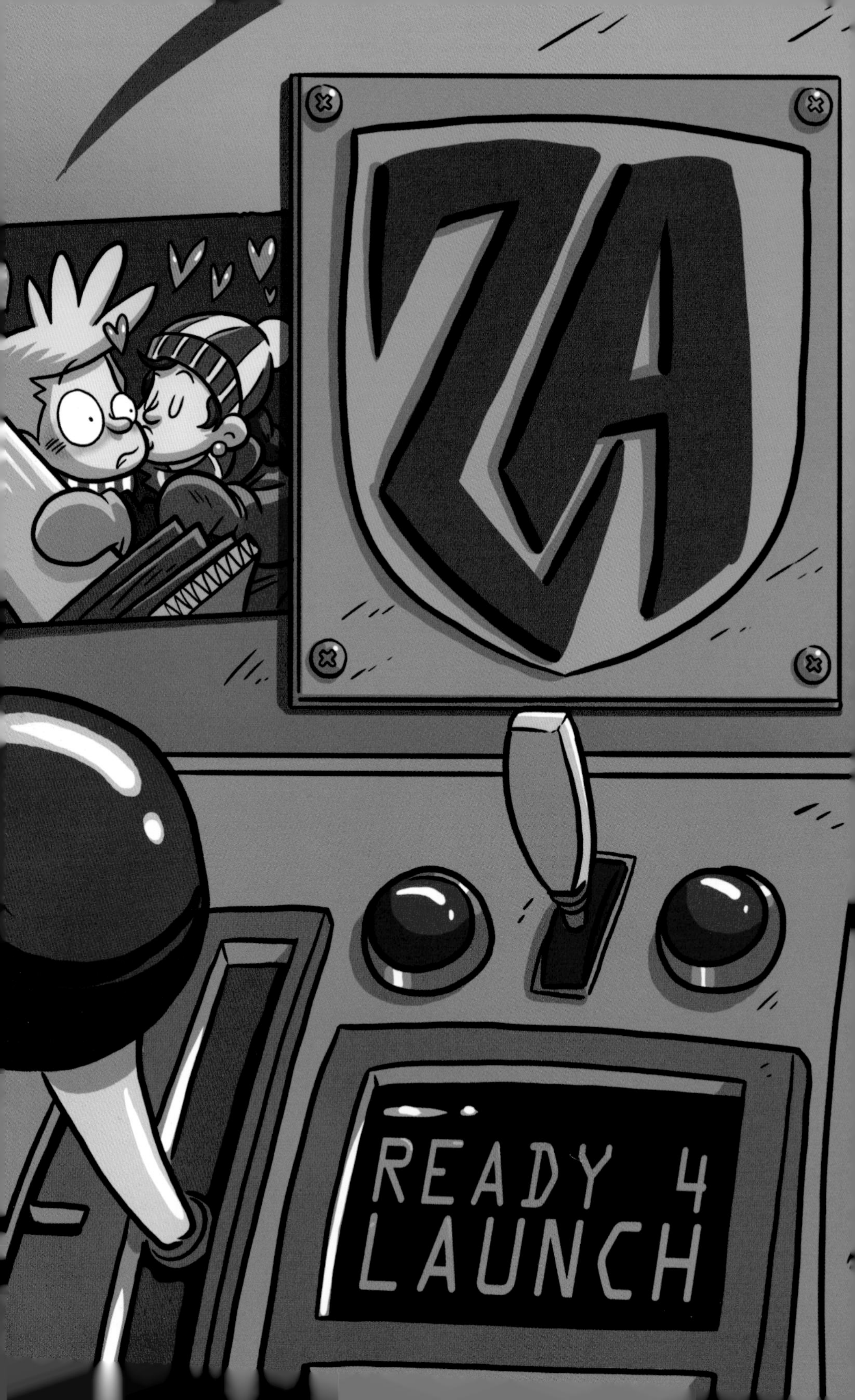
READY 4 LAUNCH

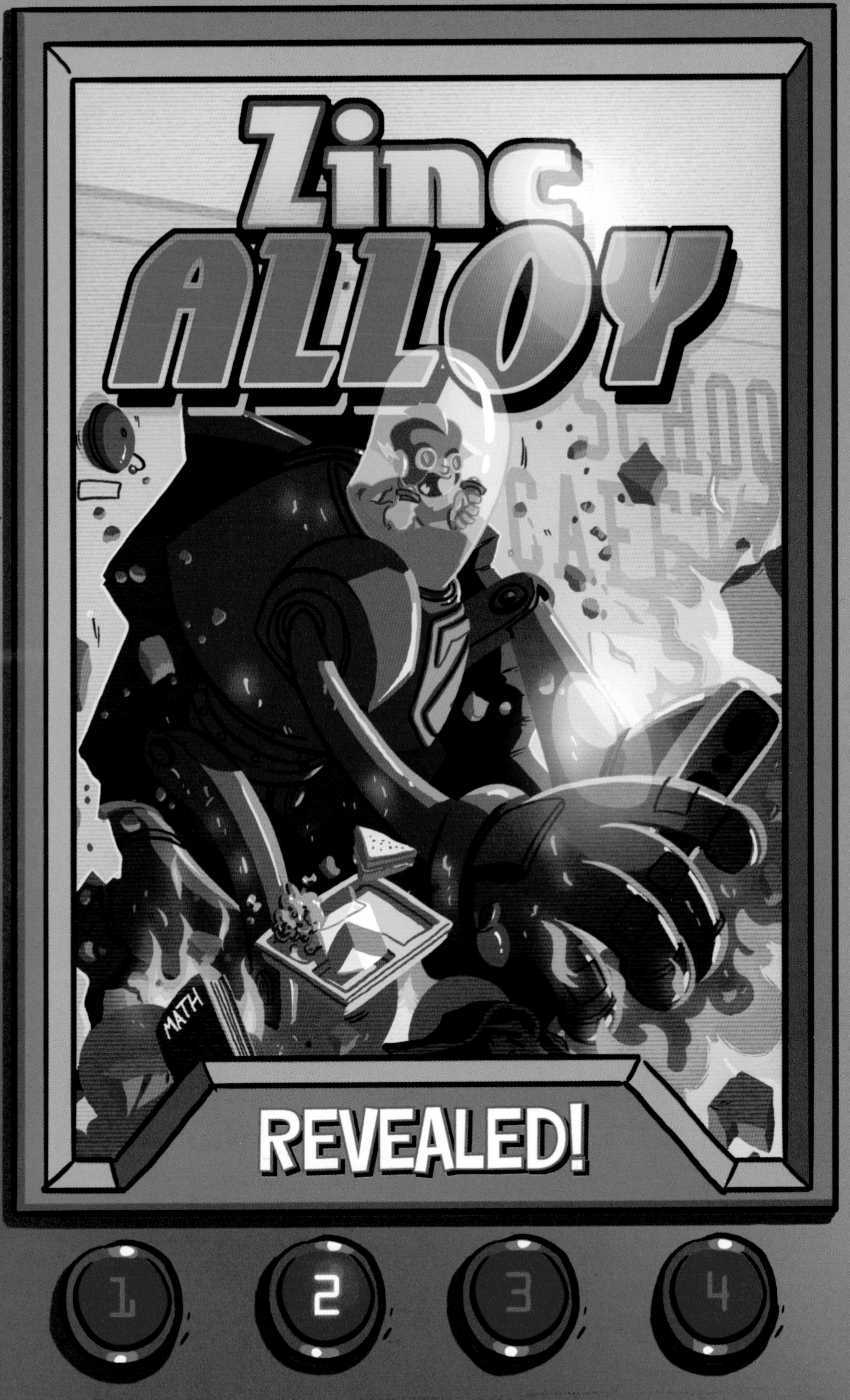
Zinc
ALLOY
MATH
REVEALED!
1
2
3
4

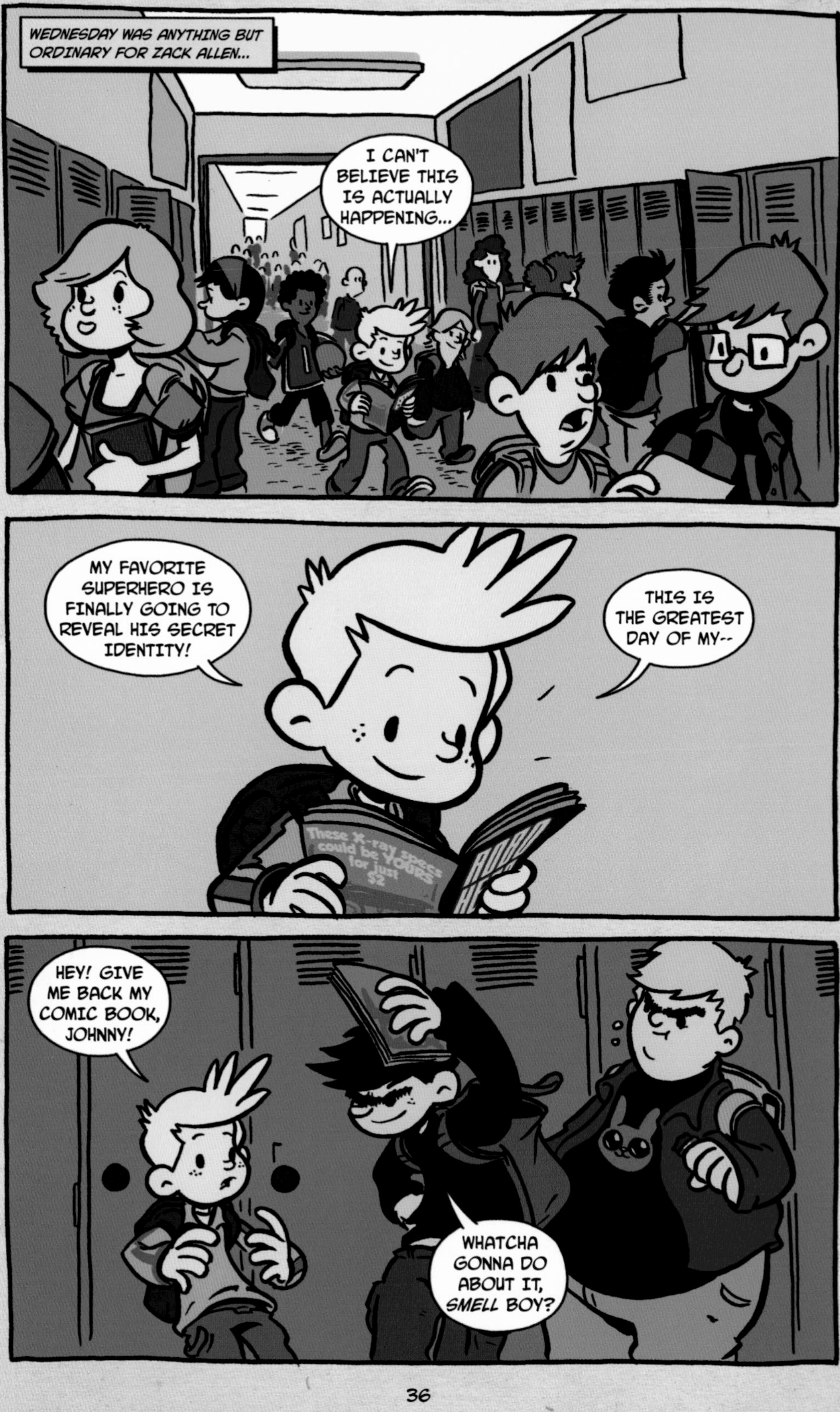
WEDNESDAY WAS ANYTHING BUT ORDINARY FOR ZACK ALLEN...
I CAN'T BELIEVE THIS IS ACTUALLY HAPPENING...
MY FAVORITE SUPERHERO IS FINALLY GOING TO REVEAL HIS SECRET IDENTITY!
THIS IS THE GREATEST DAY OF MY--
These X-ray specs could be YOURS for just $2
HEY! GIVE ME BACK MY COMIC BOOK, JOHNNY!
WHATCHA GONNA DO ABOUT IT, SMELL BOY?

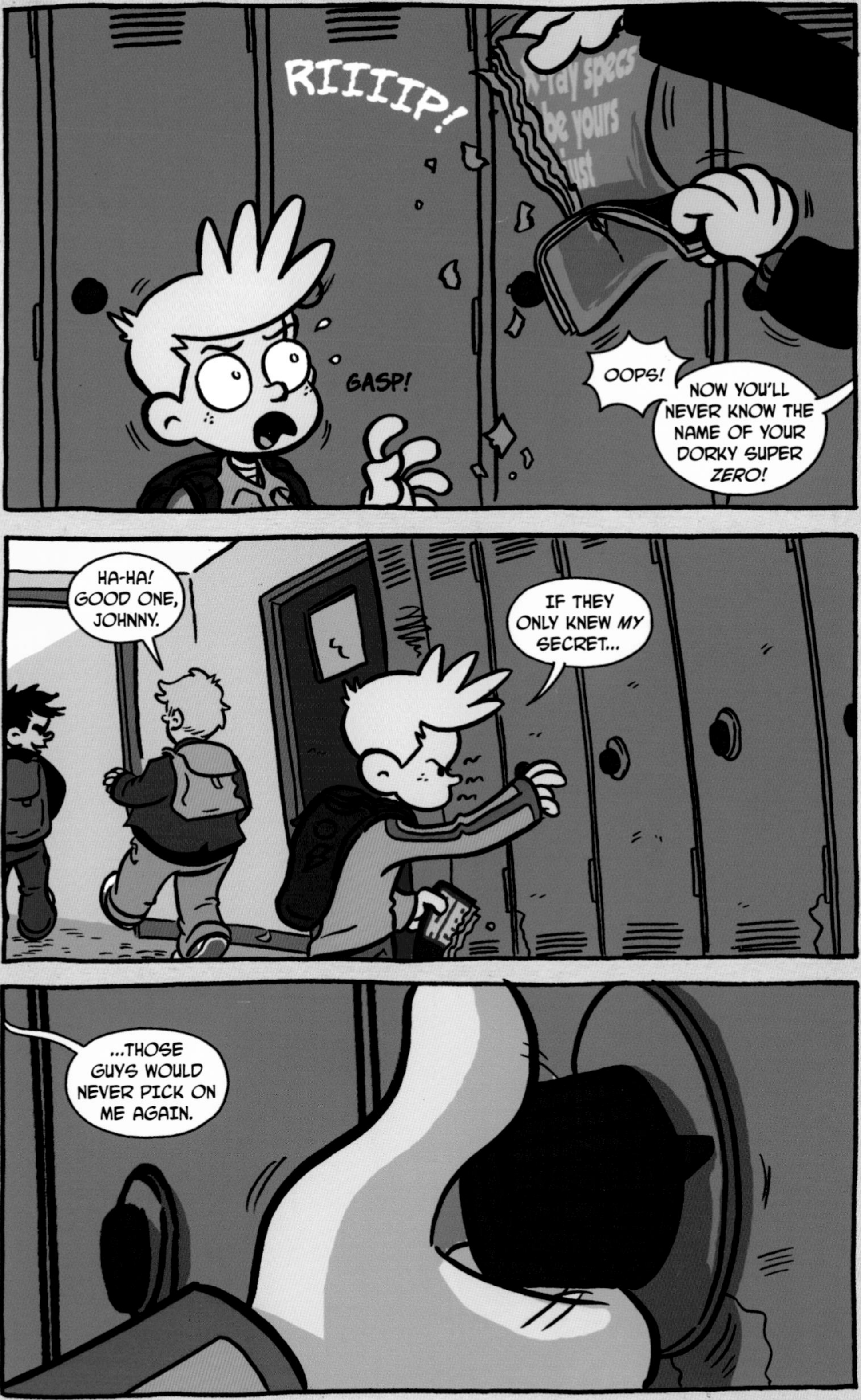
RIIIIP!
GASP!
OOPS!
NOW YOU'LL NEVER KNOW THE NAME OF YOUR DORKY SUPER ZERO!
HA-HA! GOOD ONE, JOHNNY.
IF THEY ONLY KNEW *MY* SECRET...
...THOSE GUYS WOULD NEVER PICK ON ME AGAIN.

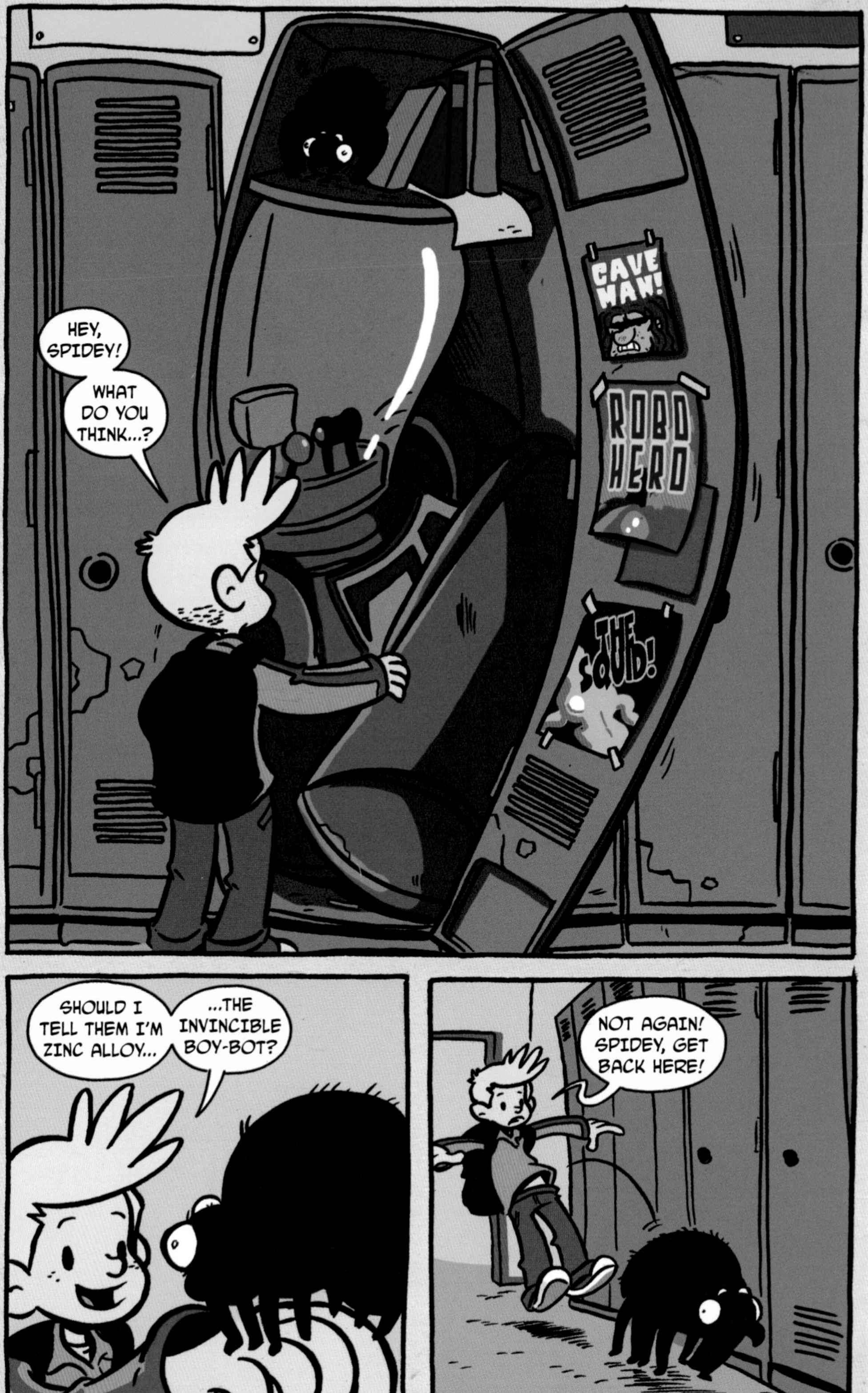
HEY, SPIDEY!
WHAT DO YOU THINK...?
CAVE MAN!
ROBO HERO
THE SQUID!
SHOULD I TELL THEM I'M ZINC ALLOY...
...THE INVINCIBLE BOY-BOT?
NOT AGAIN! SPIDEY, GET BACK HERE!

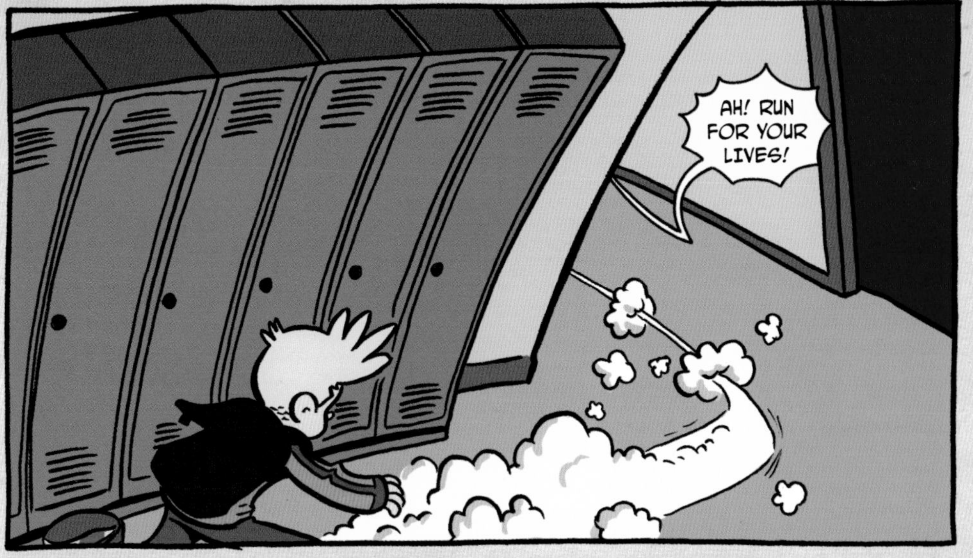
AH! RUN FOR YOUR LIVES!

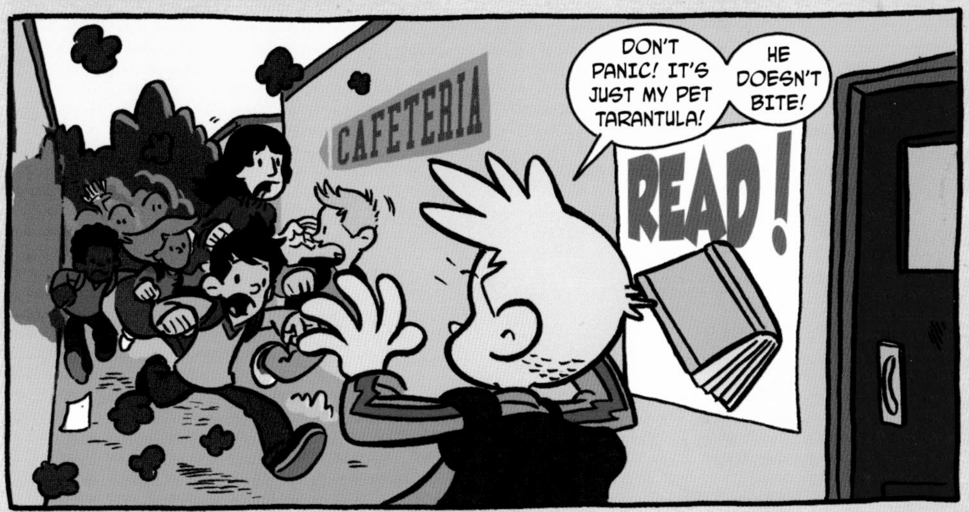
CAFETERIA
DON'T PANIC! IT'S JUST MY PET TARANTULA!
HE DOESN'T BITE!
READ!

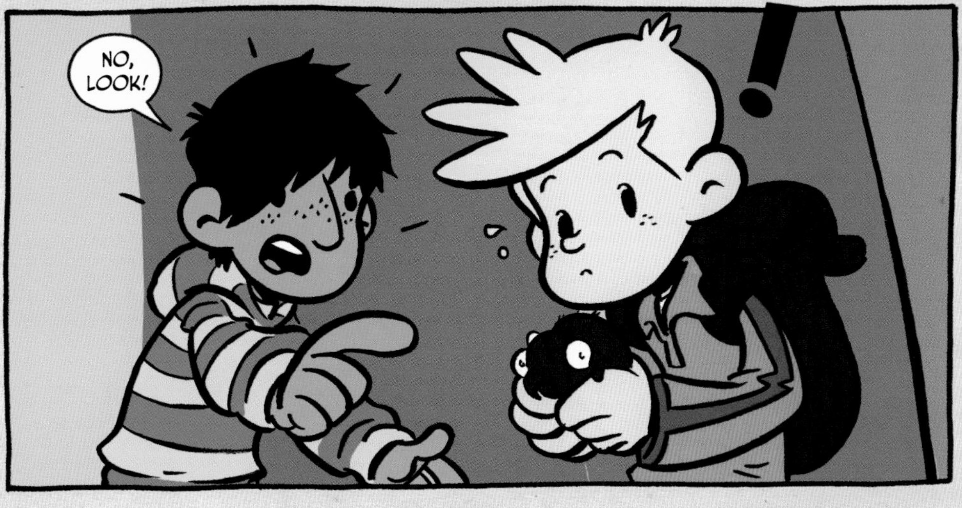
NO, LOOK!
!

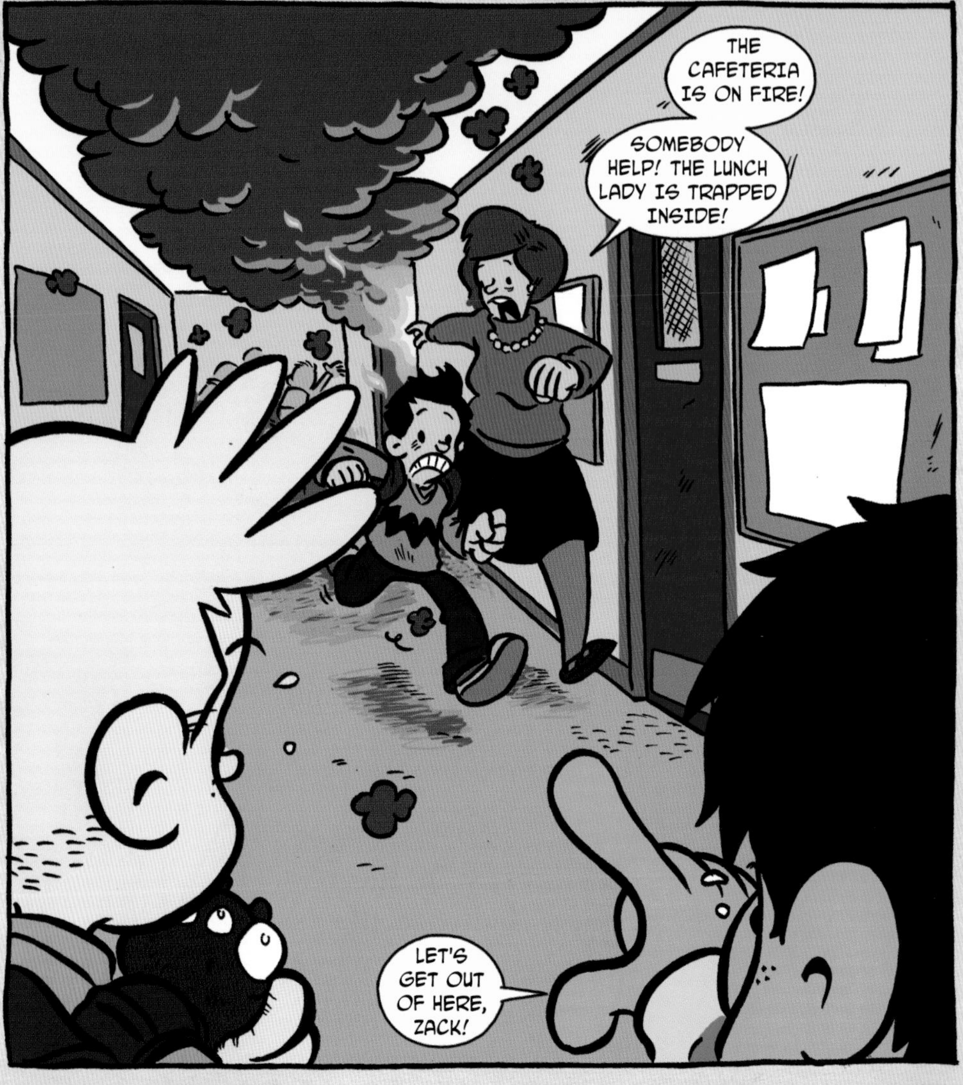
THE CAFETERIA IS ON FIRE!
SOMEBODY HELP! THE LUNCH LADY IS TRAPPED INSIDE!
LET'S GET OUT OF HERE, ZACK!

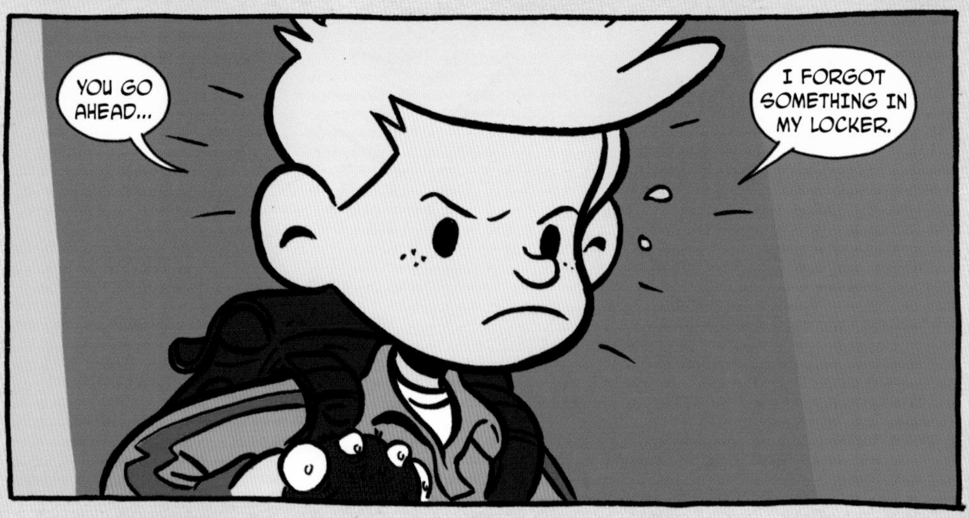
YOU GO AHEAD...
I FORGOT SOMETHING IN MY LOCKER.

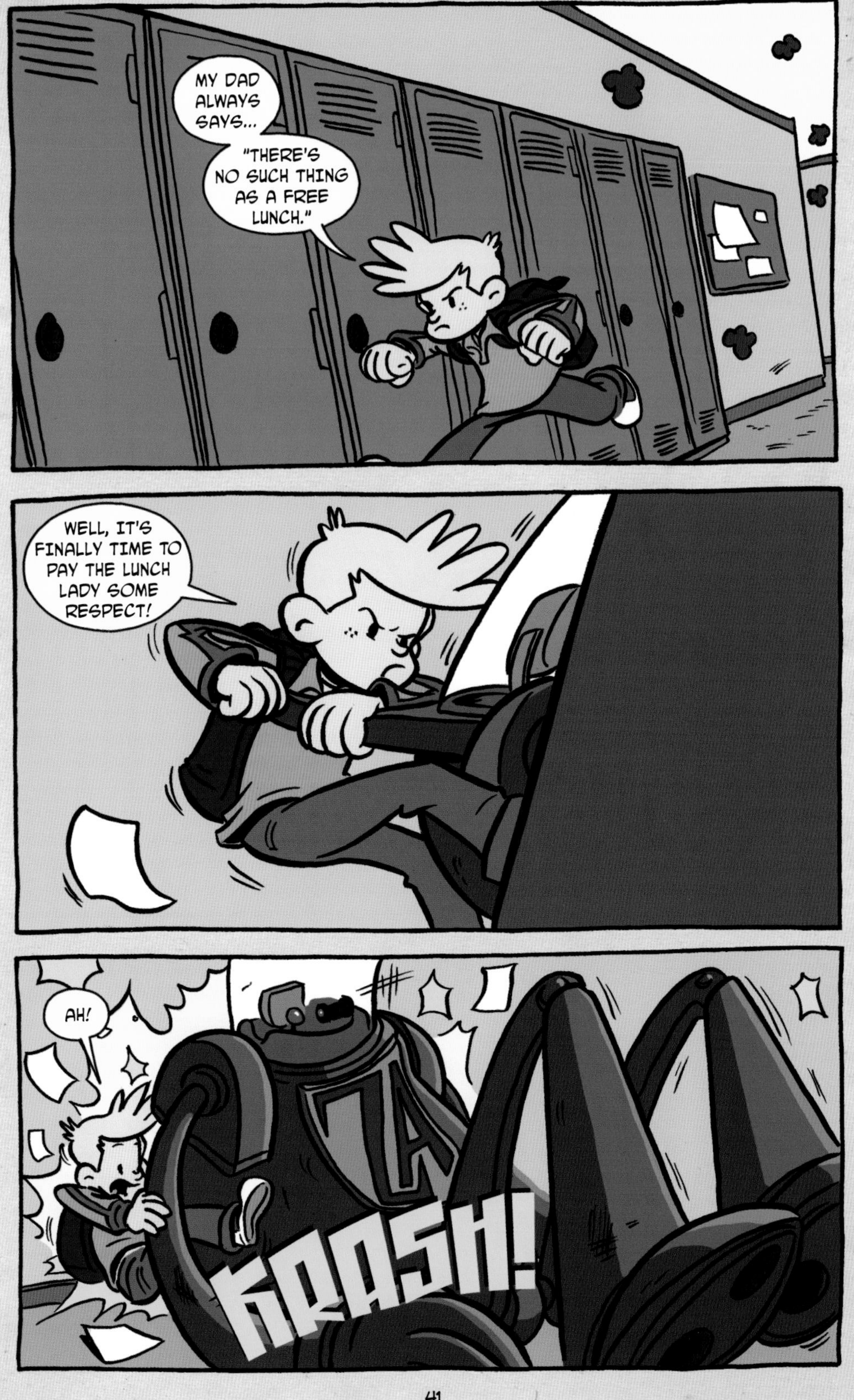
MY DAD ALWAYS SAYS...
"THERE'S NO SUCH THING AS A FREE LUNCH."
WELL, IT'S FINALLY TIME TO PAY THE LUNCH LADY SOME RESPECT!
AH!
KRASH!

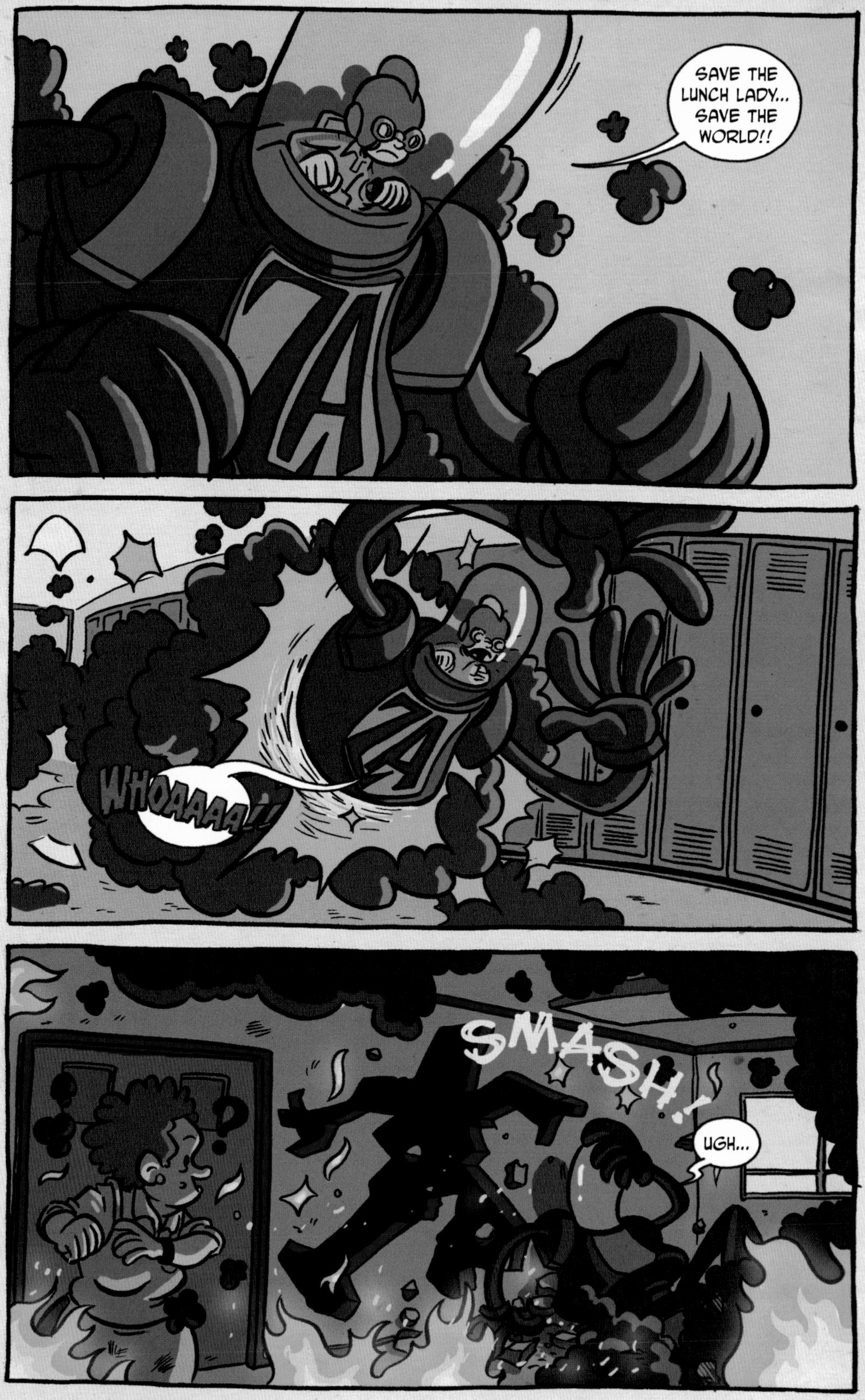
SAVE THE LUNCH LADY... SAVE THE WORLD!!
WHOAAAA!!
SMASH!
UGH...

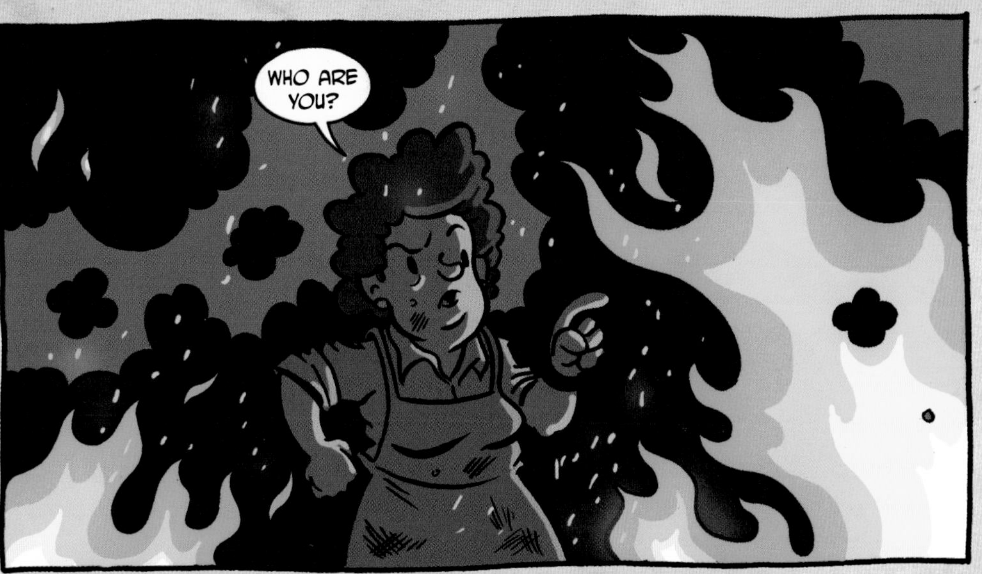
WHO ARE YOU?

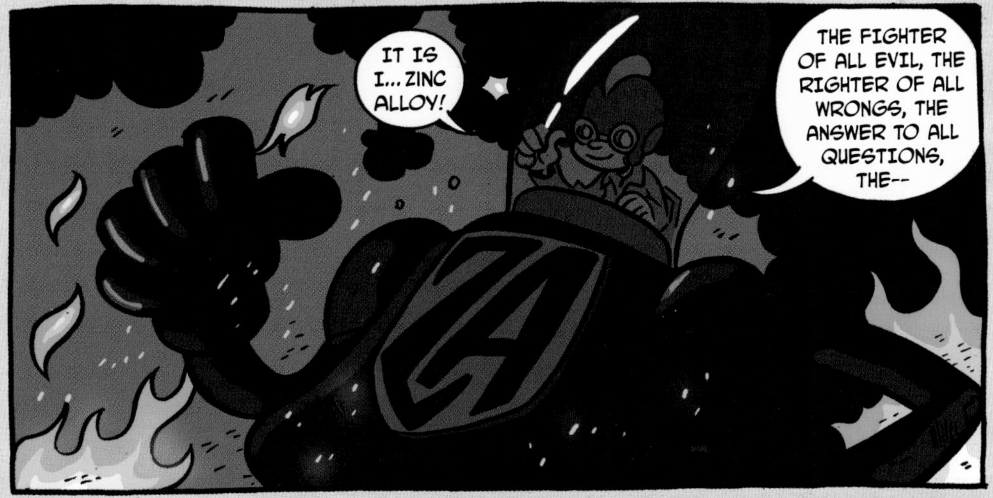
IT IS I... ZINC ALLOY!
THE FIGHTER OF ALL EVIL, THE RIGHTER OF ALL WRONGS, THE ANSWER TO ALL QUESTIONS, THE--

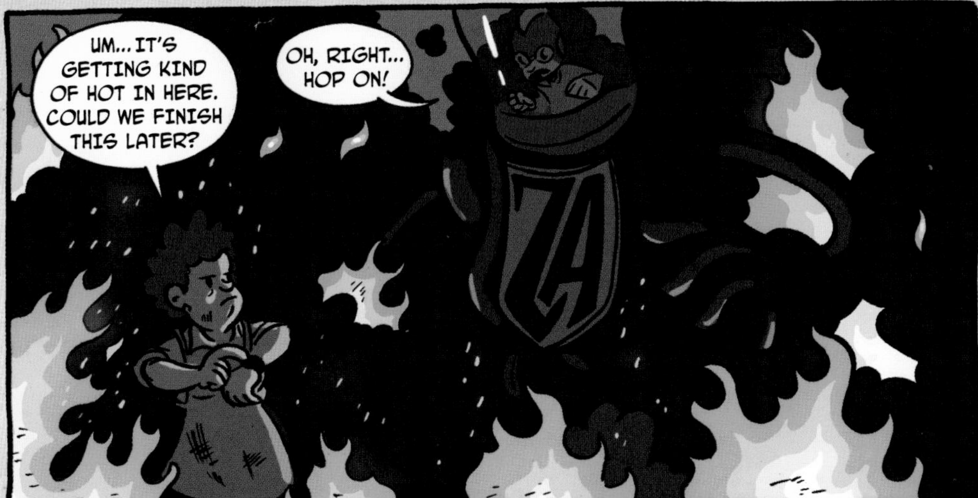
UM... IT'S GETTING KIND OF HOT IN HERE. COULD WE FINISH THIS LATER?
OH, RIGHT... HOP ON!

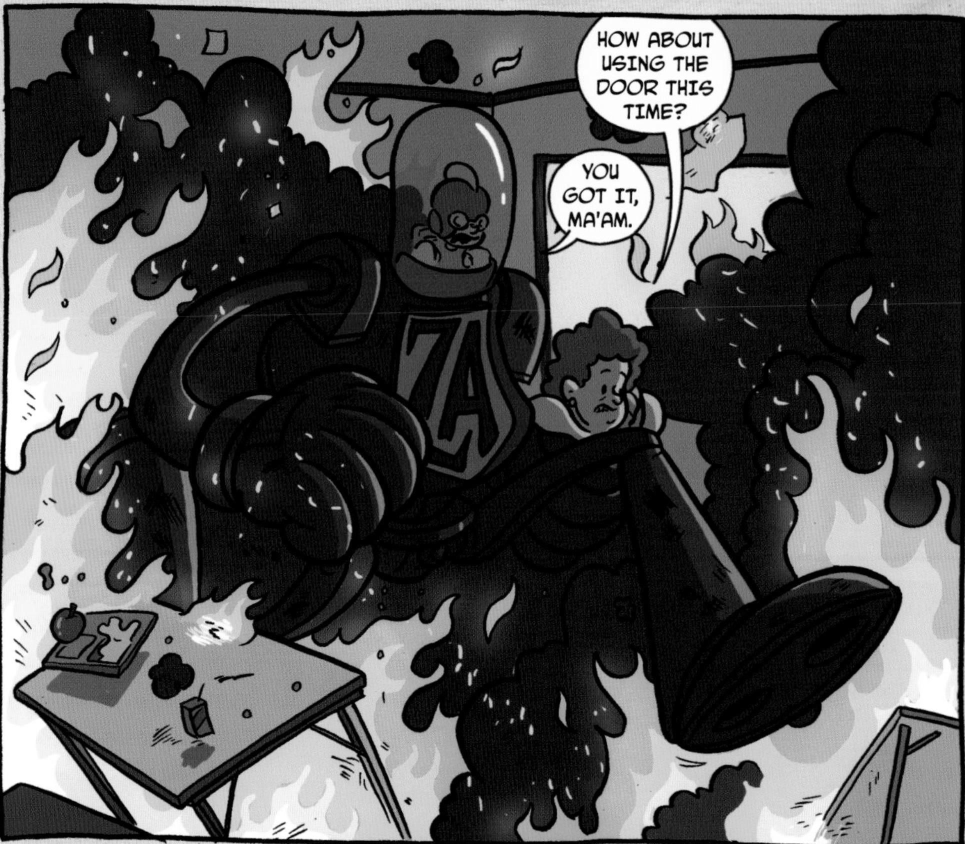
HOW ABOUT USING THE DOOR THIS TIME?
YOU GOT IT, MA'AM.

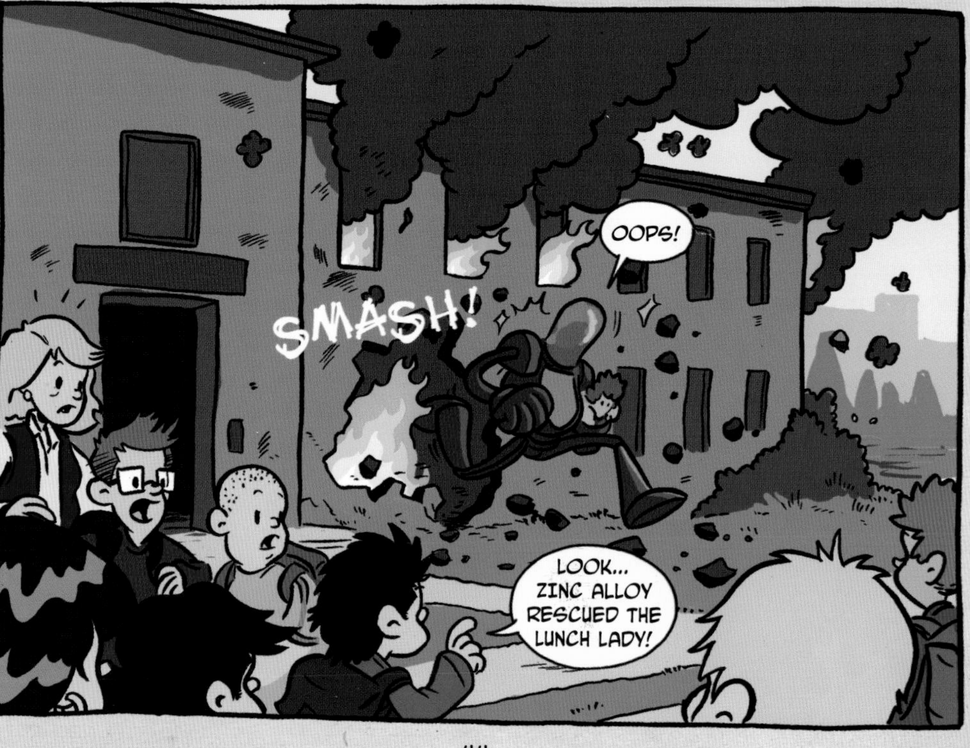
OOPS!
SMASH!
LOOK... ZINC ALLOY RESCUED THE LUNCH LADY!

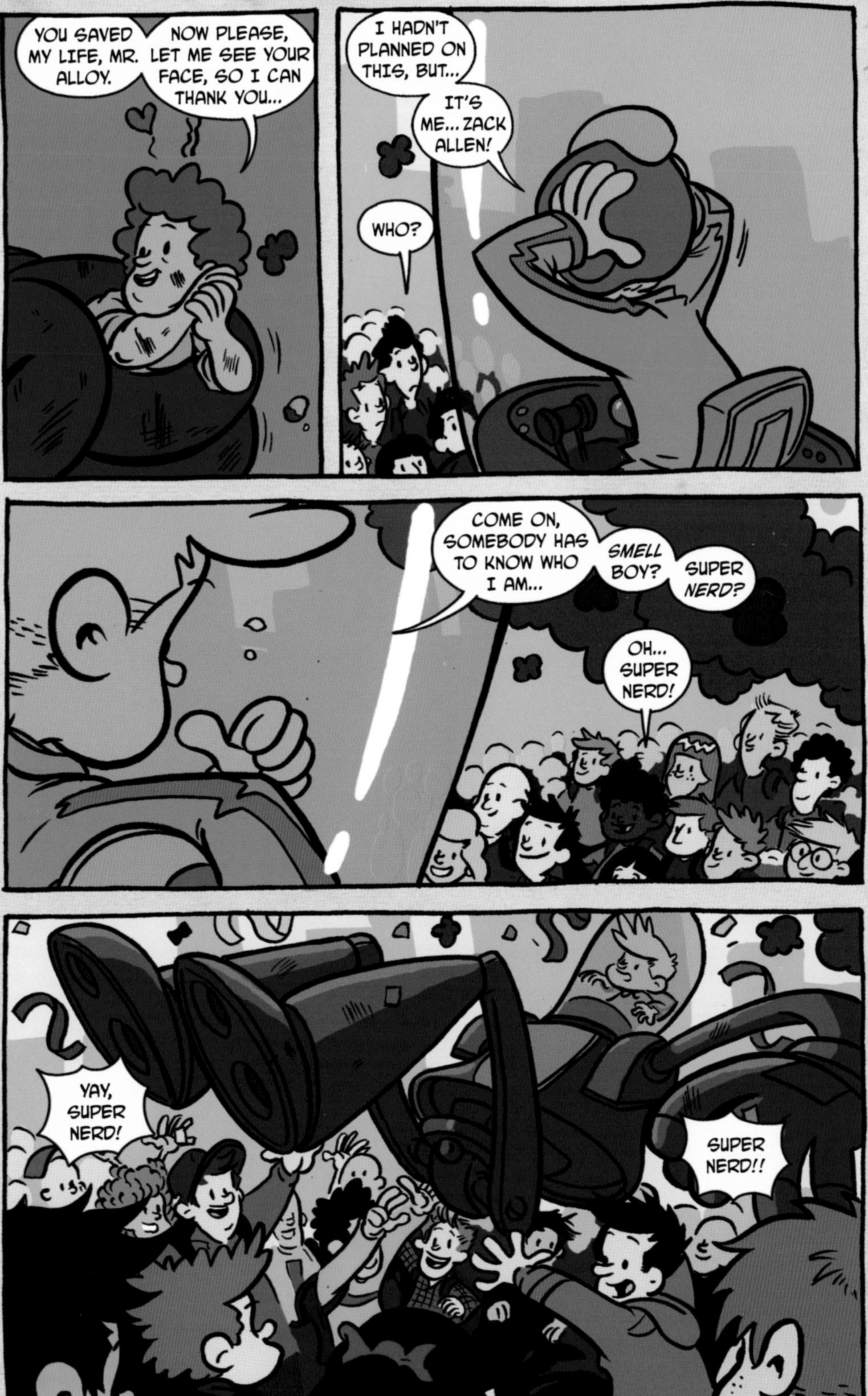
YOU SAVED MY LIFE, MR. ALLOY.
NOW PLEASE, LET ME SEE YOUR FACE, SO I CAN THANK YOU...
I HADN'T PLANNED ON THIS, BUT...
IT'S ME...ZACK ALLEN!
WHO?
COME ON, SOMEBODY HAS TO KNOW WHO I AM...
SMELL BOY?
SUPER NERD?
OH... SUPER NERD!
YAY, SUPER NERD!
SUPER NERD!!

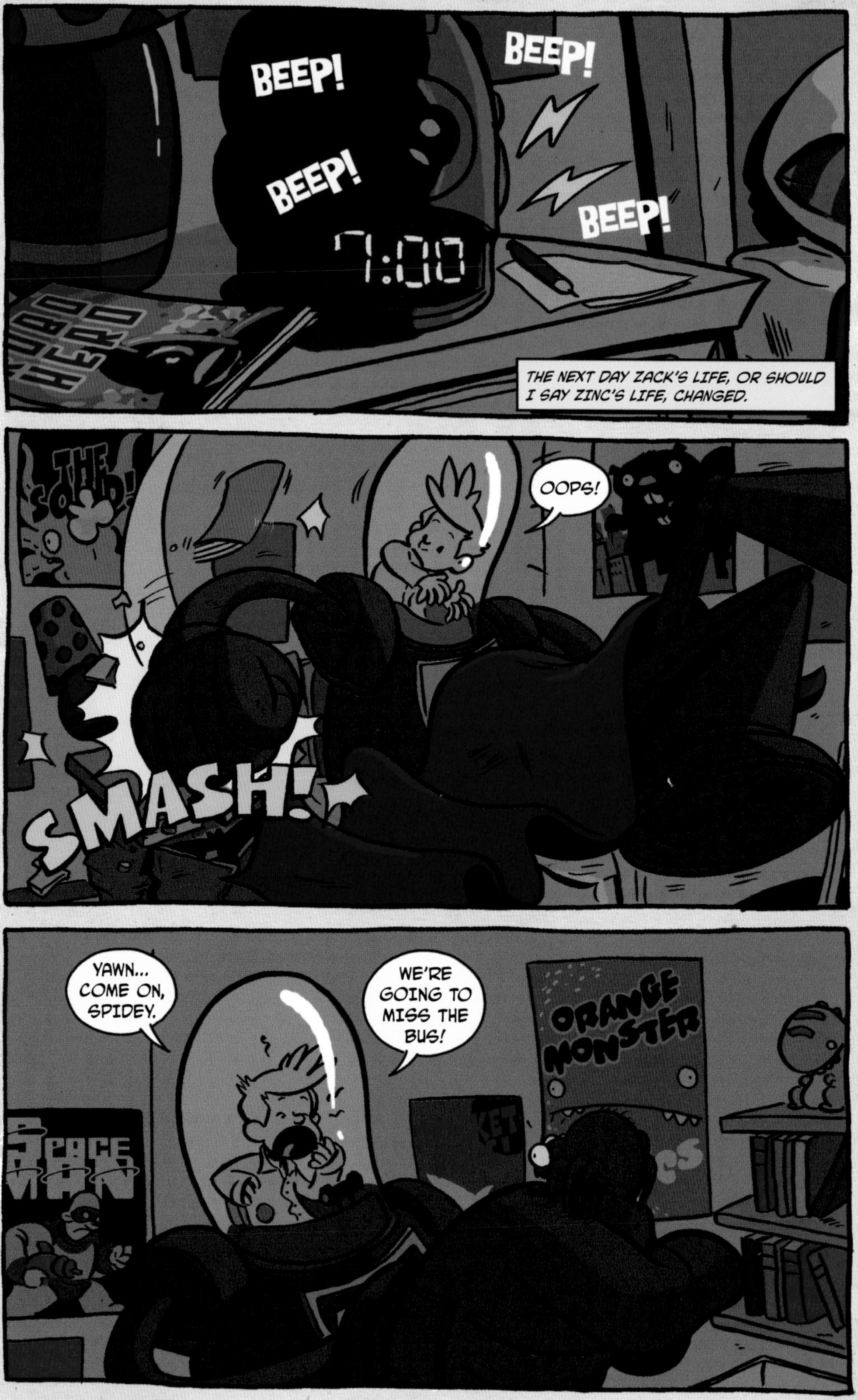
BEEP!
BEEP!
BEEP!
BEEP!
7:00
THE NEXT DAY ZACK'S LIFE, OR SHOULD I SAY ZINC'S LIFE, CHANGED.
OOPS!
SMASH!
YAWN... COME ON, SPIDEY.
WE'RE GOING TO MISS THE BUS!
ORANGE MONSTER
SPACE MAN

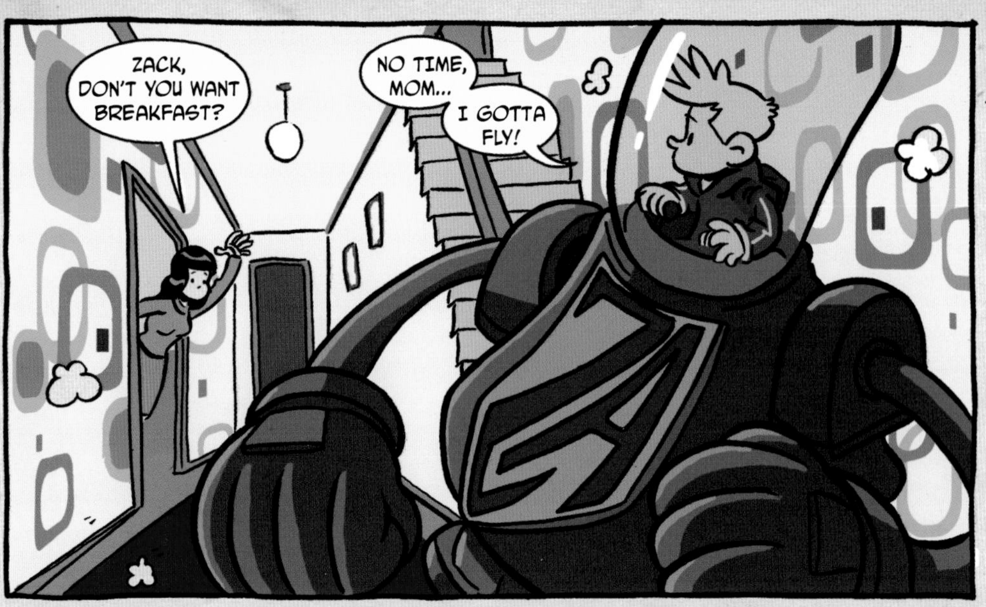
ZACK, DON'T YOU WANT BREAKFAST?
NO TIME, MOM...
I GOTTA FLY!

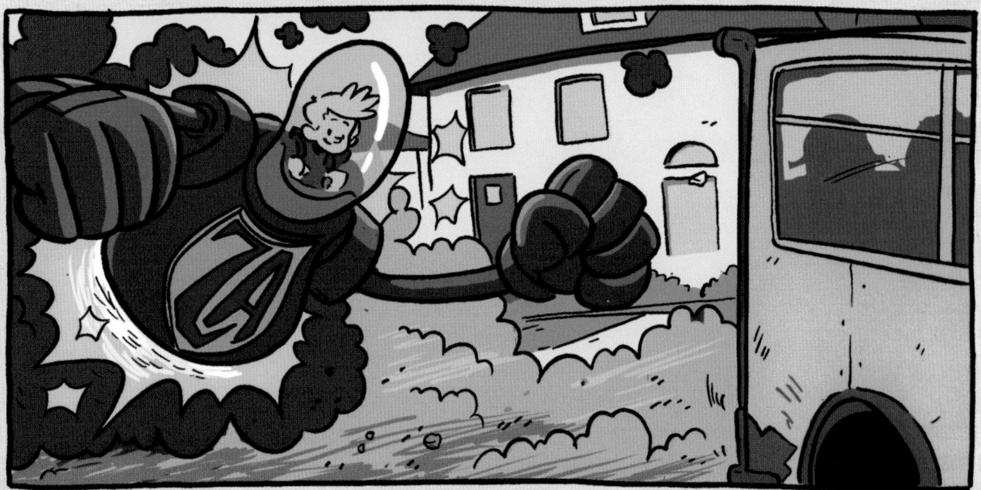

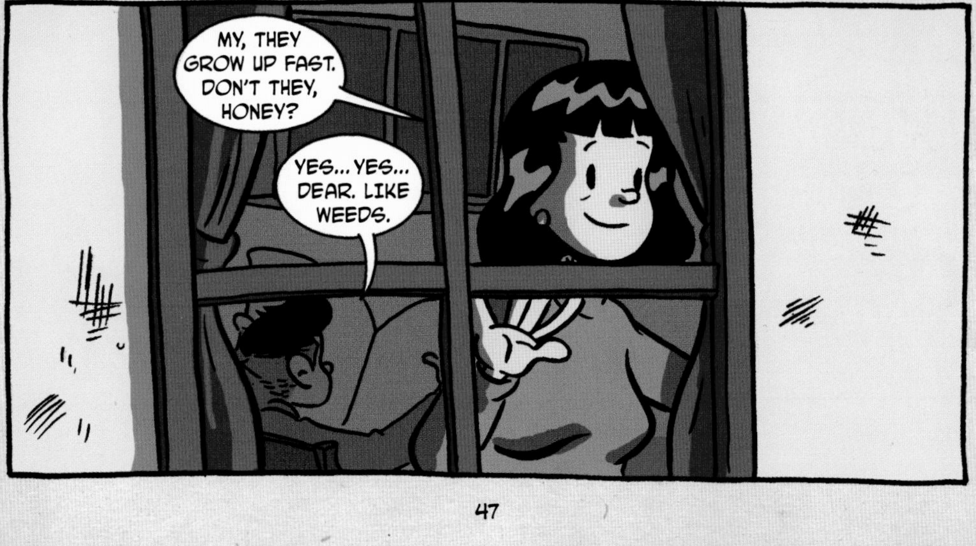
MY, THEY GROW UP FAST. DON'T THEY, HONEY?
YES... YES... DEAR. LIKE WEEDS.

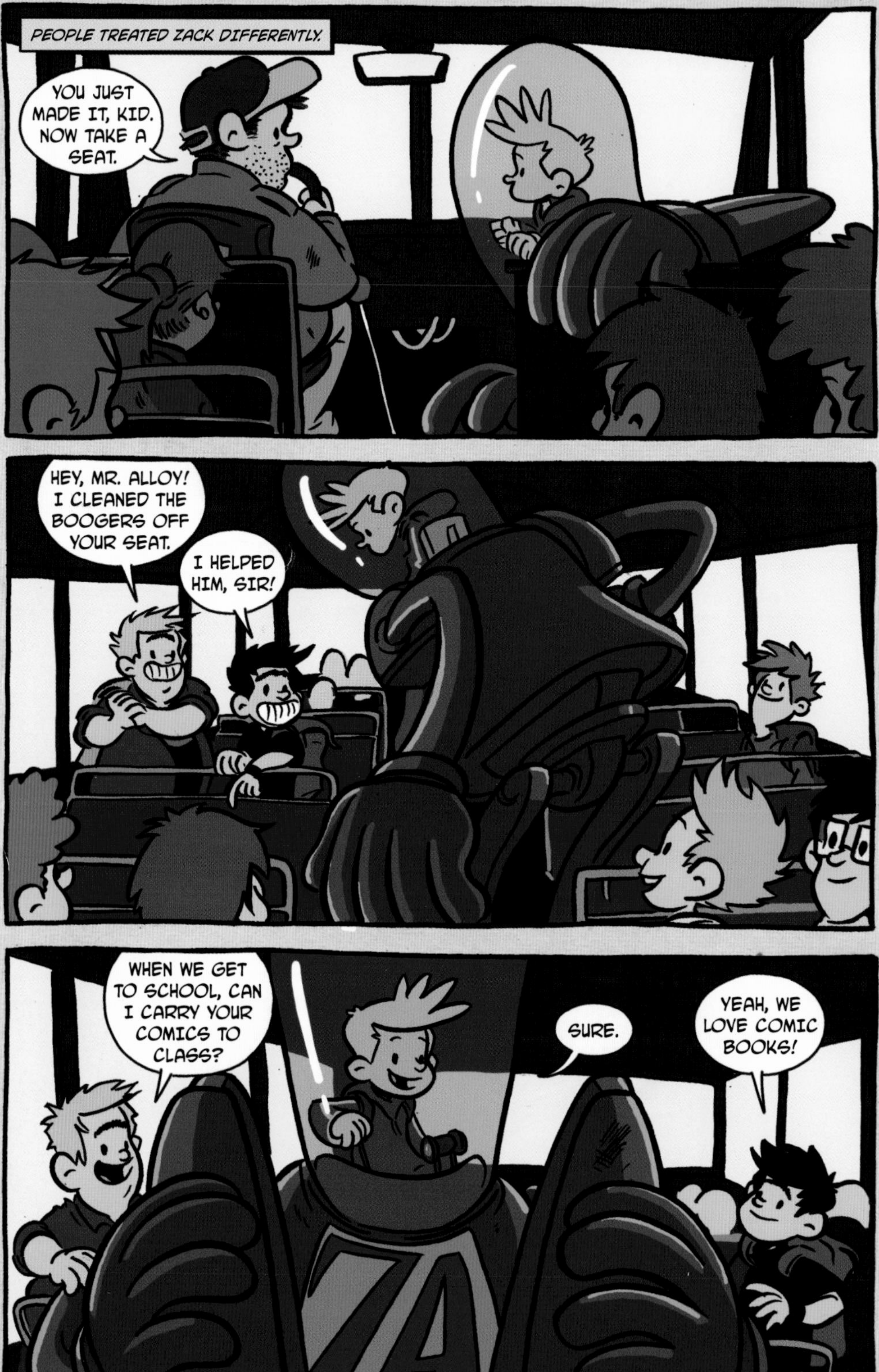
PEOPLE TREATED ZACK DIFFERENTLY.
YOU JUST MADE IT, KID. NOW TAKE A SEAT.
HEY, MR. ALLOY! I CLEANED THE BOOGERS OFF YOUR SEAT.
I HELPED HIM, SIR!
WHEN WE GET TO SCHOOL, CAN I CARRY YOUR COMICS TO CLASS?
SURE.
YEAH, WE LOVE COMIC BOOKS!

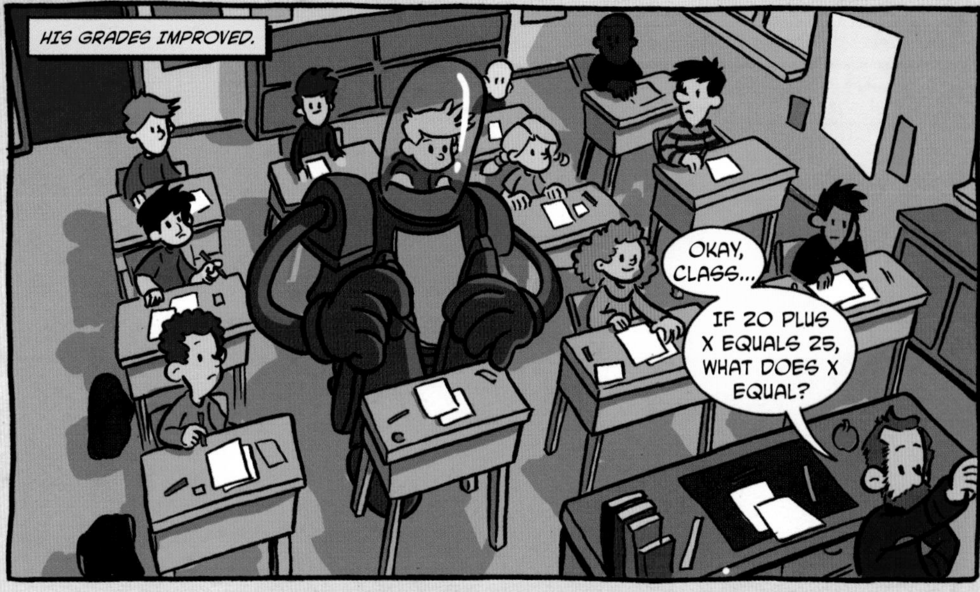
HIS GRADES IMPROVED.
OKAY, CLASS...
IF 20 PLUS X EQUALS 25, WHAT DOES X EQUAL?

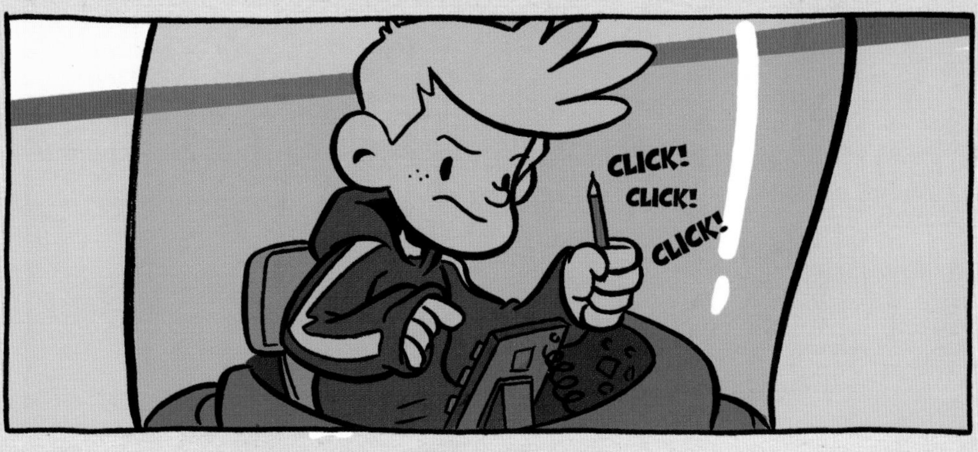
CLICK!
CLICK!
CLICK!

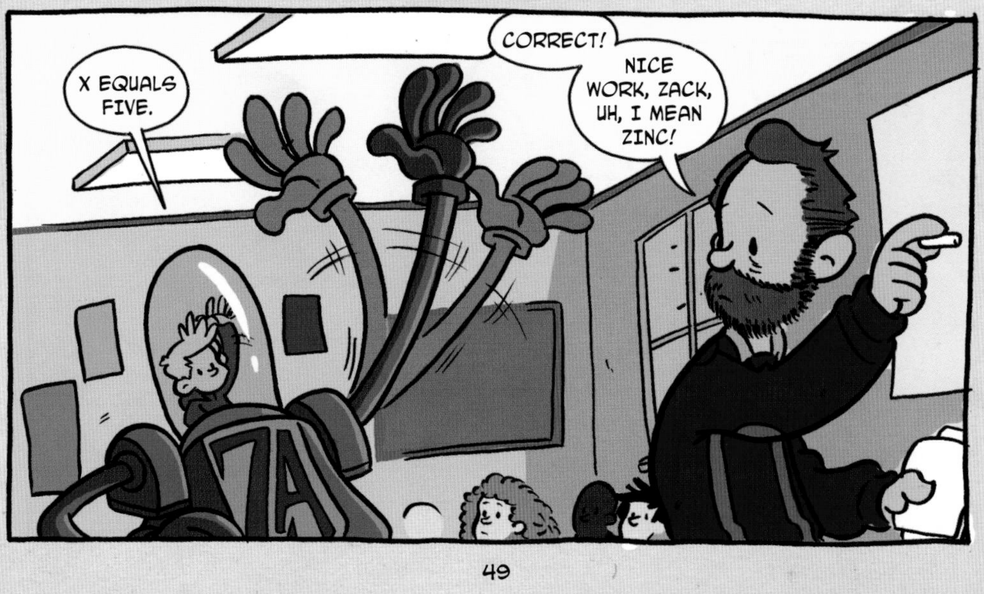
X EQUALS FIVE.
CORRECT!
NICE WORK, ZACK, UH, I MEAN ZINC!

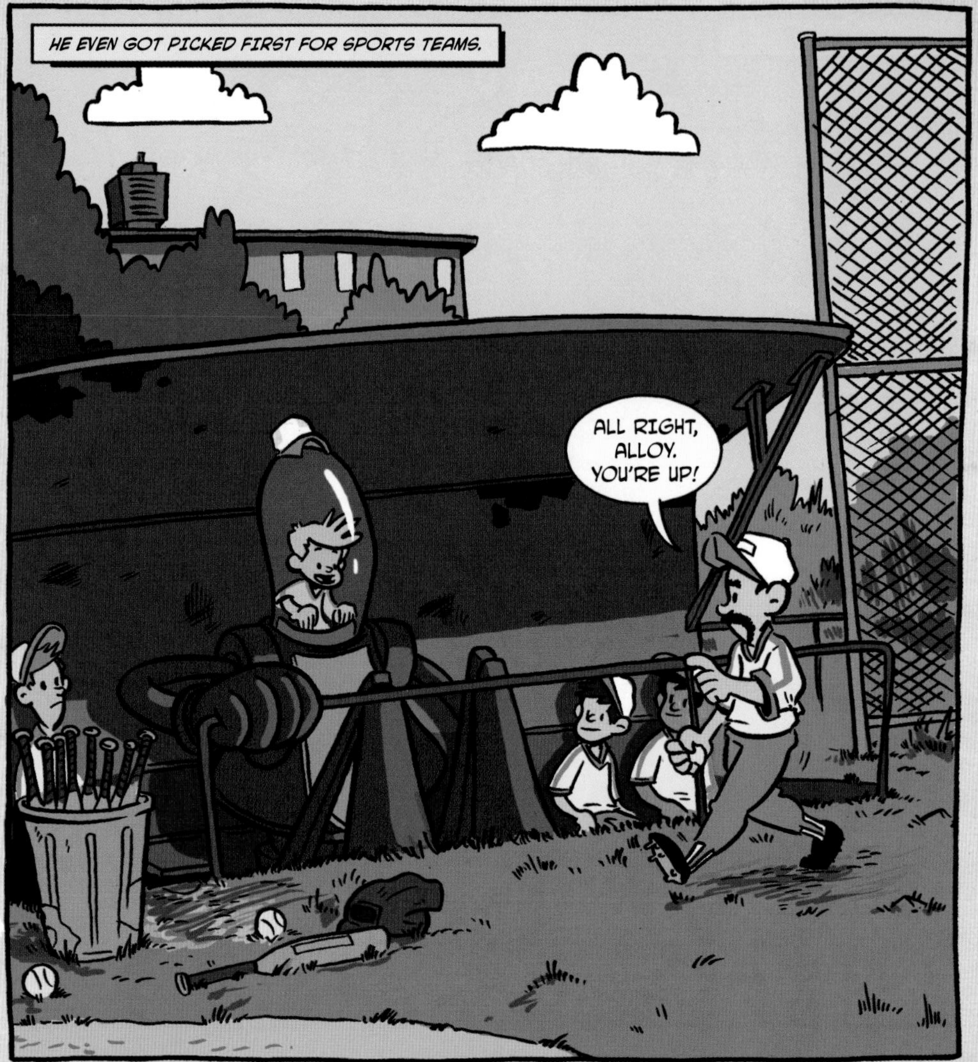
HE EVEN GOT PICKED FIRST FOR SPORTS TEAMS.
ALL RIGHT, ALLOY. YOU'RE UP!

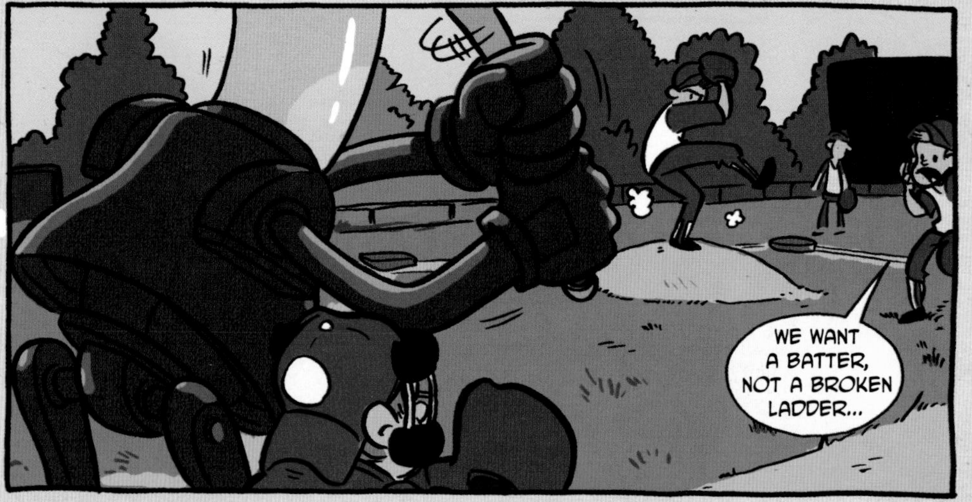
WE WANT A BATTER, NOT A BROKEN LADDER...

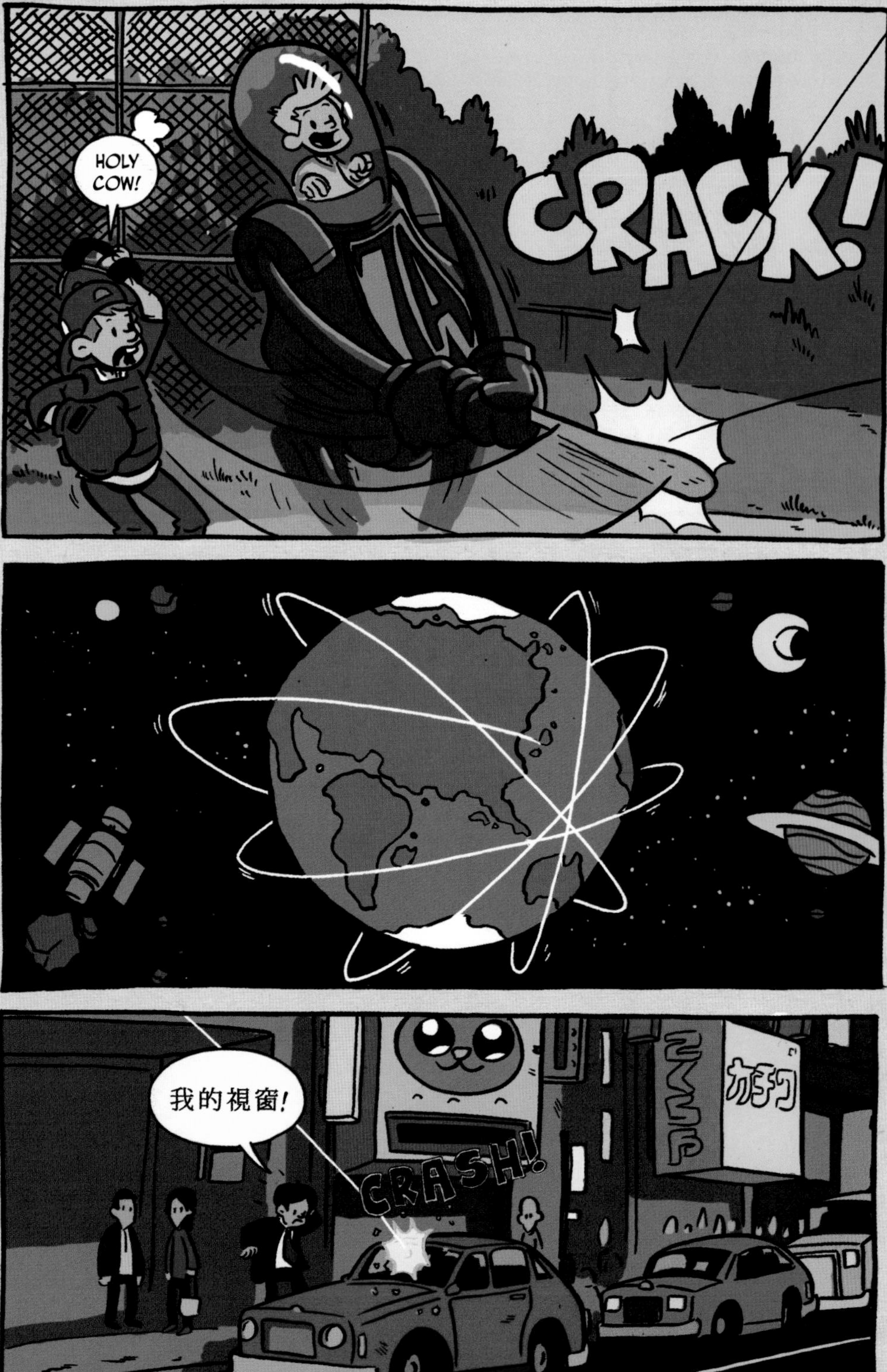
HOLY COW!
CRACK!
我的視窗!
CRASH!

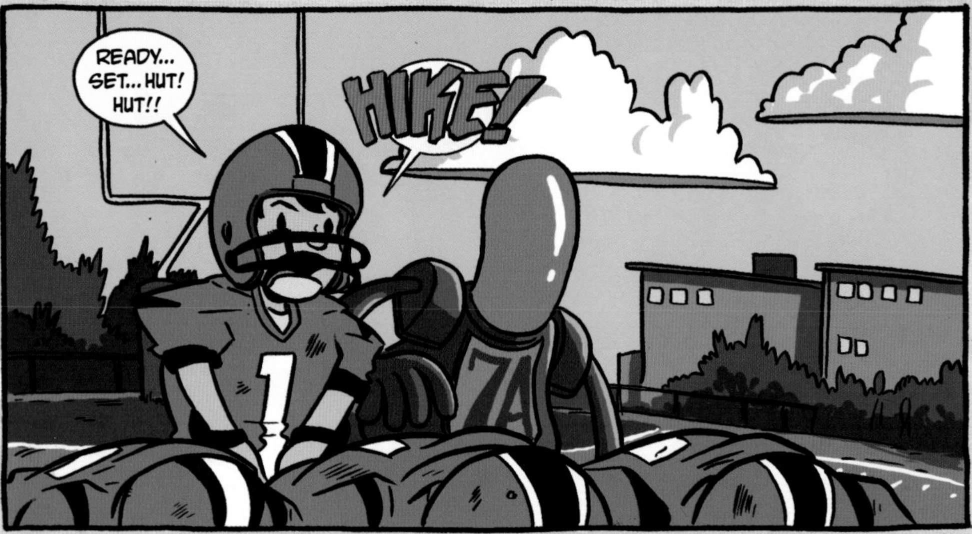
READY... SET... HUT! HUT!!
HIKE!

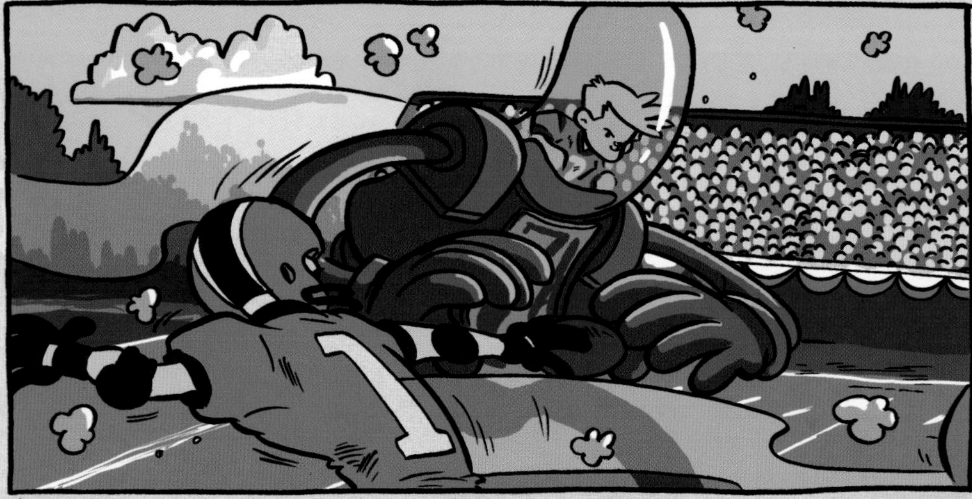

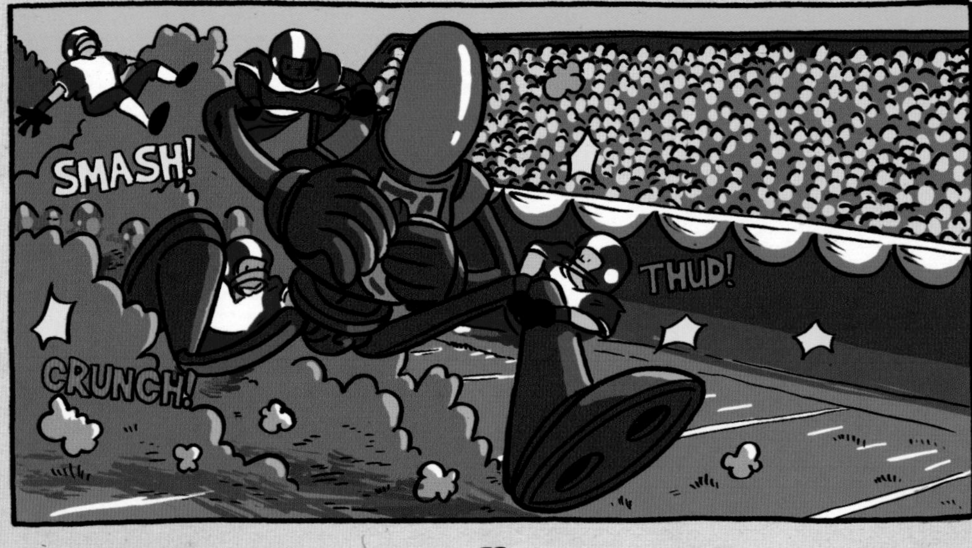
SMASH!
THUD!
CRUNCH!

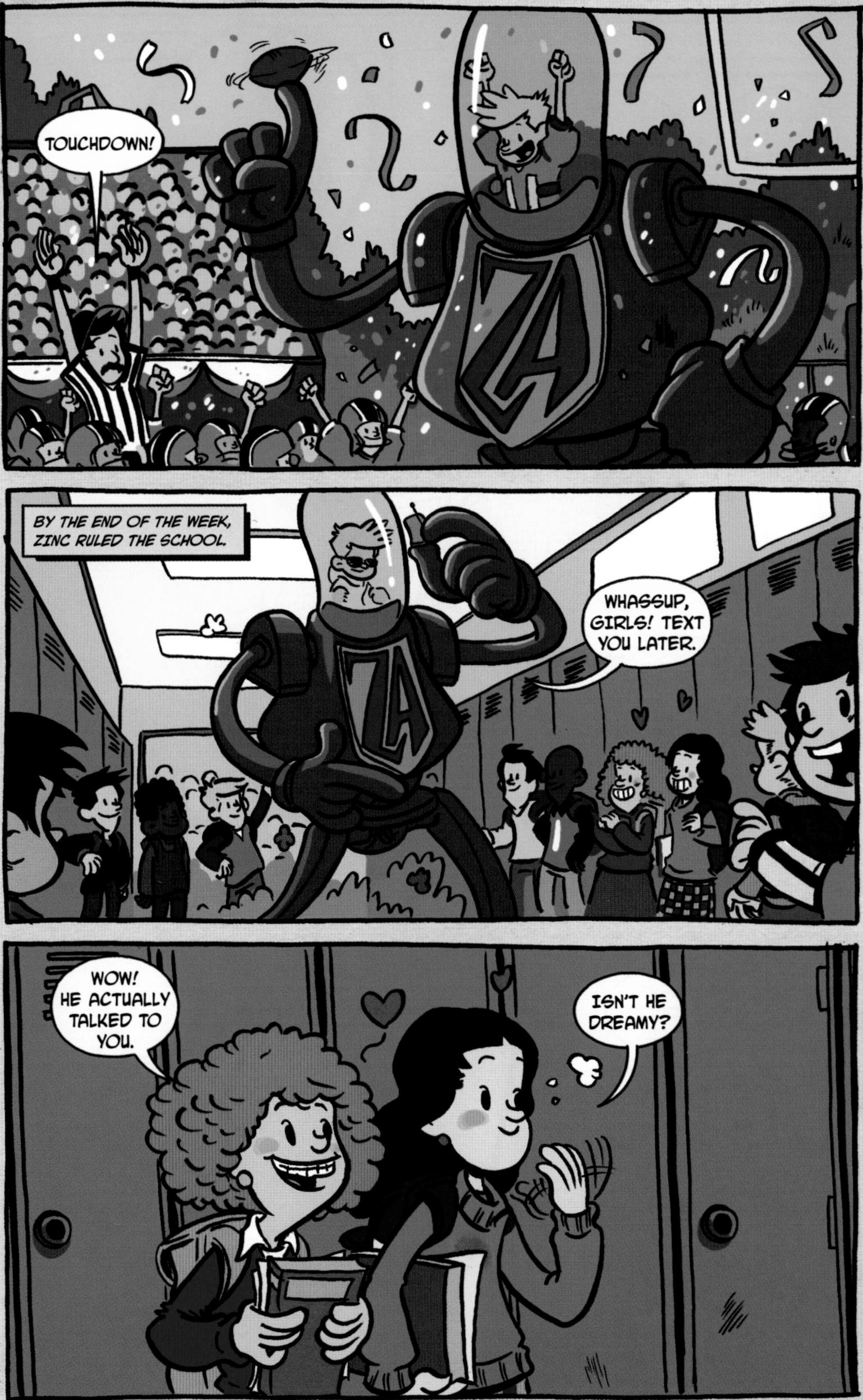
TOUCHDOWN!
BY THE END OF THE WEEK, ZINC RULED THE SCHOOL.
WHASSUP, GIRLS! TEXT YOU LATER.
WOW! HE ACTUALLY TALKED TO YOU.
ISN'T HE DREAMY?

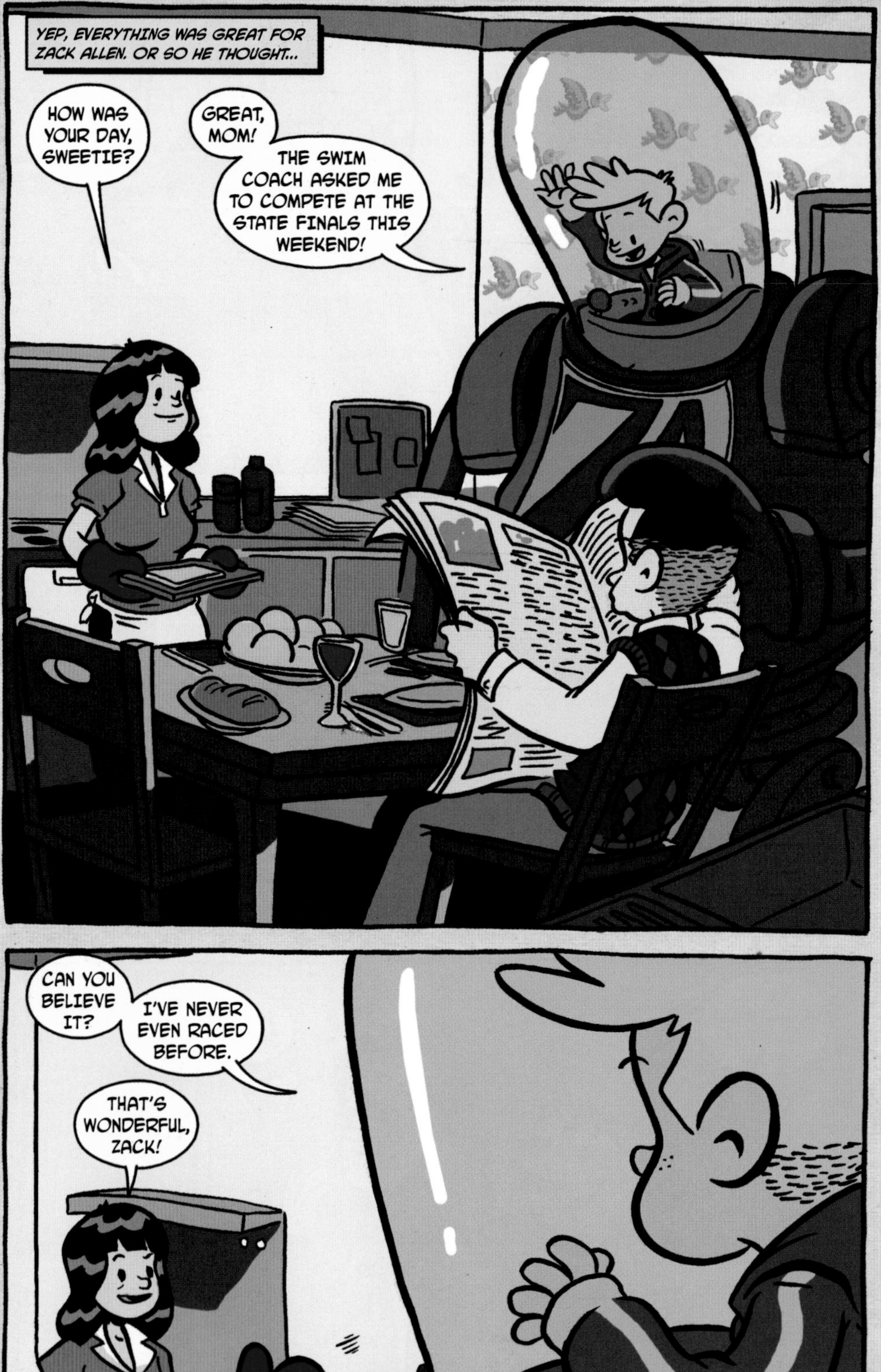
YEP, EVERYTHING WAS GREAT FOR ZACK ALLEN. OR SO HE THOUGHT...
HOW WAS YOUR DAY, SWEETIE?
GREAT, MOM!
THE SWIM COACH ASKED ME TO COMPETE AT THE STATE FINALS THIS WEEKEND!
CAN YOU BELIEVE IT?
I'VE NEVER EVEN RACED BEFORE.
THAT'S WONDERFUL, ZACK!

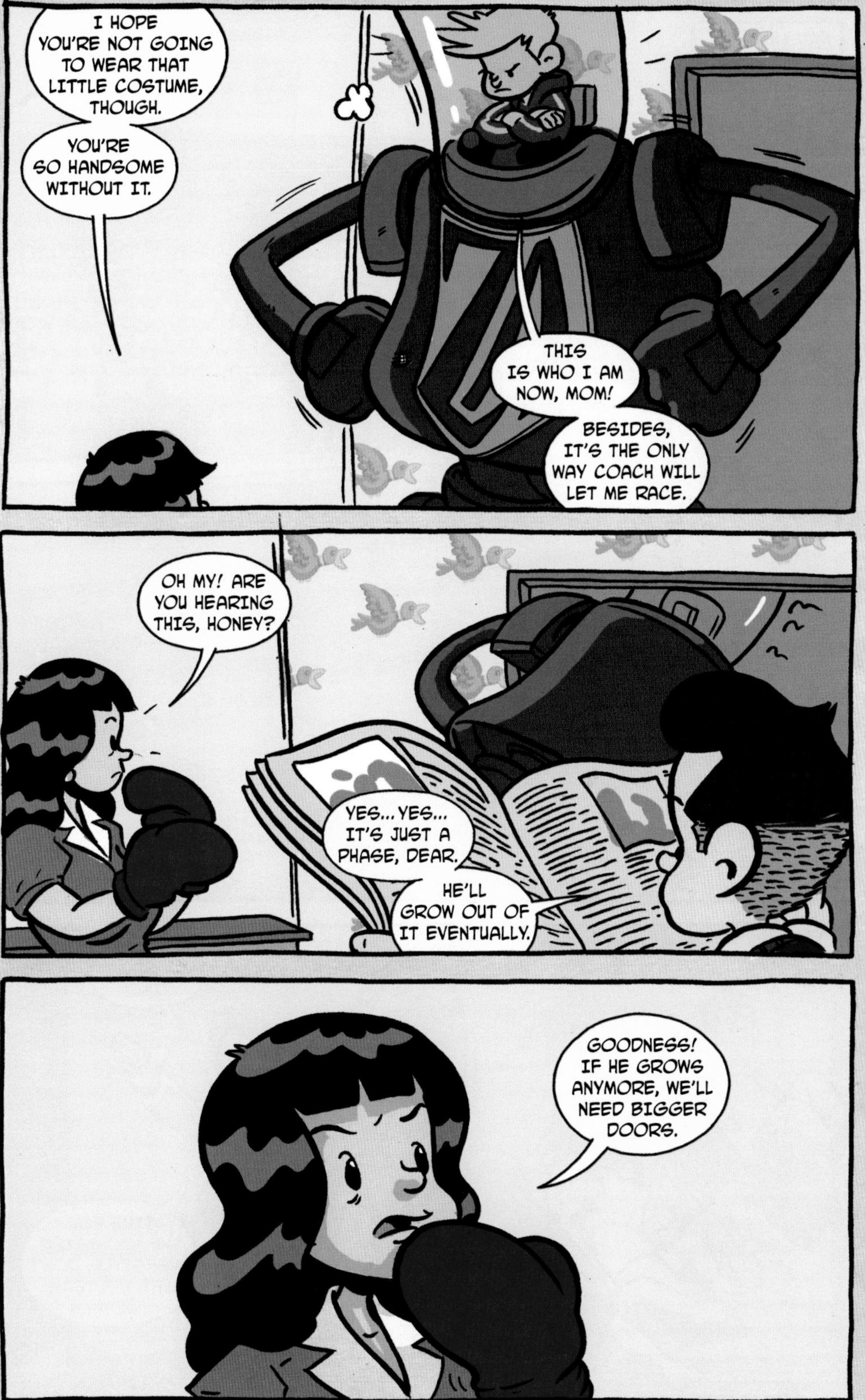
I HOPE YOU'RE NOT GOING TO WEAR THAT LITTLE COSTUME, THOUGH.
YOU'RE SO HANDSOME WITHOUT IT.
THIS IS WHO I AM NOW, MOM!
BESIDES, IT'S THE ONLY WAY COACH WILL LET ME RACE.
OH MY! ARE YOU HEARING THIS, HONEY?
YES... YES... IT'S JUST A PHASE, DEAR.
HE'LL GROW OUT OF IT EVENTUALLY.
GOODNESS! IF HE GROWS ANYMORE, WE'LL NEED BIGGER DOORS.

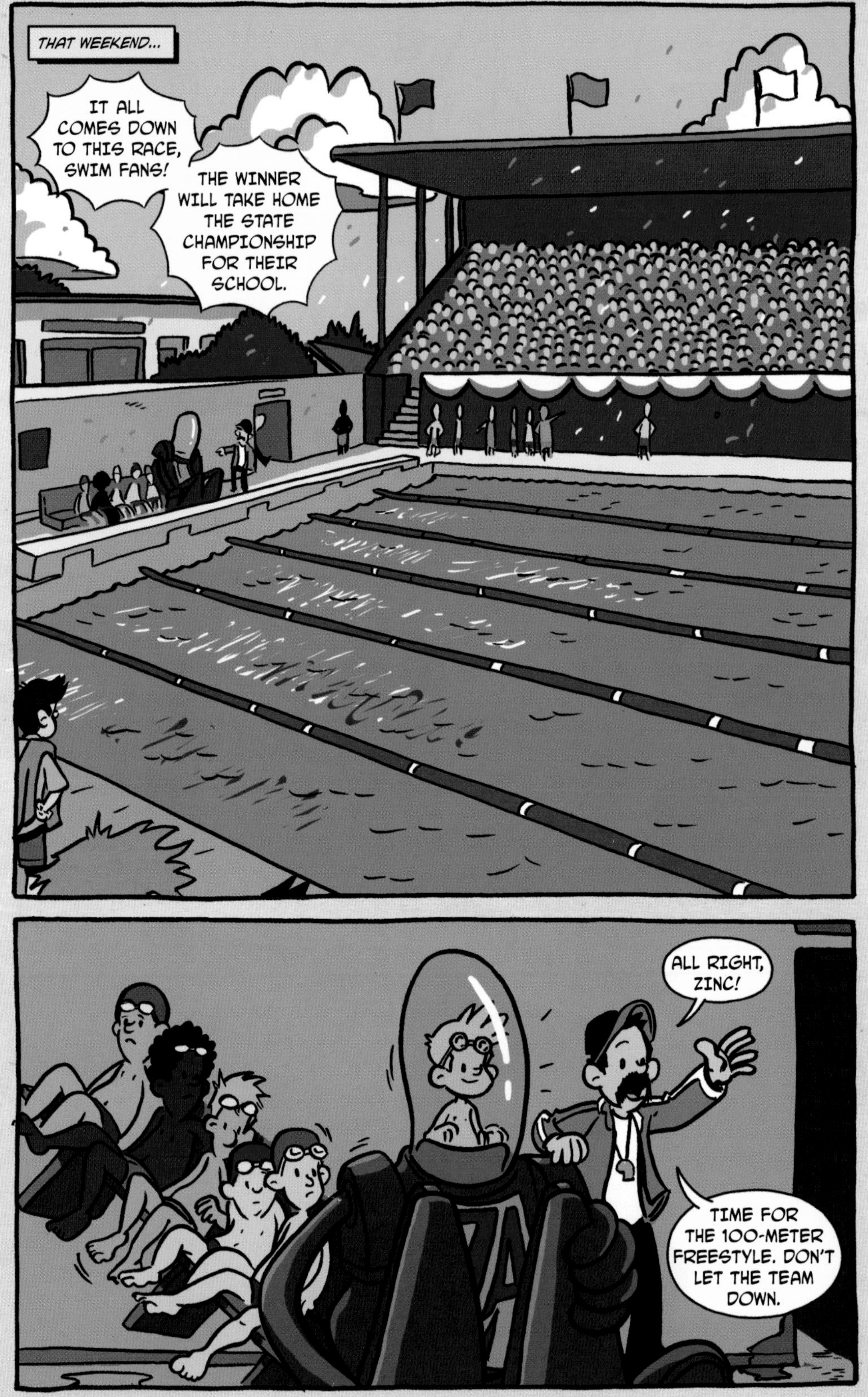
THAT WEEKEND...
IT ALL COMES DOWN TO THIS RACE, SWIM FANS!
THE WINNER WILL TAKE HOME THE STATE CHAMPIONSHIP FOR THEIR SCHOOL.
ALL RIGHT, ZINC!
TIME FOR THE 100-METER FREESTYLE. DON'T LET THE TEAM DOWN.

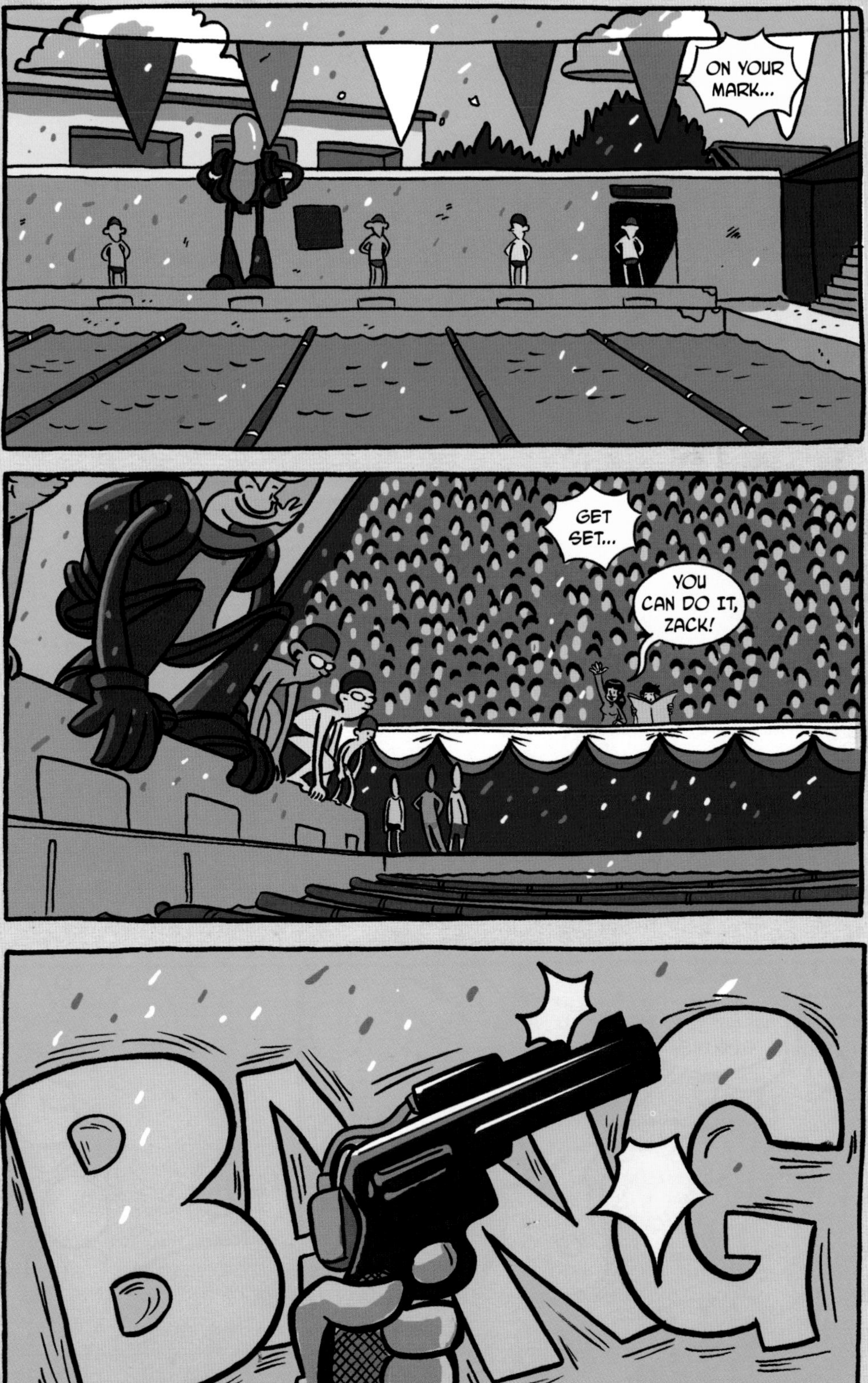
ON YOUR MARK...
GET SET...
YOU CAN DO IT, ZACK!
BANG

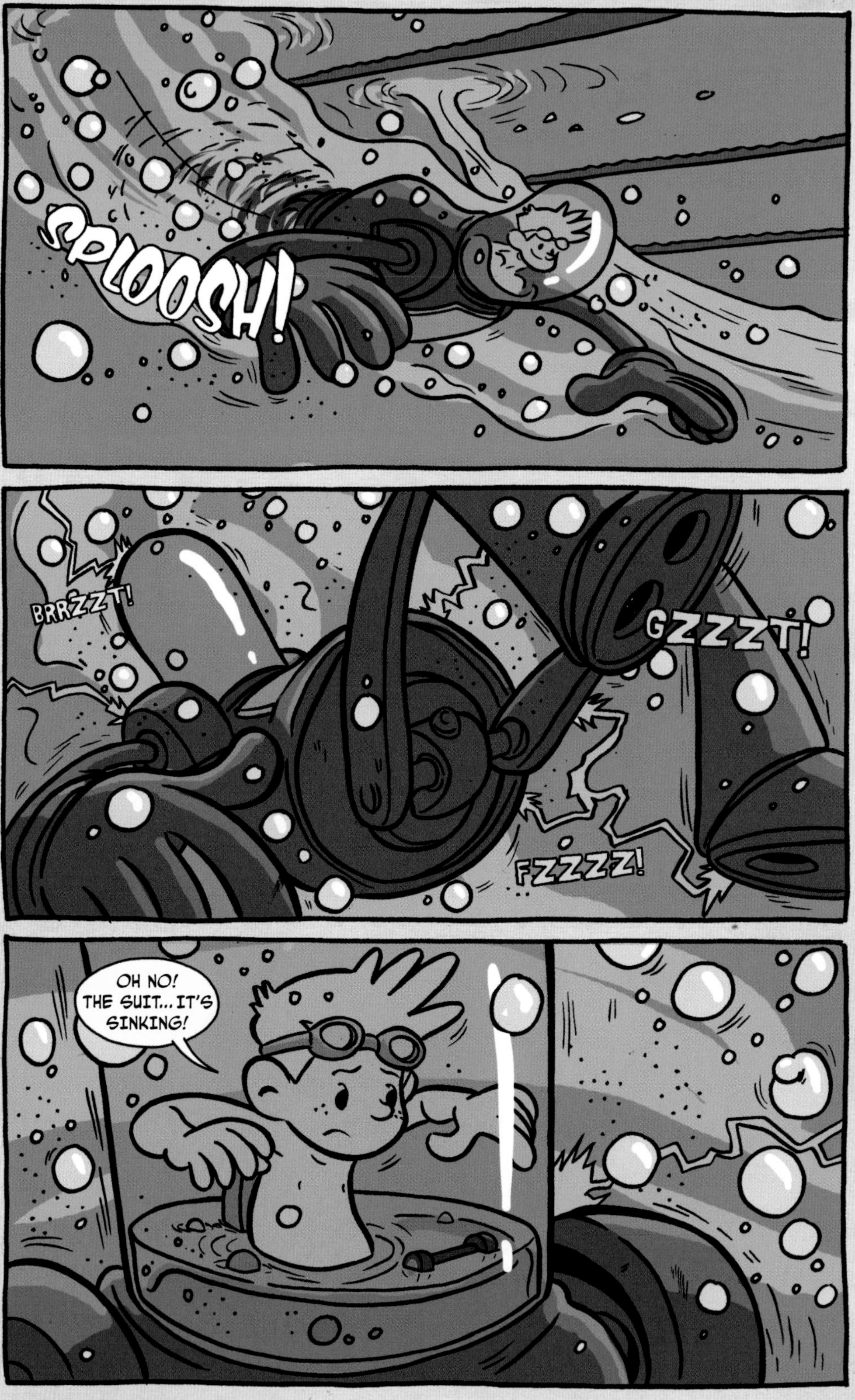
SPLOOSH!
BRRZZZT!
GZZZZT!
FZZZZ!
OH NO! THE SUIT... IT'S SINKING!

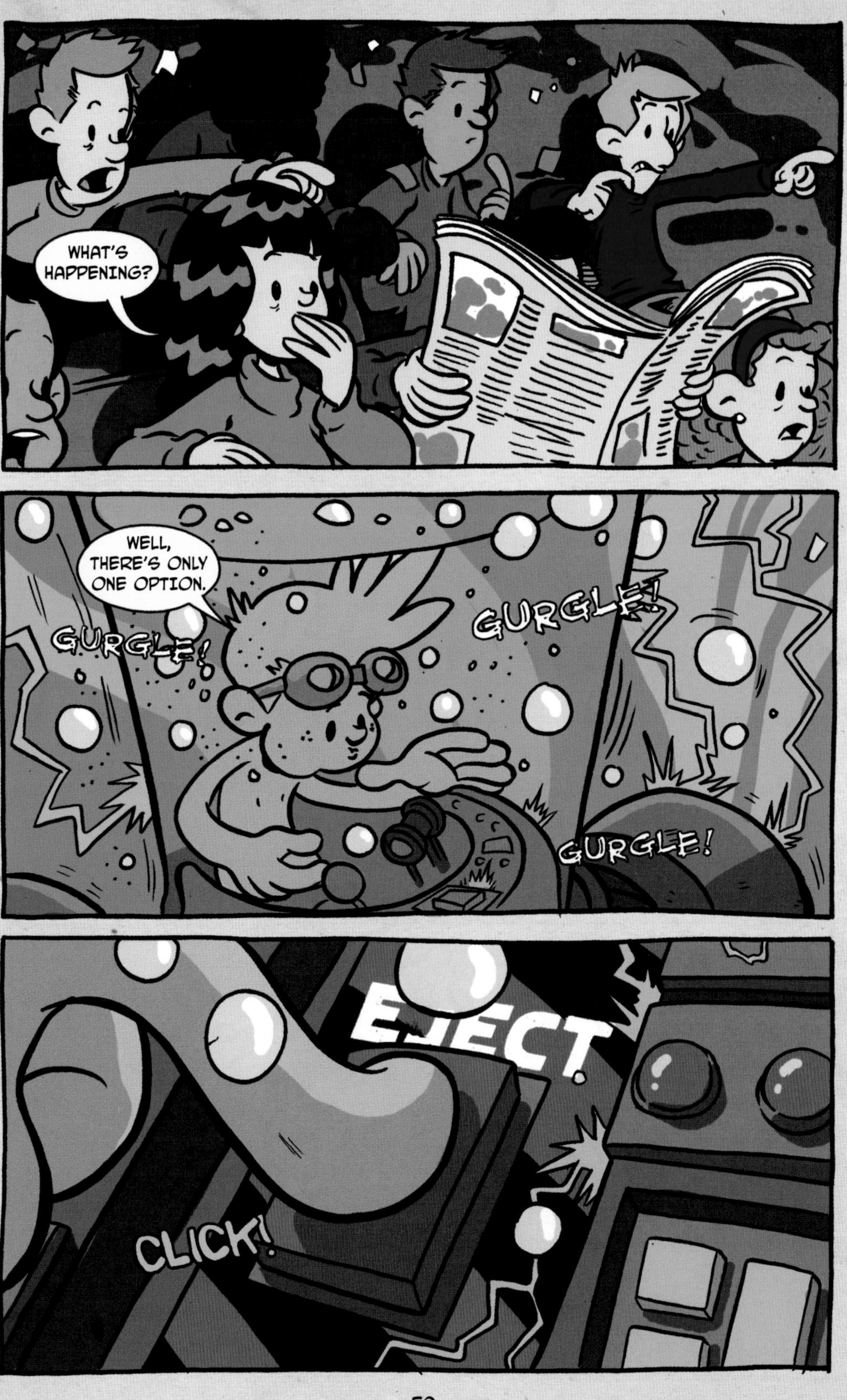
WHAT'S HAPPENING?
WELL, THERE'S ONLY ONE OPTION.
GURGLE!
GURGLE!
GURGLE!
EJECT
CLICK!

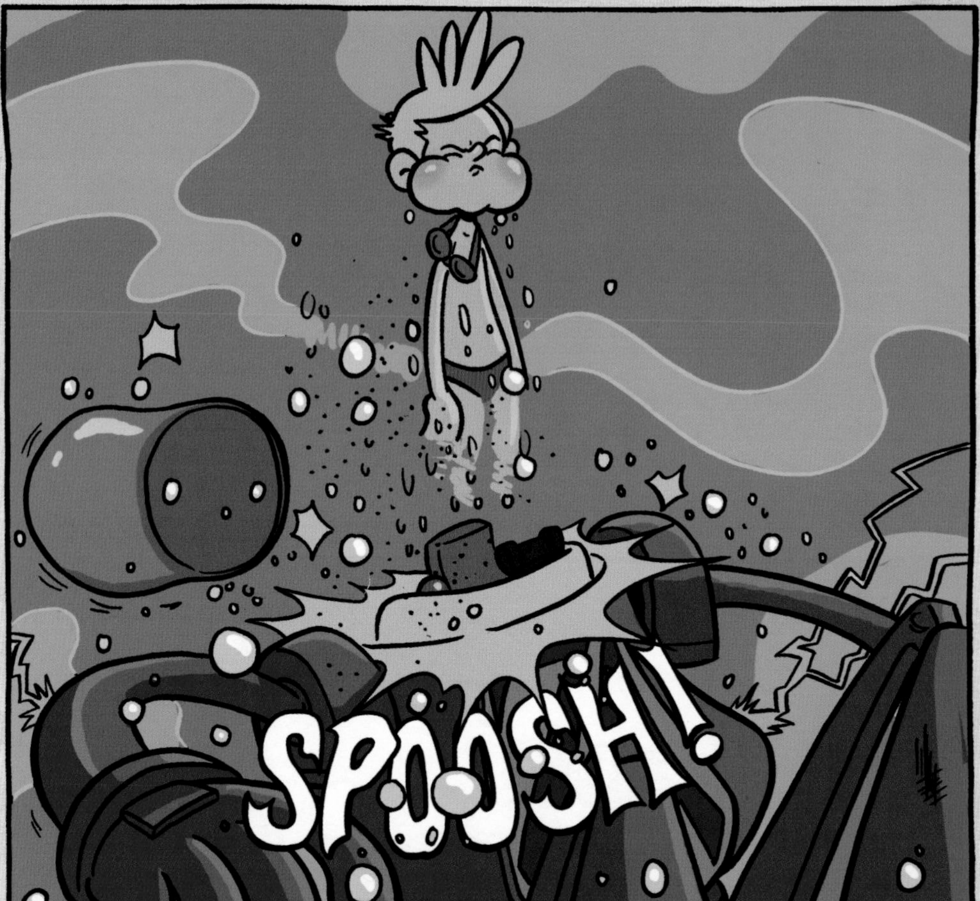
SPOOSH!

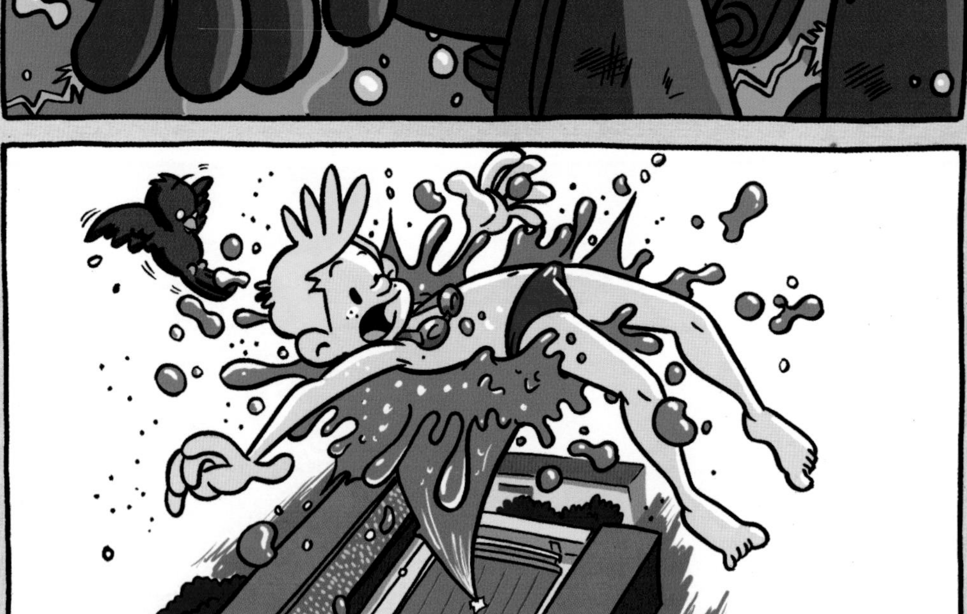

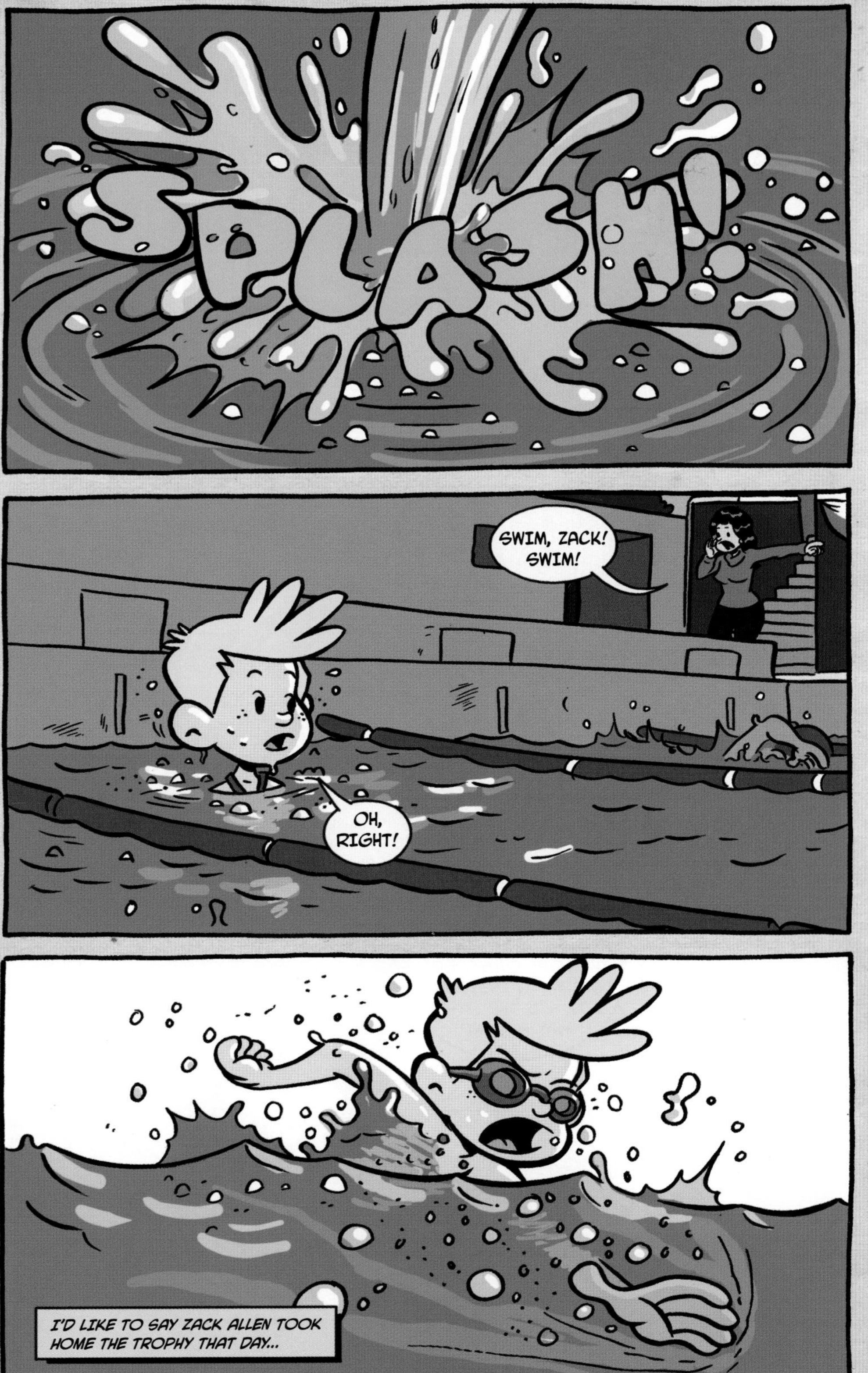
SPLASH!
SWIM, ZACK! SWIM!
OH, RIGHT!
I'D LIKE TO SAY ZACK ALLEN TOOK HOME THE TROPHY THAT DAY...

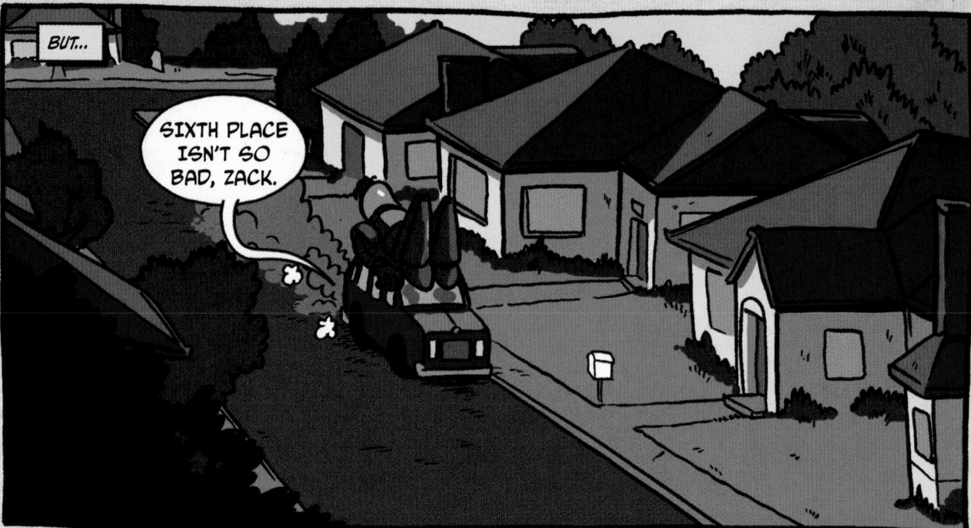
BUT...
SIXTH PLACE ISN'T SO BAD, ZACK.

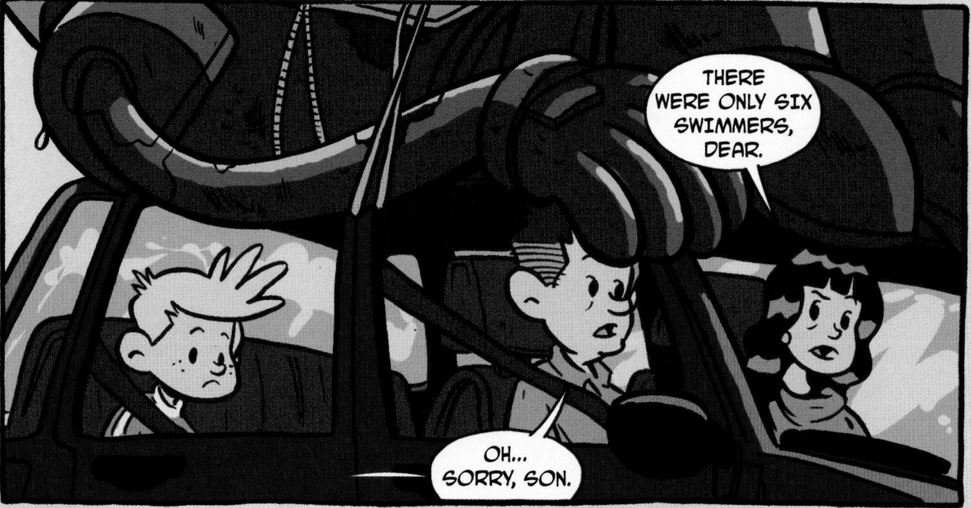
THERE WERE ONLY SIX SWIMMERS, DEAR.
OH... SORRY, SON.

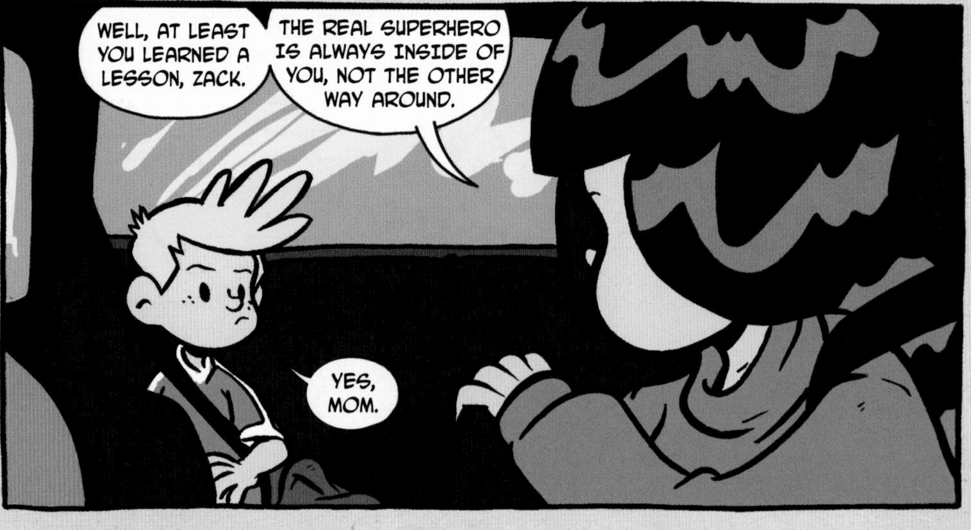
WELL, AT LEAST YOU LEARNED A LESSON, ZACK.
THE REAL SUPERHERO IS ALWAYS INSIDE OF YOU, NOT THE OTHER WAY AROUND.
YES, MOM.

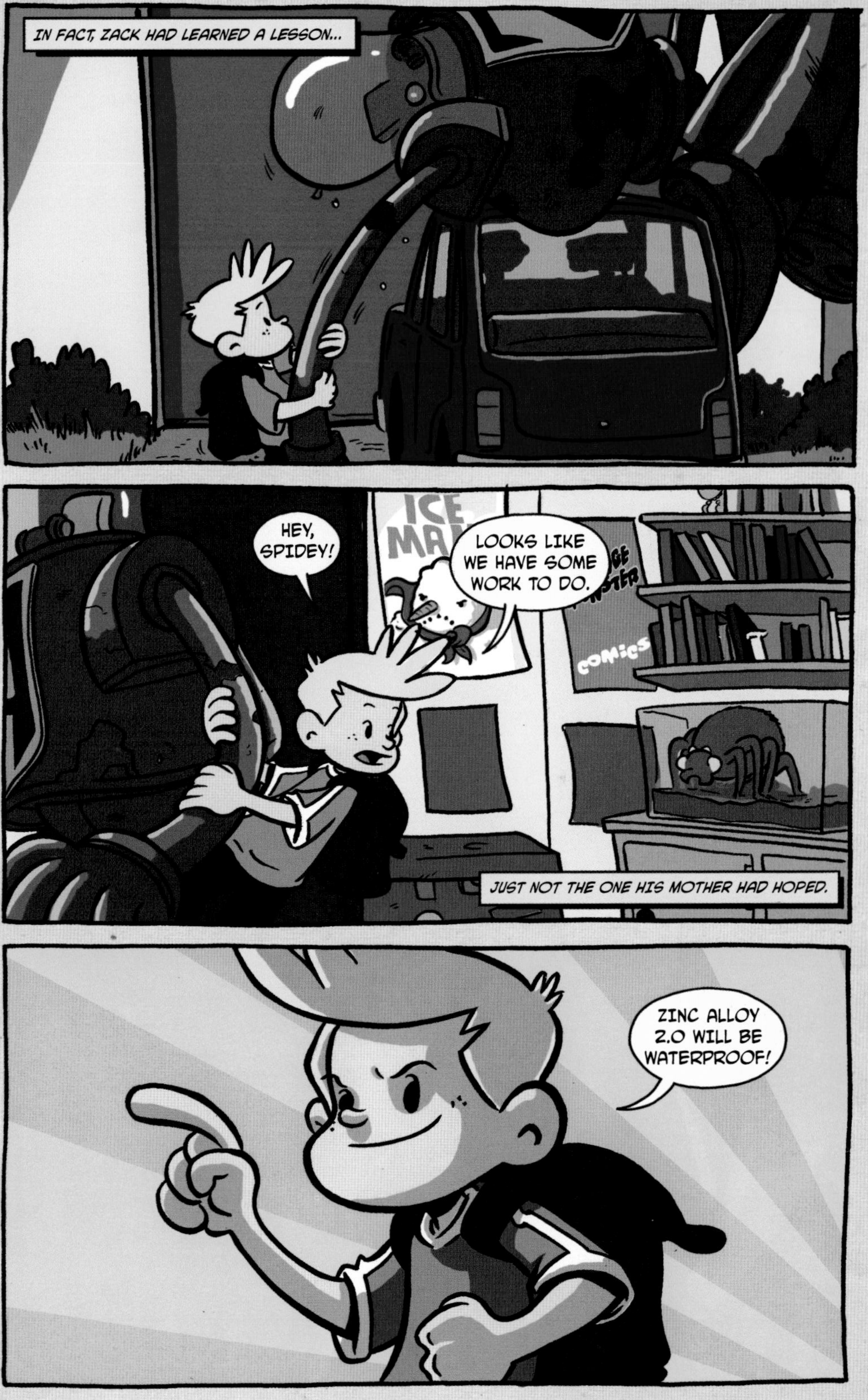
IN FACT, ZACK HAD LEARNED A LESSON...
HEY, SPIDEY!
LOOKS LIKE WE HAVE SOME WORK TO DO.
COMICS
JUST NOT THE ONE HIS MOTHER HAD HOPED.
ZINC ALLOY 2.0 WILL BE WATERPROOF!

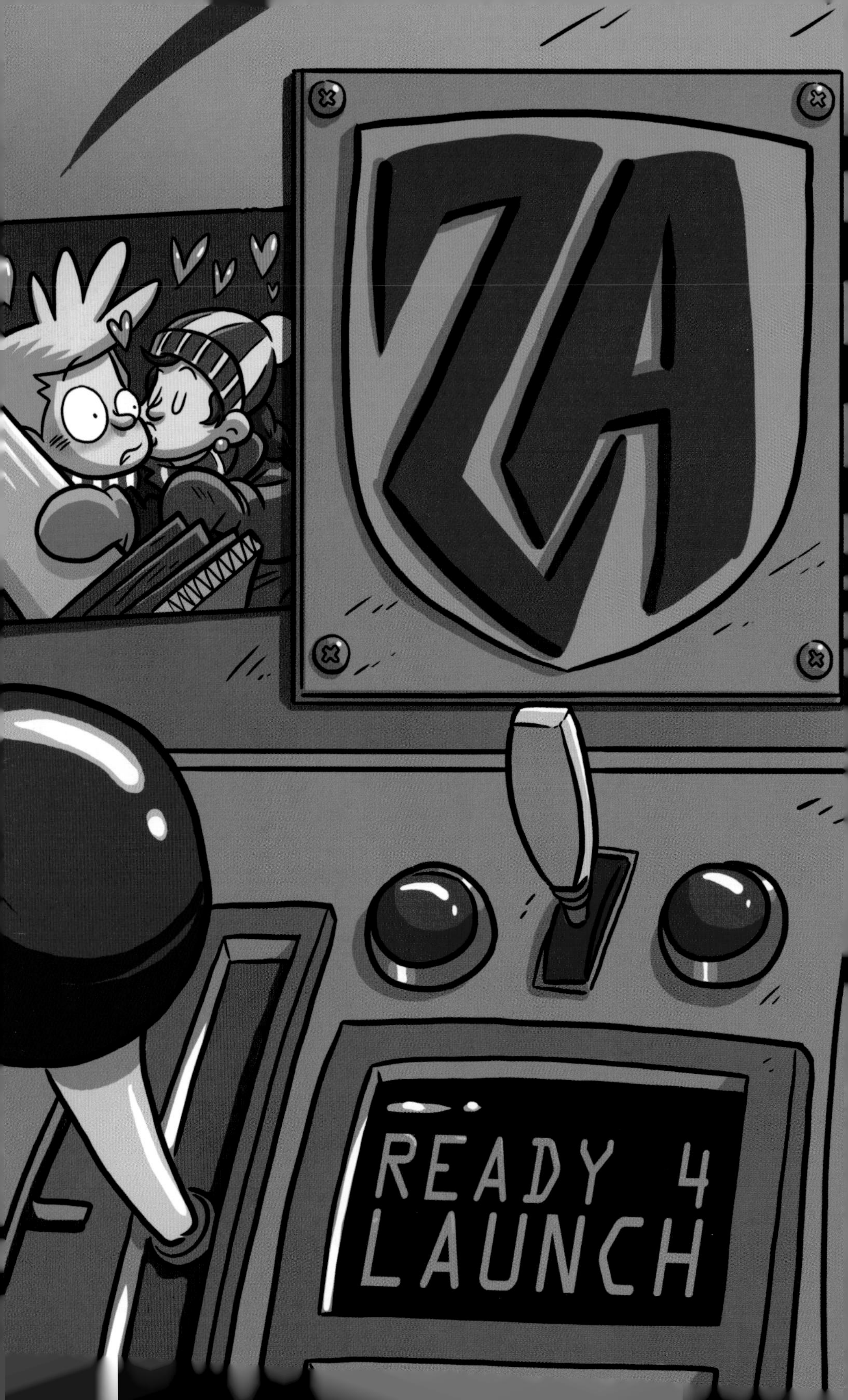
ZA
READY 4 LAUNCH

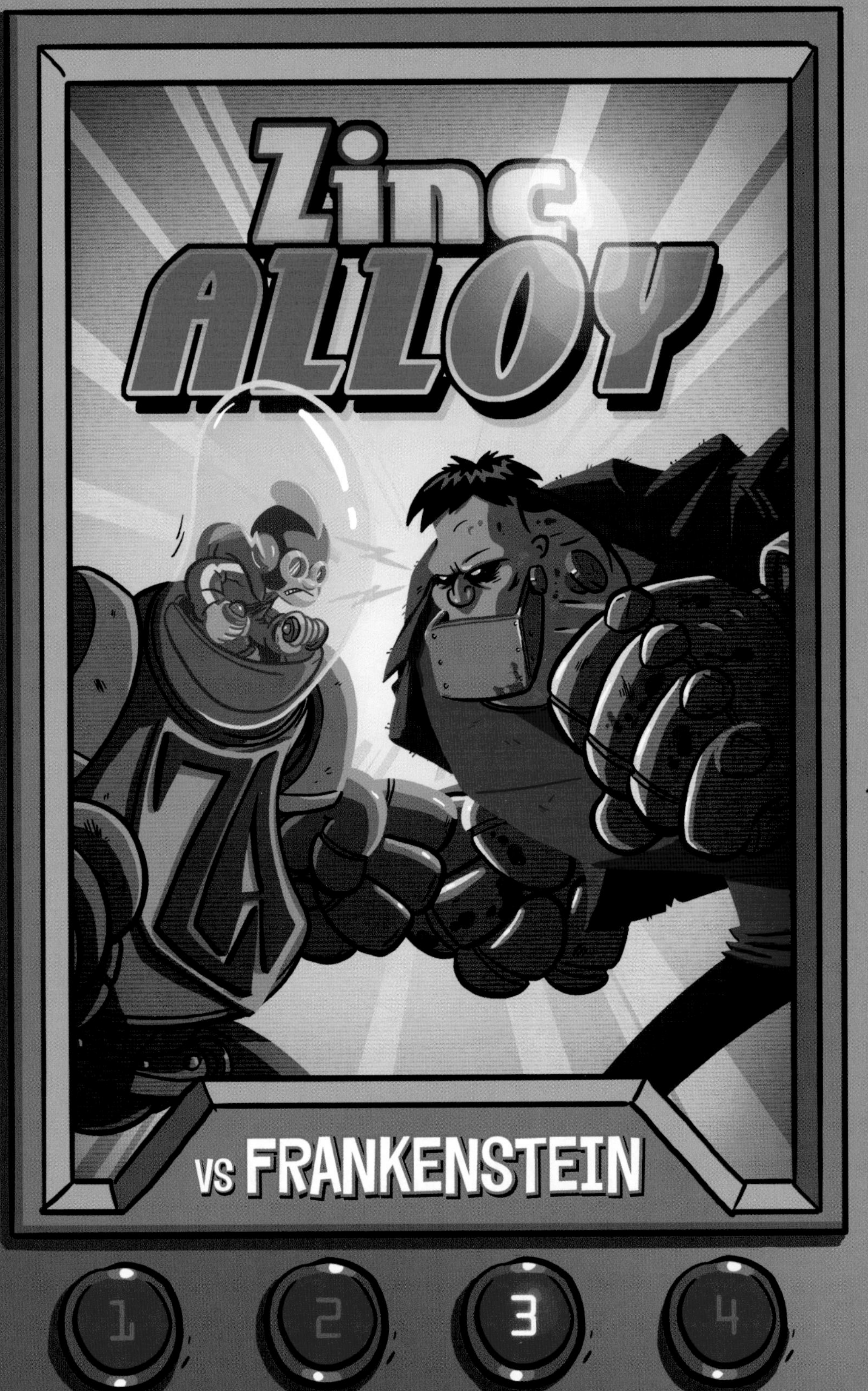
Zinc ALLOY
vs FRANKENSTEIN
1
2
3
4

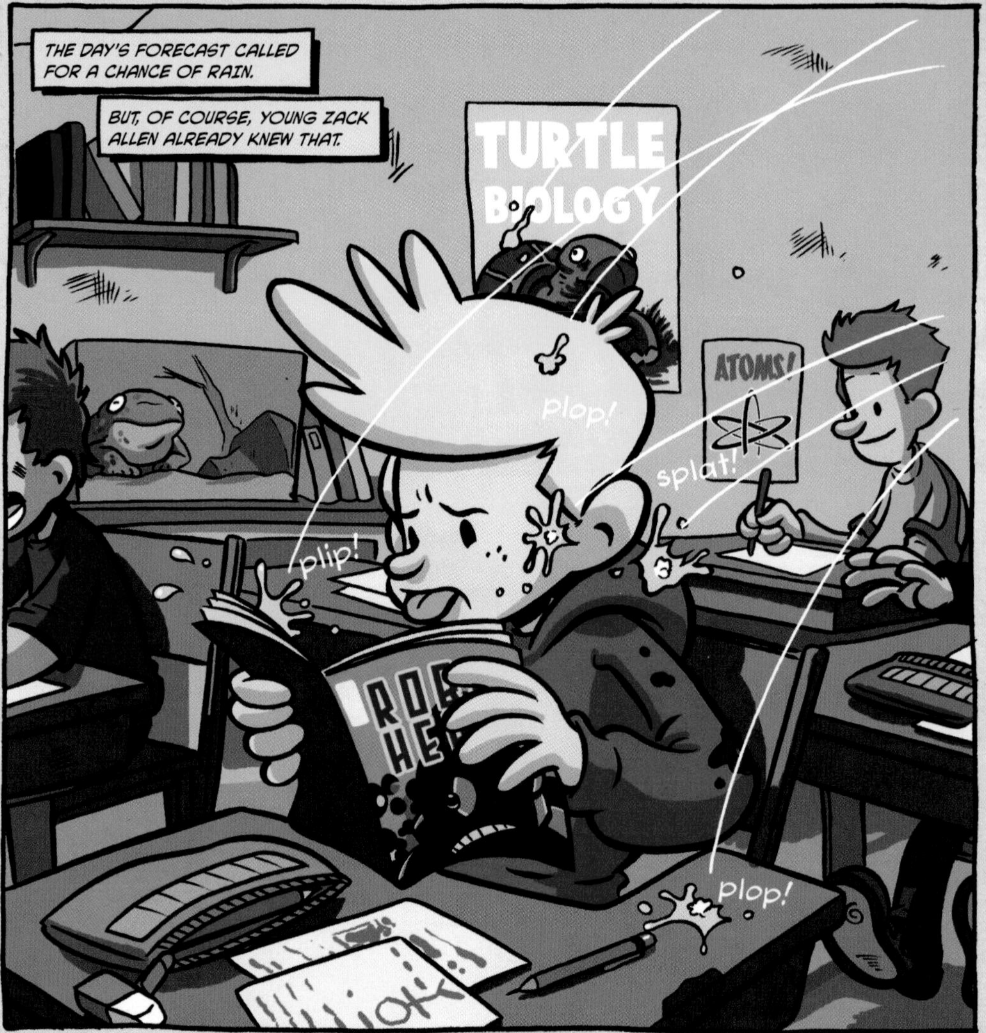
THE DAY'S FORECAST CALLED FOR A CHANCE OF RAIN.
BUT, OF COURSE, YOUNG ZACK ALLEN ALREADY KNEW THAT.
TURTLE BIOLOGY
ATOMS!
plop!
splat!
plip!
plop!

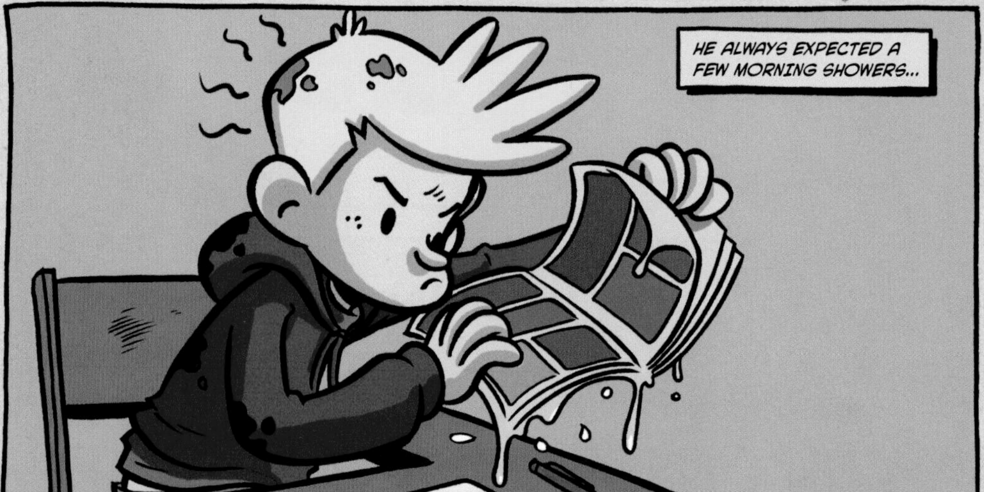
HE ALWAYS EXPECTED A FEW MORNING SHOWERS...

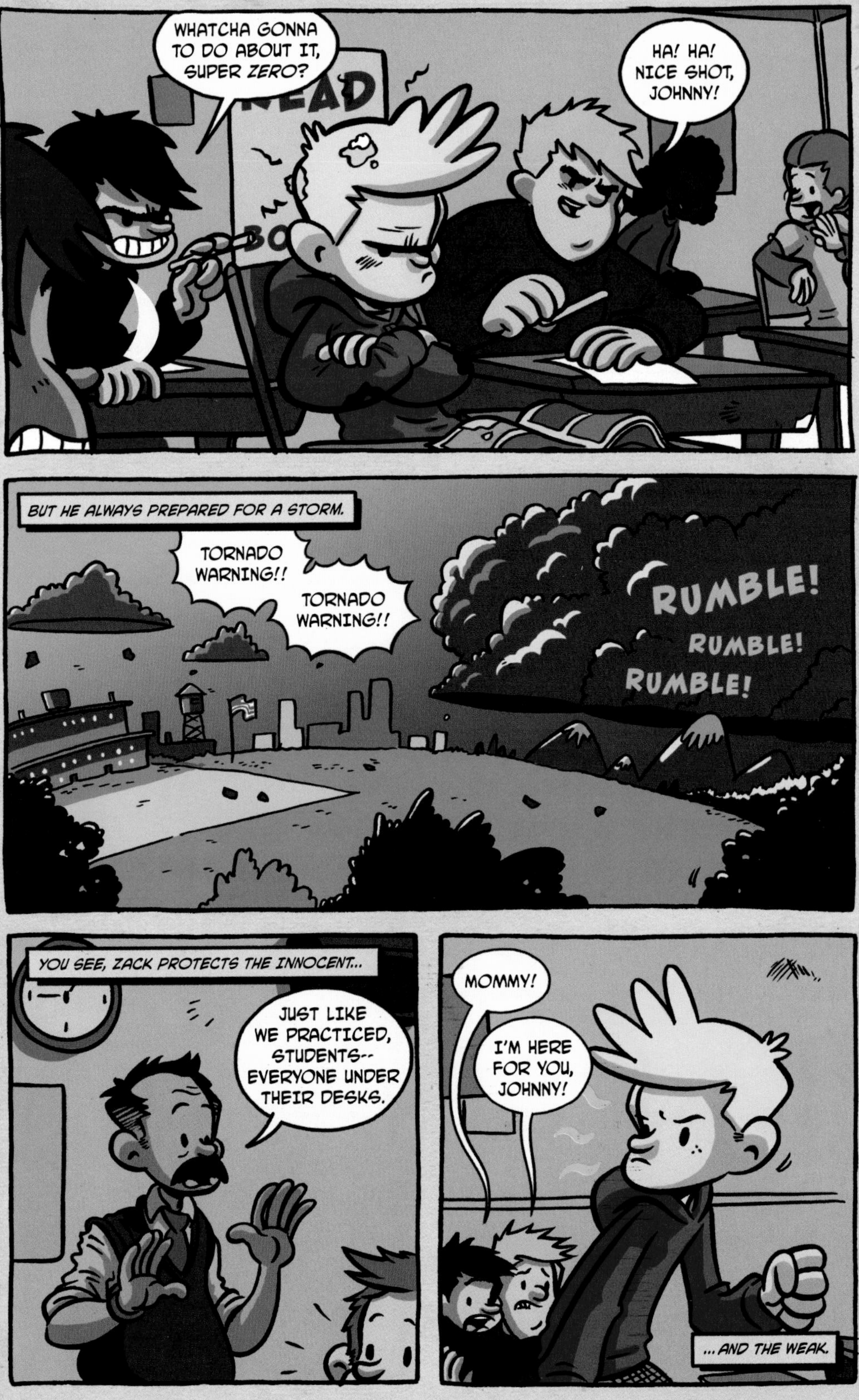
WHATCHA GONNA TO DO ABOUT IT, SUPER ZERO?
HA! HA! NICE SHOT, JOHNNY!
BUT HE ALWAYS PREPARED FOR A STORM.
TORNADO WARNING!!
TORNADO WARNING!!
RUMBLE!
RUMBLE!
RUMBLE!
YOU SEE, ZACK PROTECTS THE INNOCENT...
JUST LIKE WE PRACTICED, STUDENTS-- EVERYONE UNDER THEIR DESKS.
MOMMY!
I'M HERE FOR YOU, JOHNNY!
...AND THE WEAK.

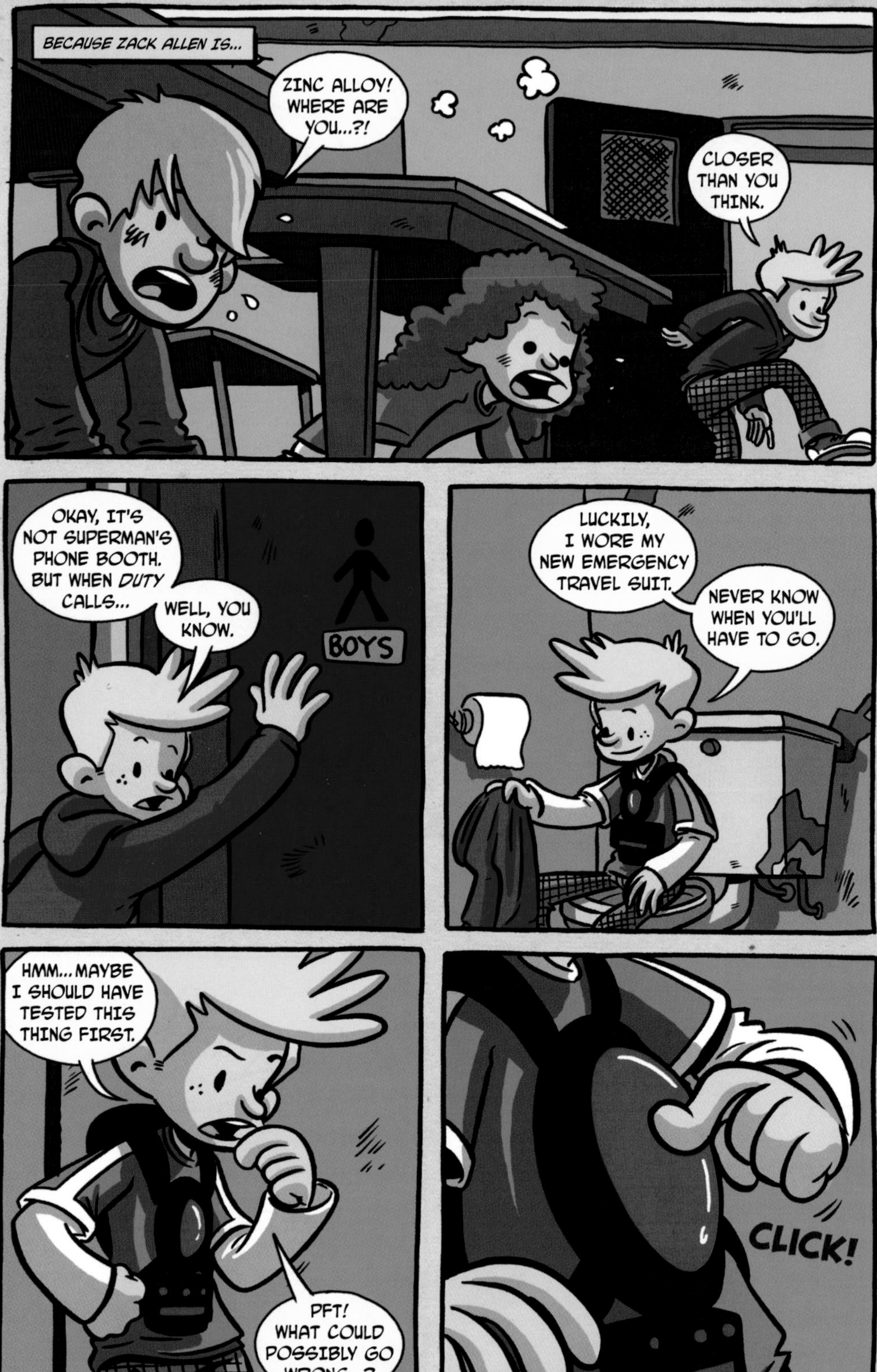
BECAUSE ZACK ALLEN IS...
ZINC ALLOY! WHERE ARE YOU...?!
CLOSER THAN YOU THINK.
OKAY, IT'S NOT SUPERMAN'S PHONE BOOTH. BUT WHEN DUTY CALLS...
WELL, YOU KNOW.
BOYS
LUCKILY, I WORE MY NEW EMERGENCY TRAVEL SUIT.
NEVER KNOW WHEN YOU'LL HAVE TO GO.
HMM... MAYBE I SHOULD HAVE TESTED THIS THING FIRST.
PFT! WHAT COULD POSSIBLY GO WRONG...?
CLICK!

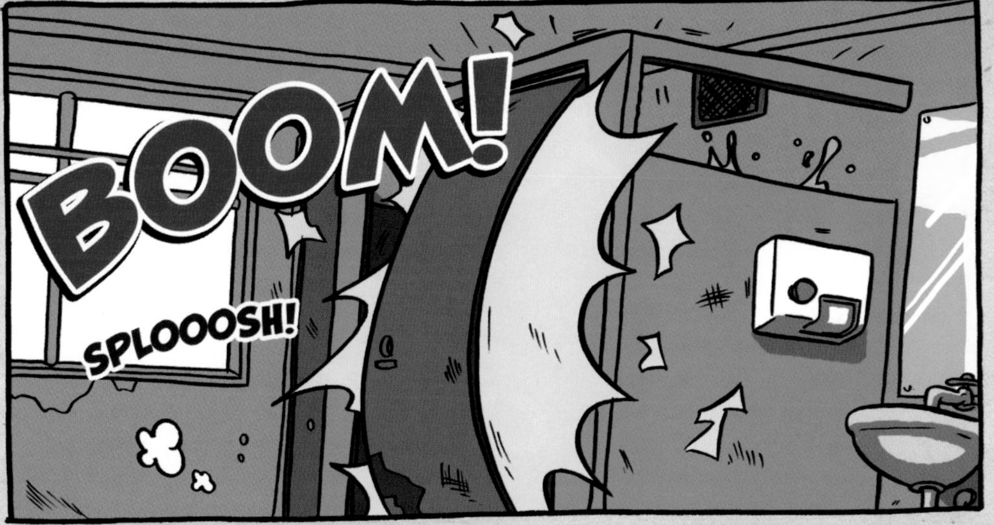
BOOM!
SPLOOOSH!

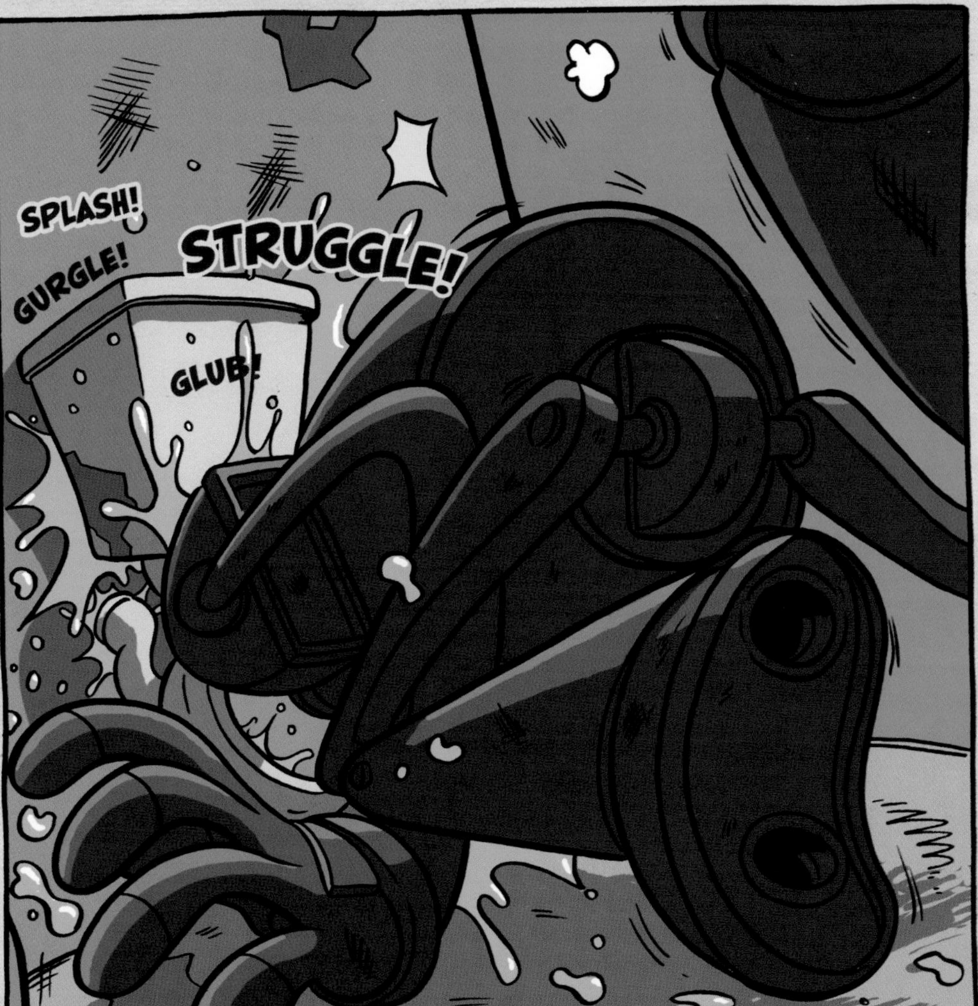
SPLASH!
GURGLE!
STRUGGLE!
GLUB!

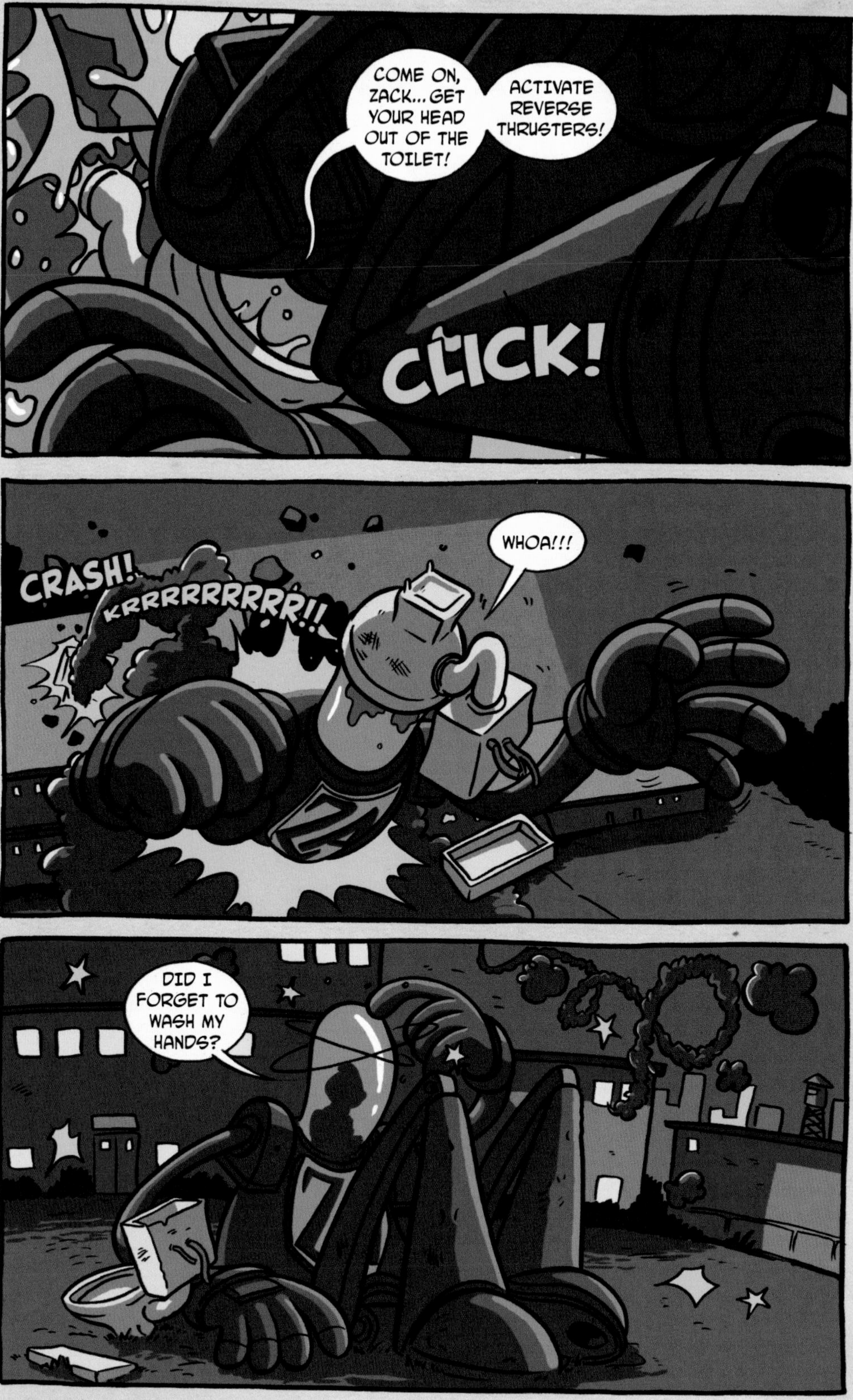
COME ON, ZACK... GET YOUR HEAD OUT OF THE TOILET!
ACTIVATE REVERSE THRUSTERS!
CLICK!
CRASH!
KRRRRRRRRR!!
WHOA!!!
DID I FORGET TO WASH MY HANDS?

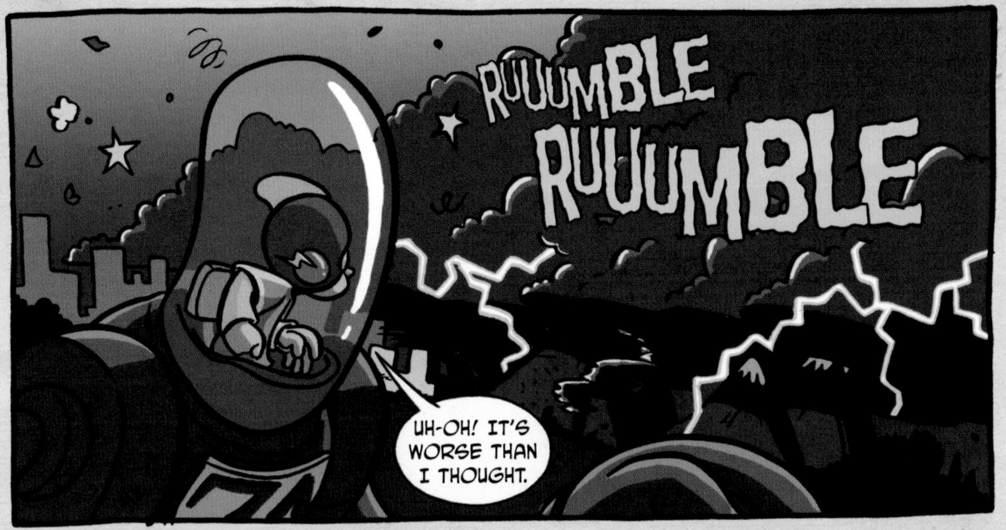
RUUUMBLE
RUUUMBLE
UH-OH! IT'S WORSE THAN I THOUGHT.

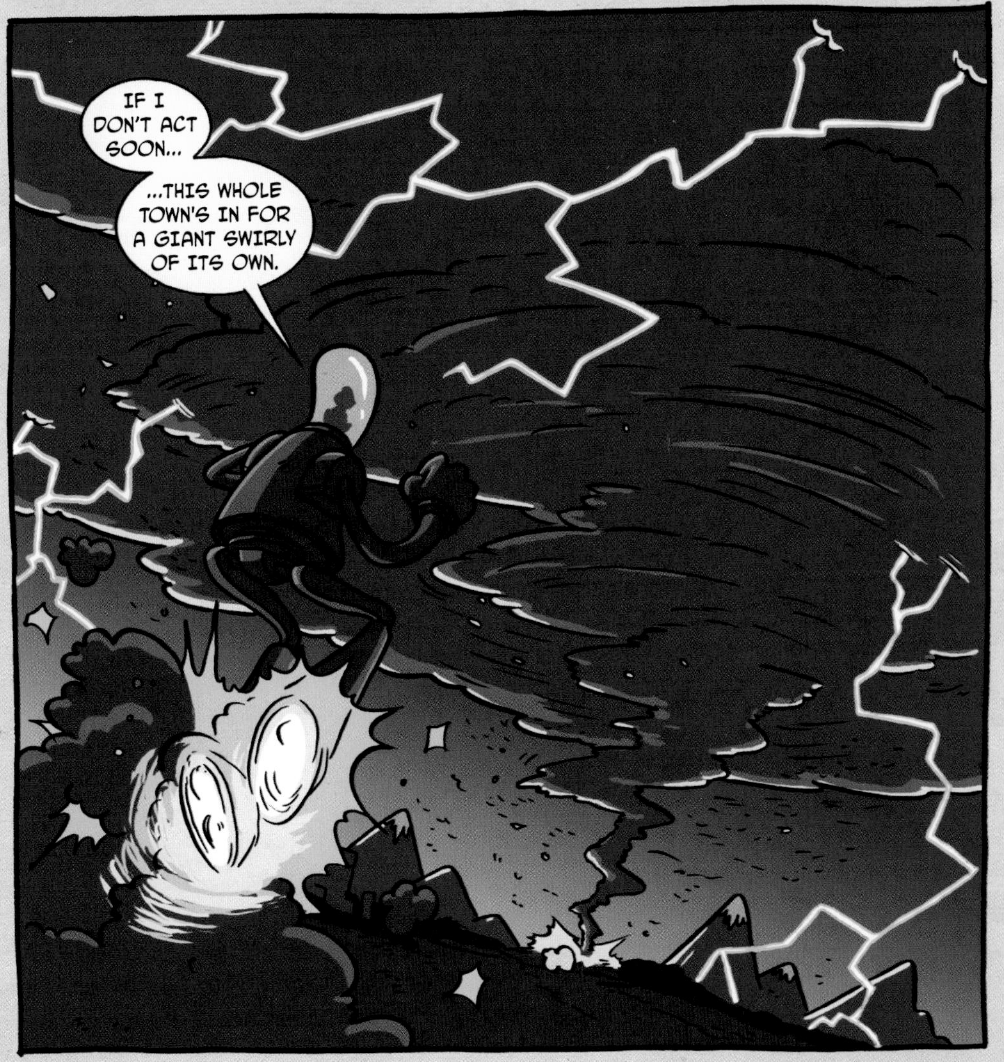
IF I DON'T ACT SOON...
...THIS WHOLE TOWN'S IN FOR A GIANT SWIRLY OF ITS OWN.

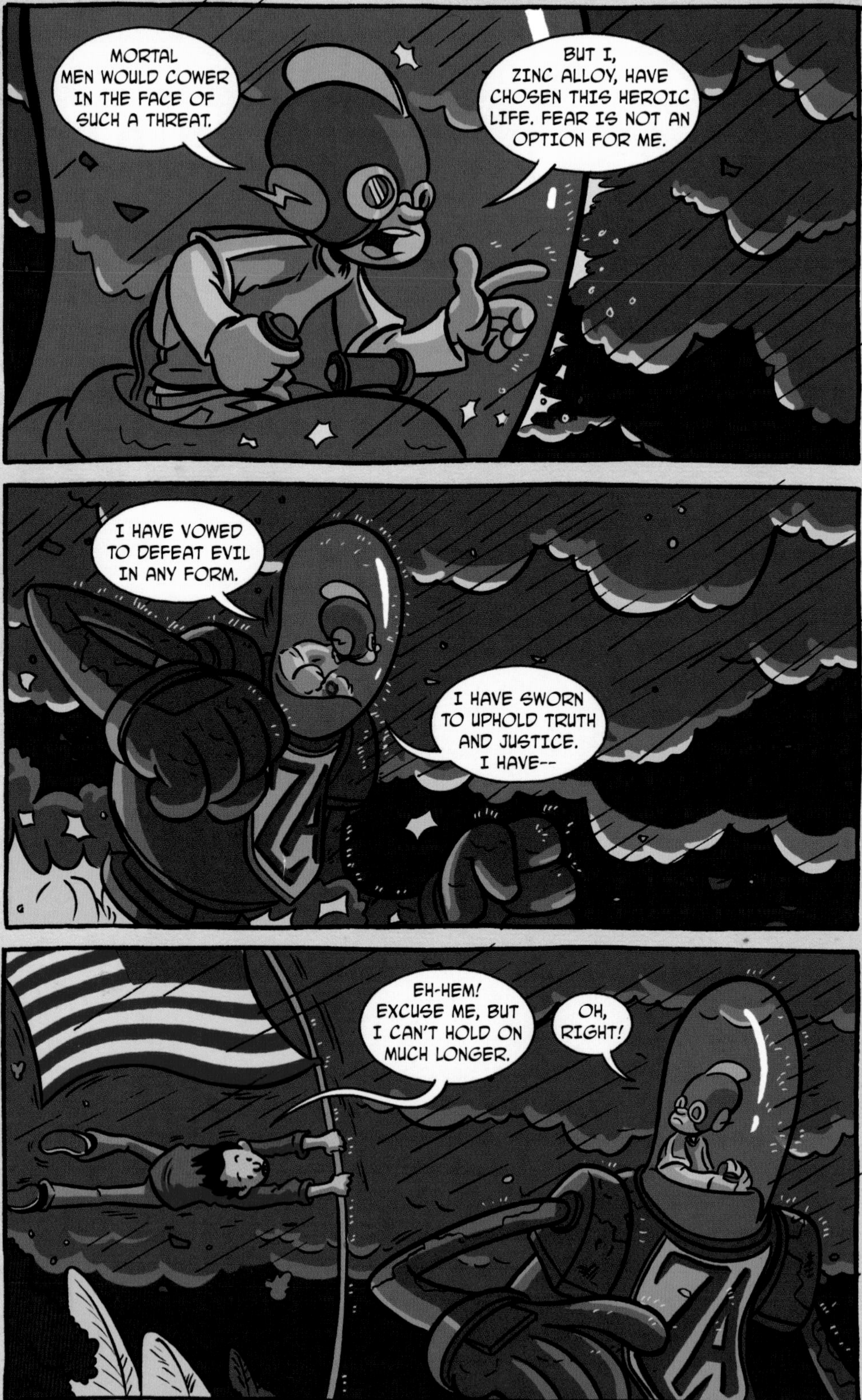
MORTAL MEN WOULD COWER IN THE FACE OF SUCH A THREAT.
BUT I, ZINC ALLOY, HAVE CHOSEN THIS HEROIC LIFE. FEAR IS NOT AN OPTION FOR ME.
I HAVE VOWED TO DEFEAT EVIL IN ANY FORM.
I HAVE SWORN TO UPHOLD TRUTH AND JUSTICE. I HAVE--
EH-HEM! EXCUSE ME, BUT I CAN'T HOLD ON MUCH LONGER.
OH, RIGHT!

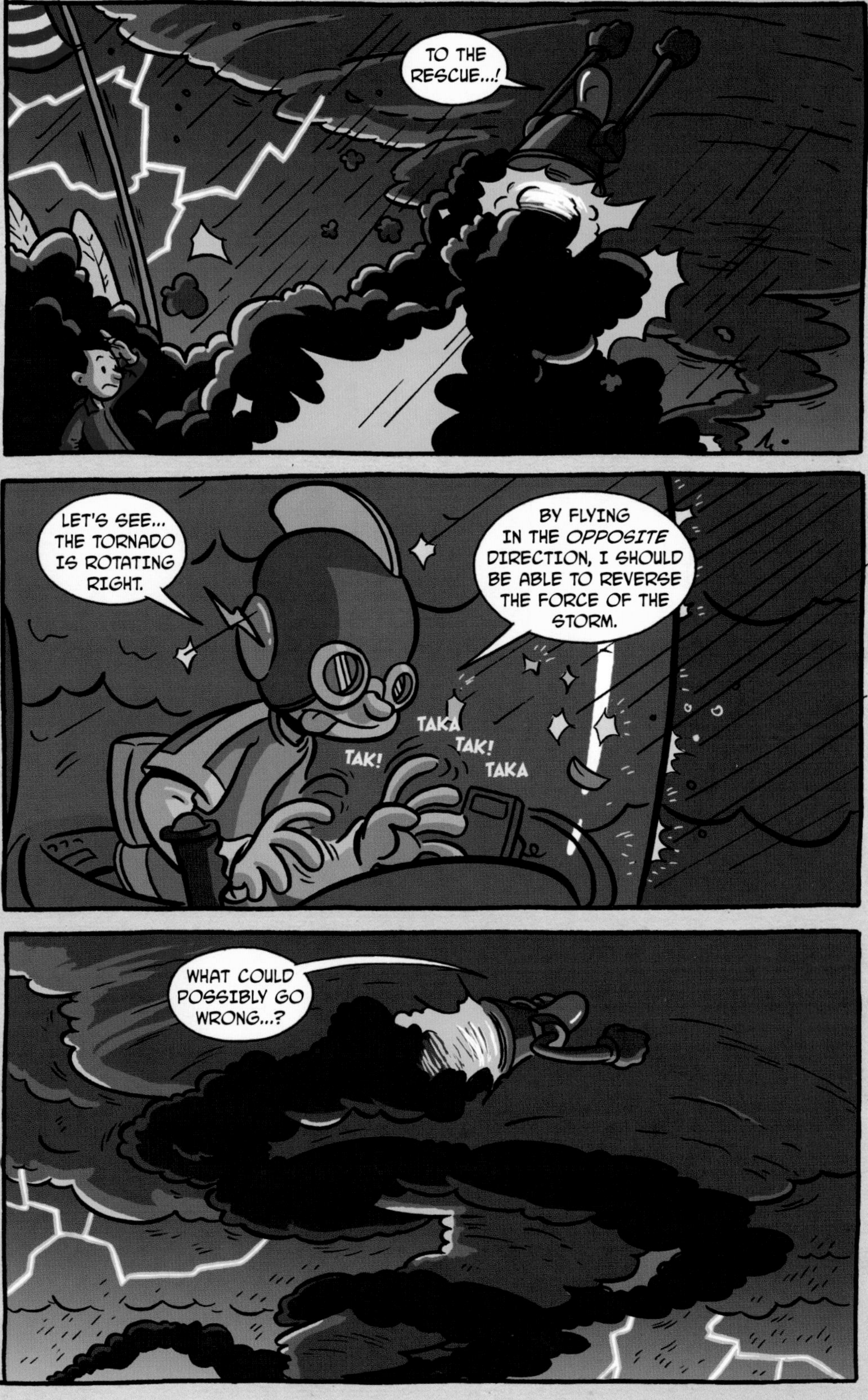
TO THE RESCUE...!
LET'S SEE... THE TORNADO IS ROTATING RIGHT.
BY FLYING IN THE *OPPOSITE* DIRECTION, I SHOULD BE ABLE TO REVERSE THE FORCE OF THE STORM.
TAKA
TAK!
TAK!
TAKA
WHAT COULD POSSIBLY GO WRONG...?

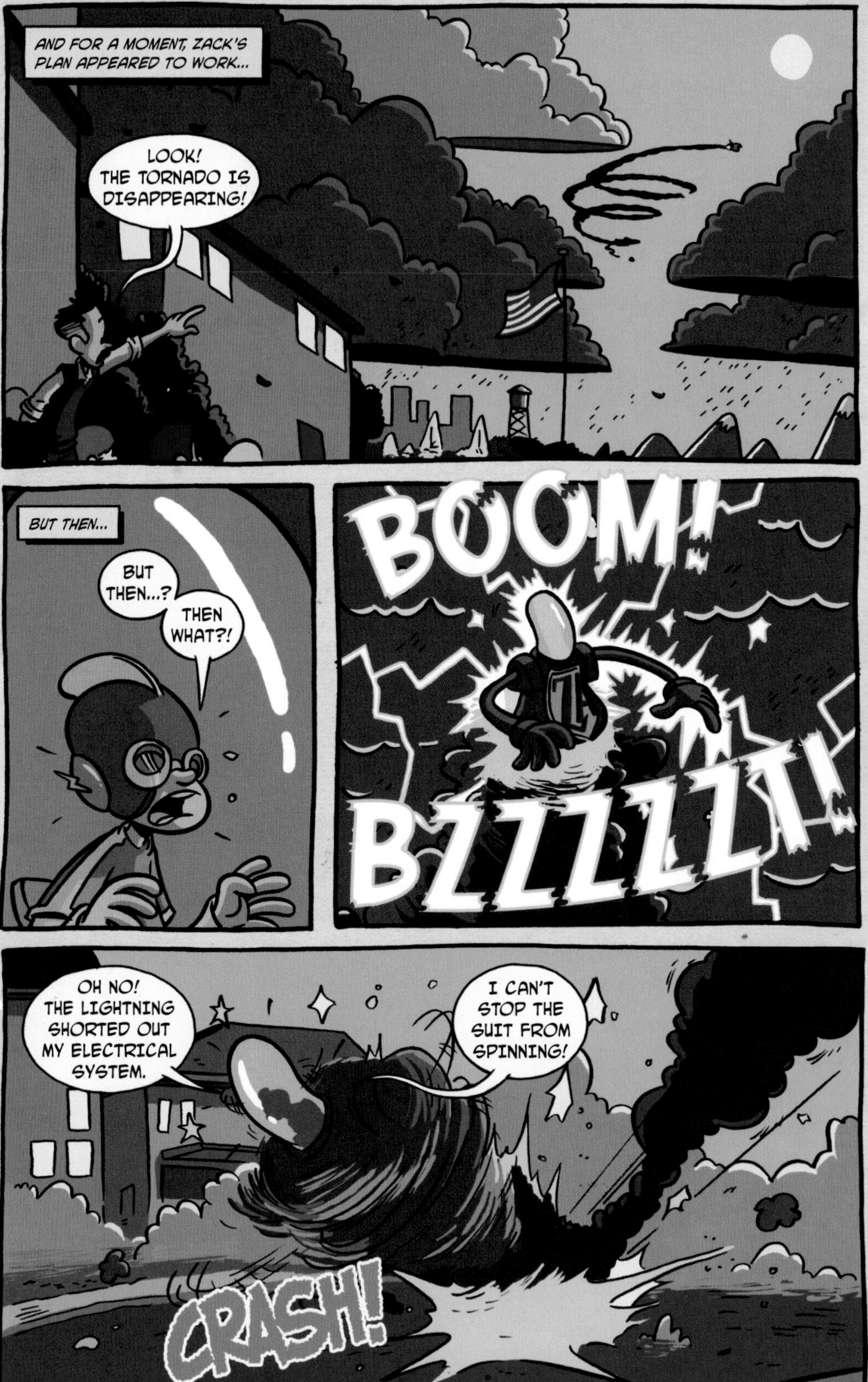
AND FOR A MOMENT, ZACK'S PLAN APPEARED TO WORK...
LOOK! THE TORNADO IS DISAPPEARING!
BUT THEN...
BUT THEN...?
THEN WHAT?!
BOOM!
BZZZZZT!
OH NO! THE LIGHTNING SHORTED OUT MY ELECTRICAL SYSTEM.
I CAN'T STOP THE SUIT FROM SPINNING!
CRASH!

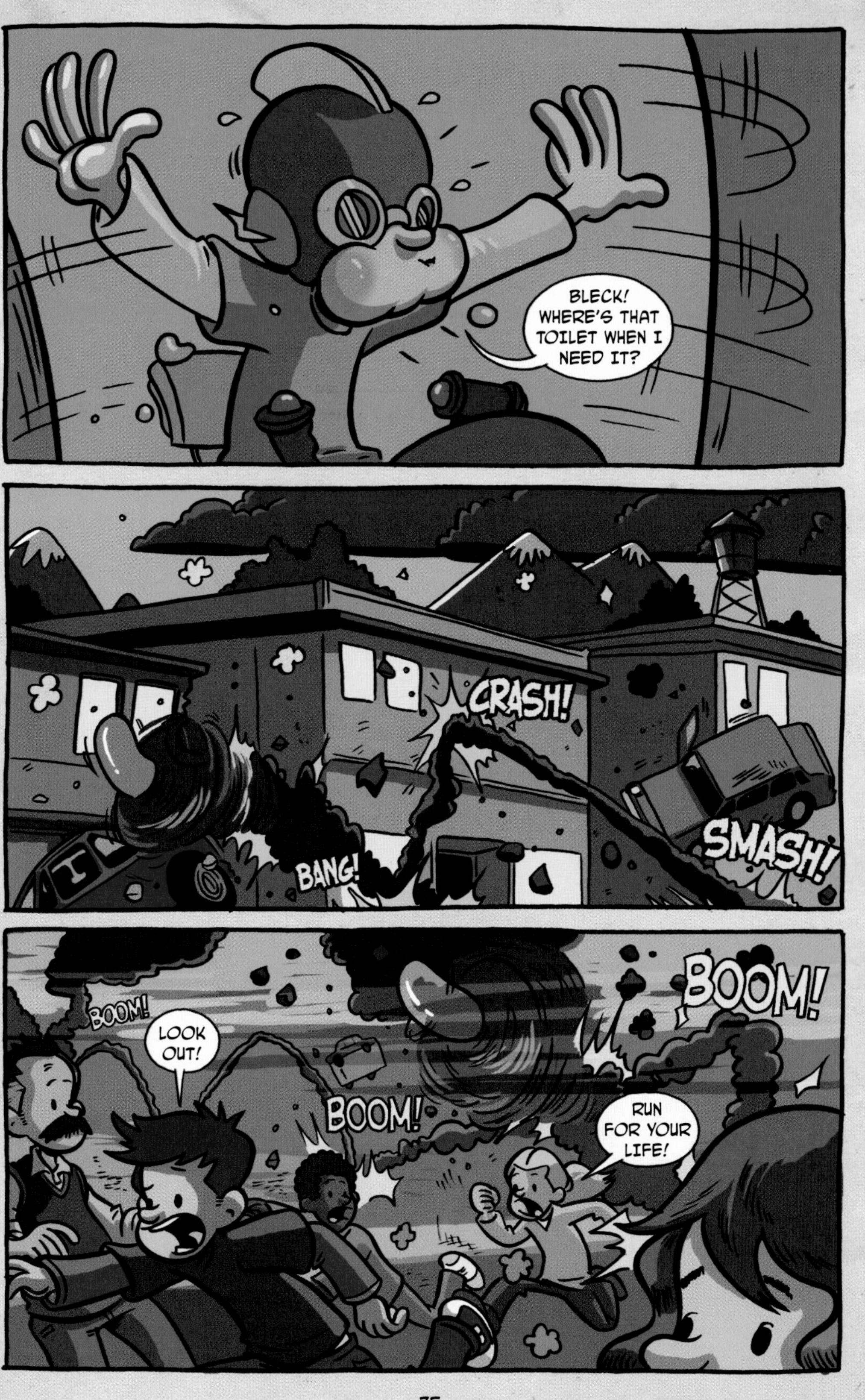
BLECK! WHERE'S THAT TOILET WHEN I NEED IT?
CRASH!
SMASH!
BANG!
BOOM!
BOOM!
LOOK OUT!
BOOM!
RUN FOR YOUR LIFE!

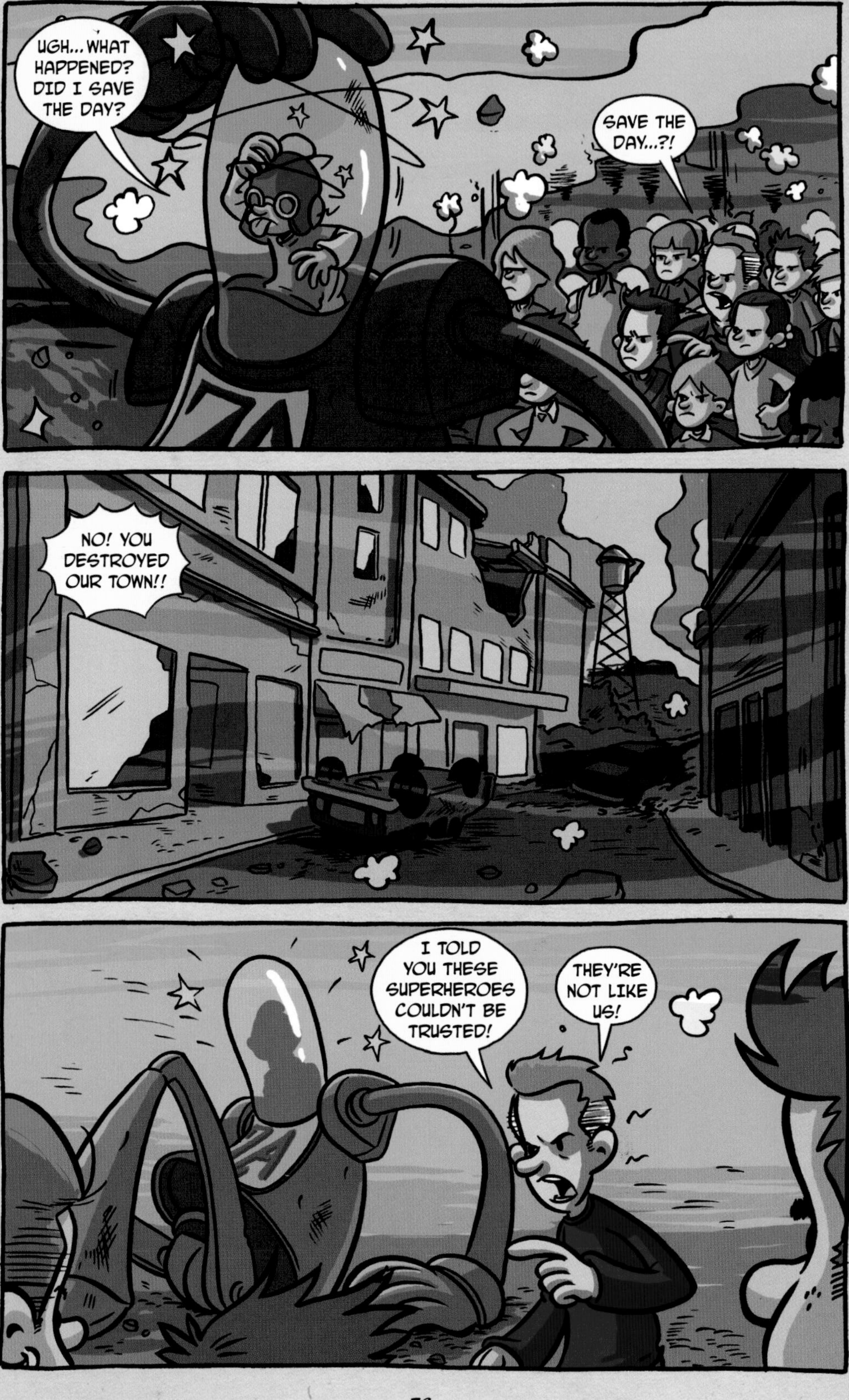
UGH... WHAT HAPPENED? DID I SAVE THE DAY?
SAVE THE DAY...?!
NO! YOU DESTROYED OUR TOWN!!
I TOLD YOU THESE SUPERHEROES COULDN'T BE TRUSTED!
THEY'RE NOT LIKE US!

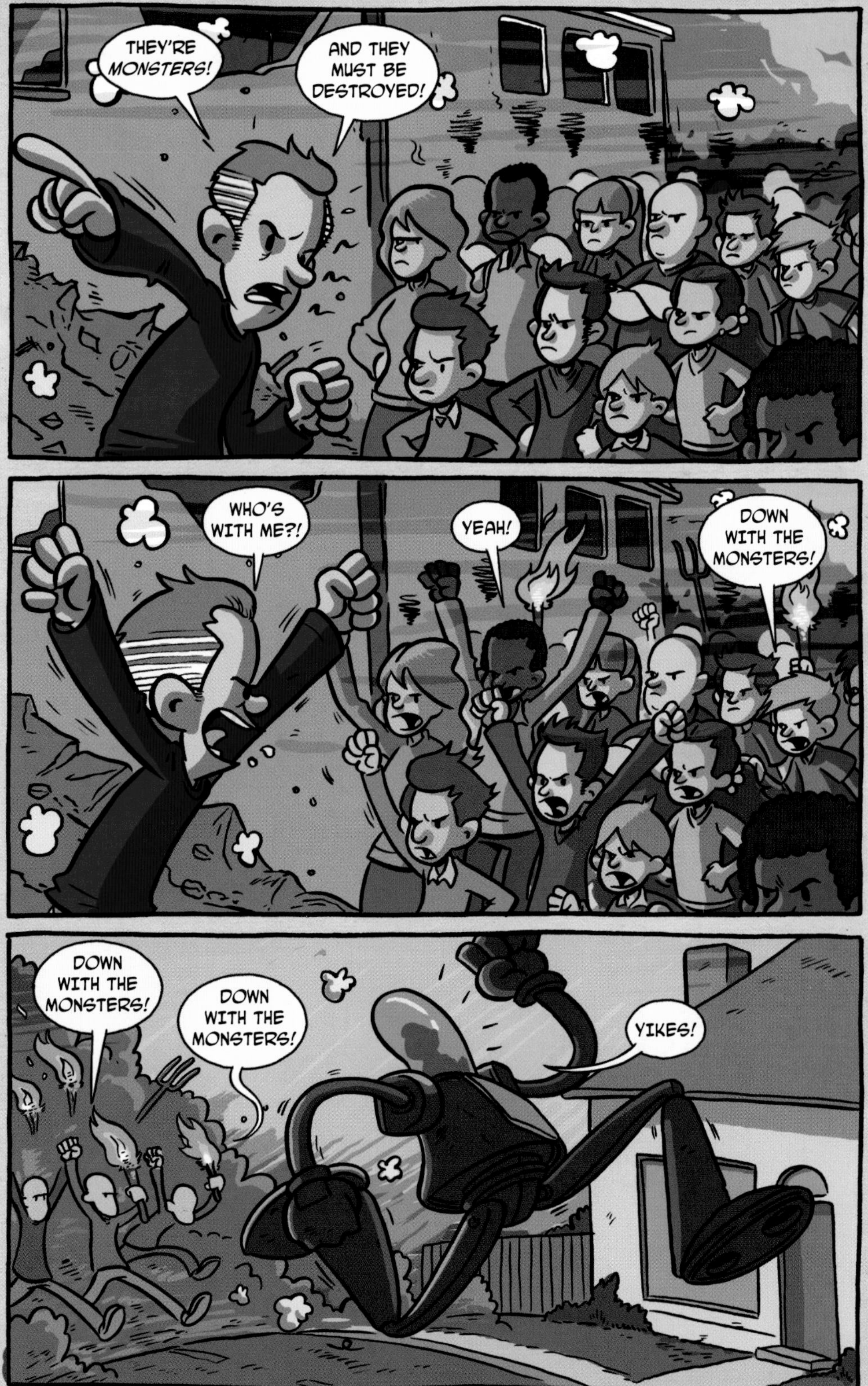
THEY'RE *MONSTERS!*
AND THEY MUST BE DESTROYED!
WHO'S WITH ME?!
YEAH!
DOWN WITH THE MONSTERS!
DOWN WITH THE MONSTERS!
DOWN WITH THE MONSTERS!
YIKES!

78

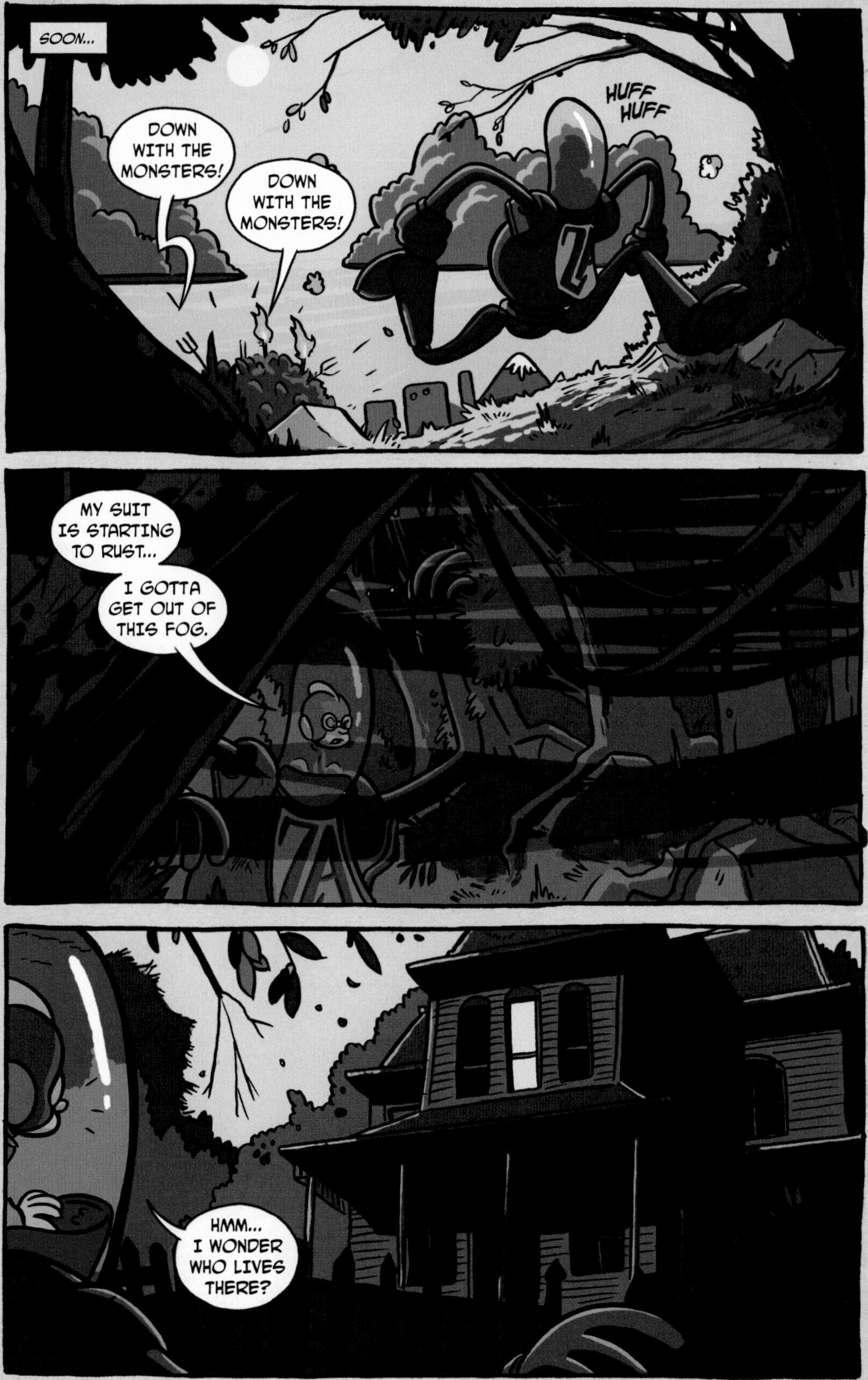
SOON...
DOWN WITH THE MONSTERS!
DOWN WITH THE MONSTERS!
HUFF HUFF
MY SUIT IS STARTING TO RUST...
I GOTTA GET OUT OF THIS FOG.
HMM... I WONDER WHO LIVES THERE?

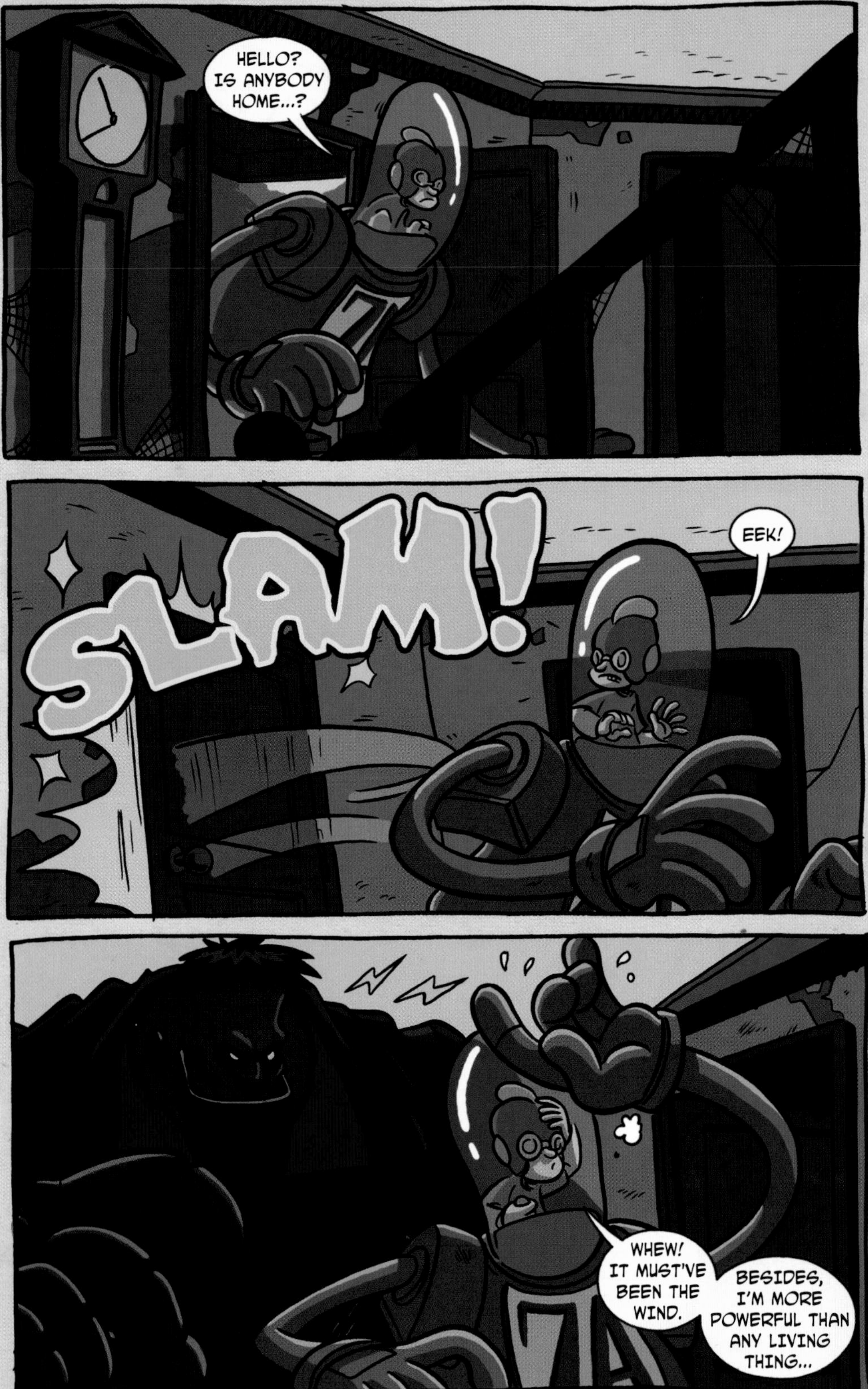
HELLO? IS ANYBODY HOME...?
SLAM!
EEK!
WHEW! IT MUST'VE BEEN THE WIND.
BESIDES, I'M MORE POWERFUL THAN ANY LIVING THING...

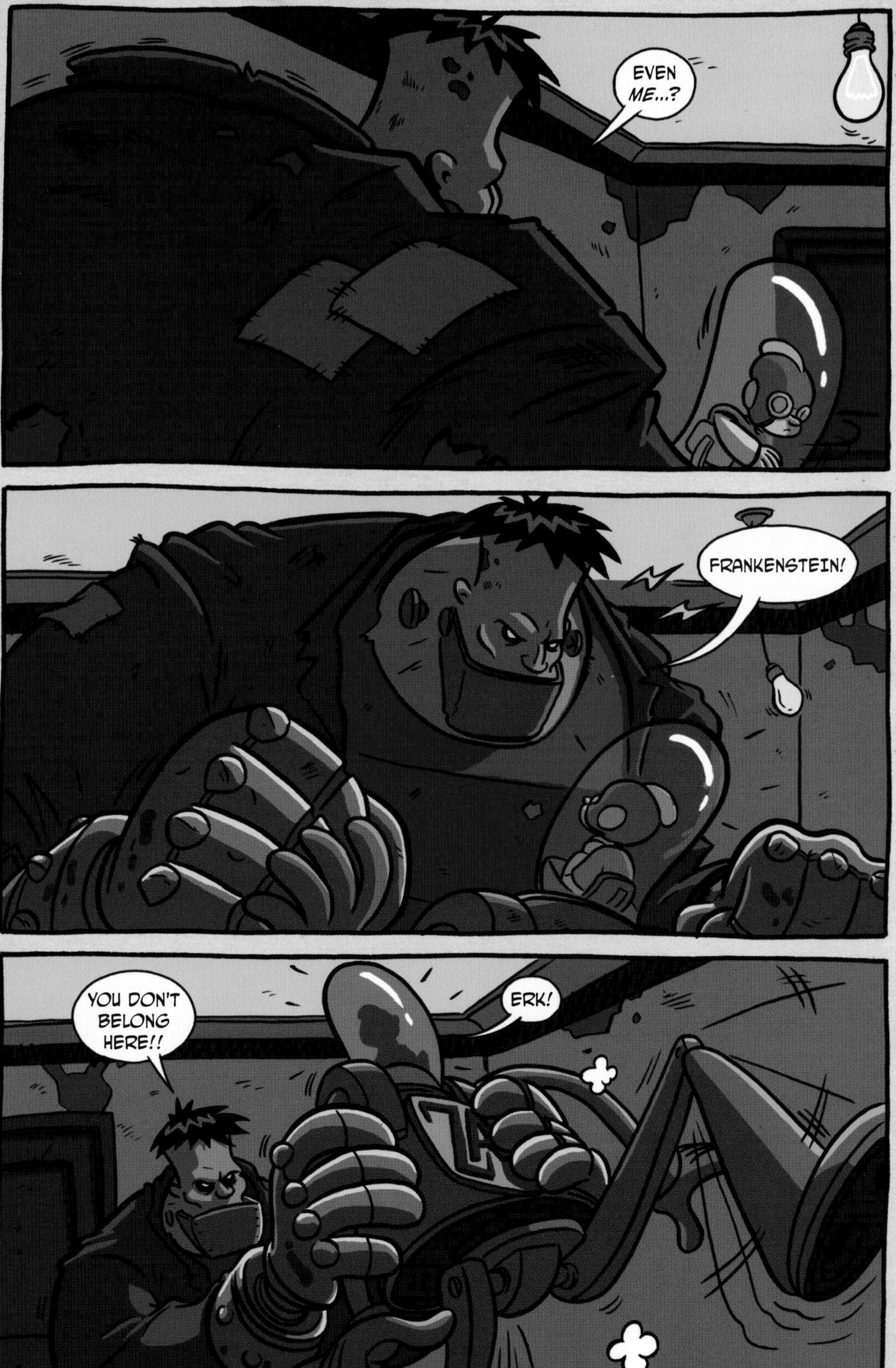
EVEN ME...?
FRANKENSTEIN!
YOU DON'T BELONG HERE!!
ERK!

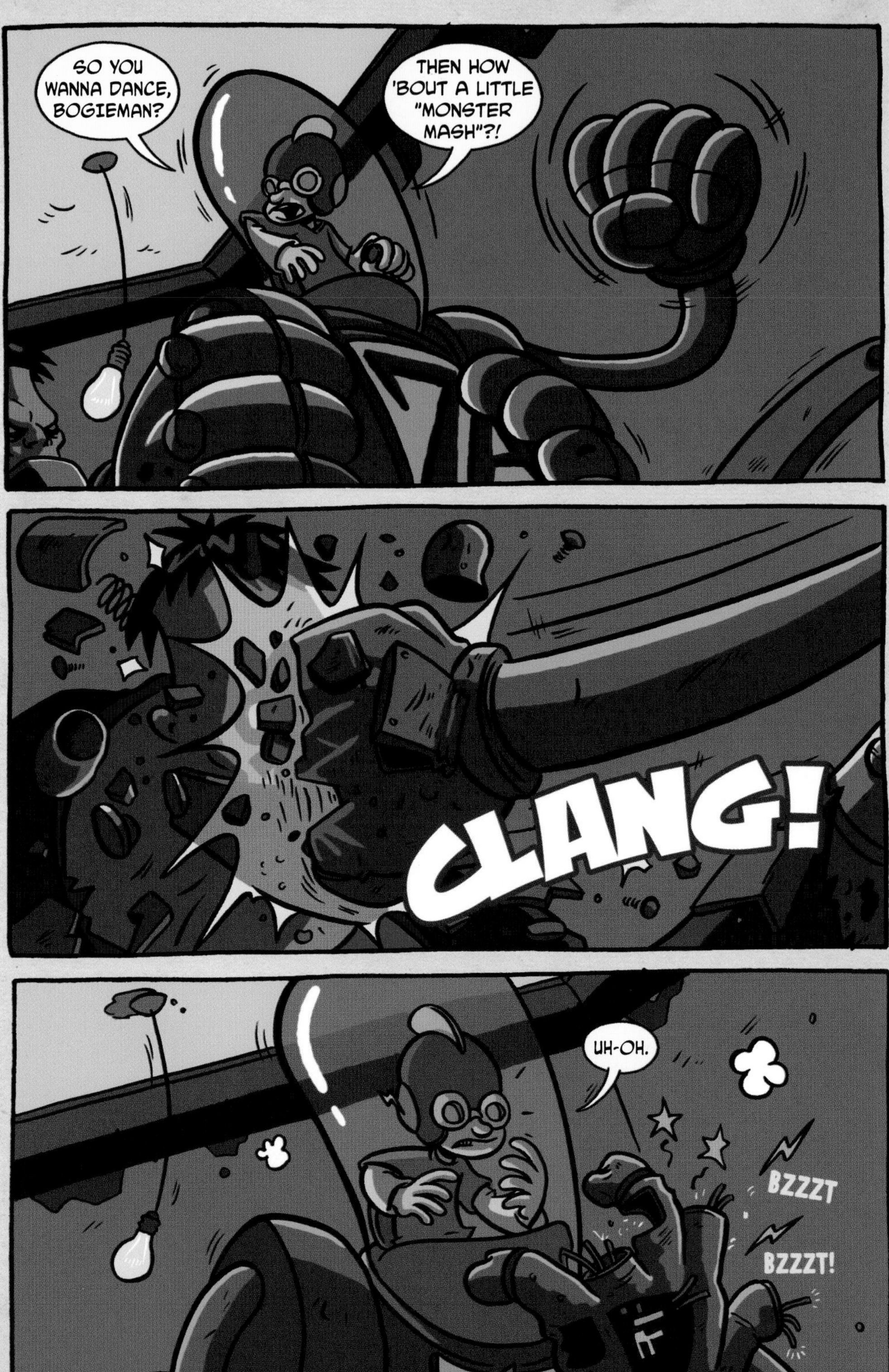
SO YOU WANNA DANCE, BOGIEMAN?
THEN HOW 'BOUT A LITTLE "MONSTER MASH"?!
CLANG!
UH-OH.
BZZZT
BZZZT!

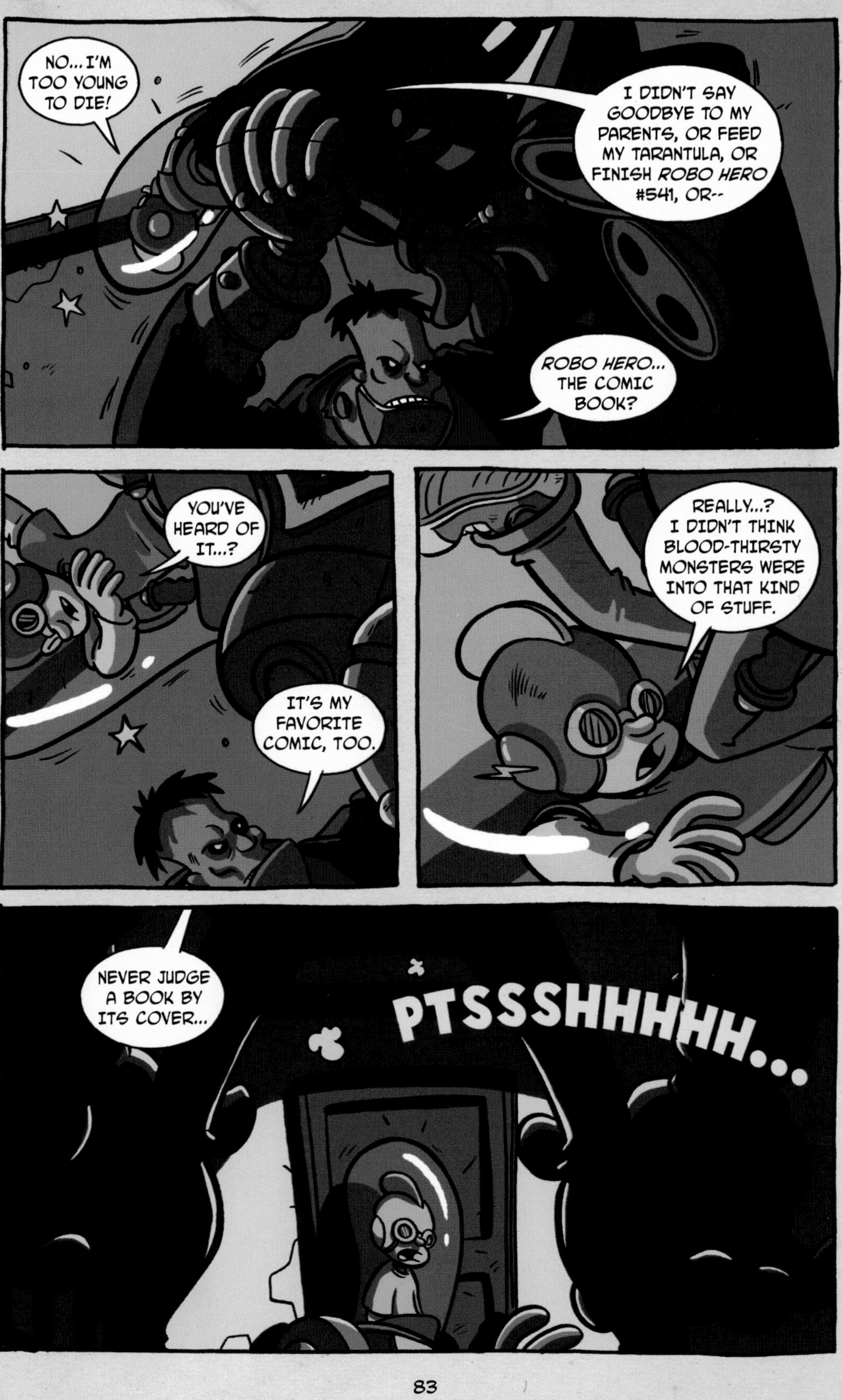
NO... I'M TOO YOUNG TO DIE!
I DIDN'T SAY GOODBYE TO MY PARENTS, OR FEED MY TARANTULA, OR FINISH *ROBO HERO* #541, OR--
ROBO HERO... THE COMIC BOOK?
YOU'VE HEARD OF IT...?
IT'S MY FAVORITE COMIC, TOO.
REALLY...? I DIDN'T THINK BLOOD-THIRSTY MONSTERS WERE INTO THAT KIND OF STUFF.
NEVER JUDGE A BOOK BY ITS COVER...
PTSSSHHHHH...

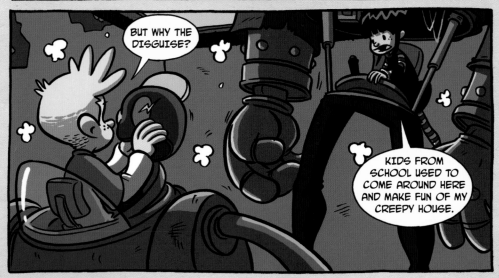

84

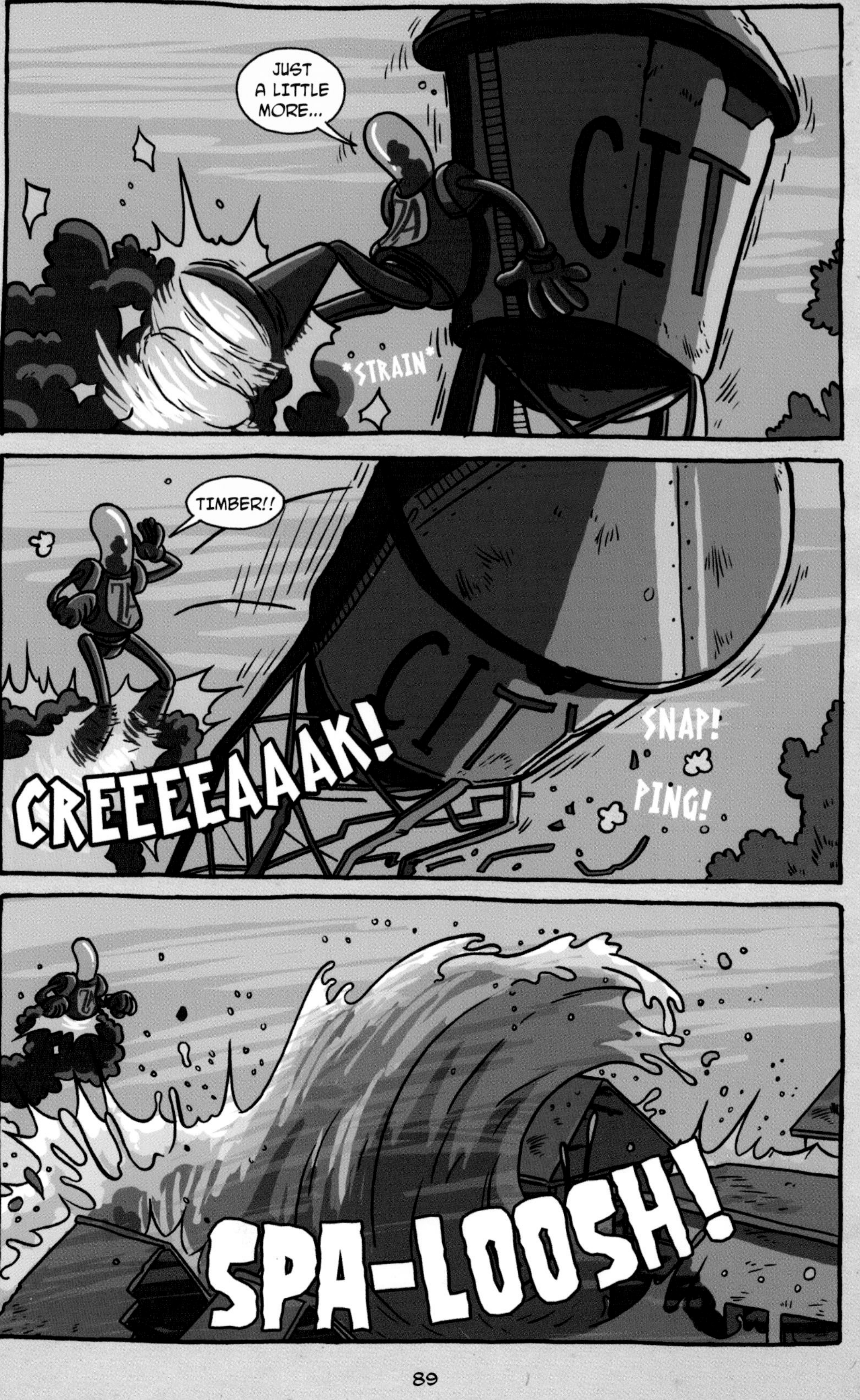
JUST A LITTLE MORE...
CIT
STRAIN
TIMBER!!
CIT
CREEEEAAAK!
SNAP!
PING!
SPA-LOOSH!

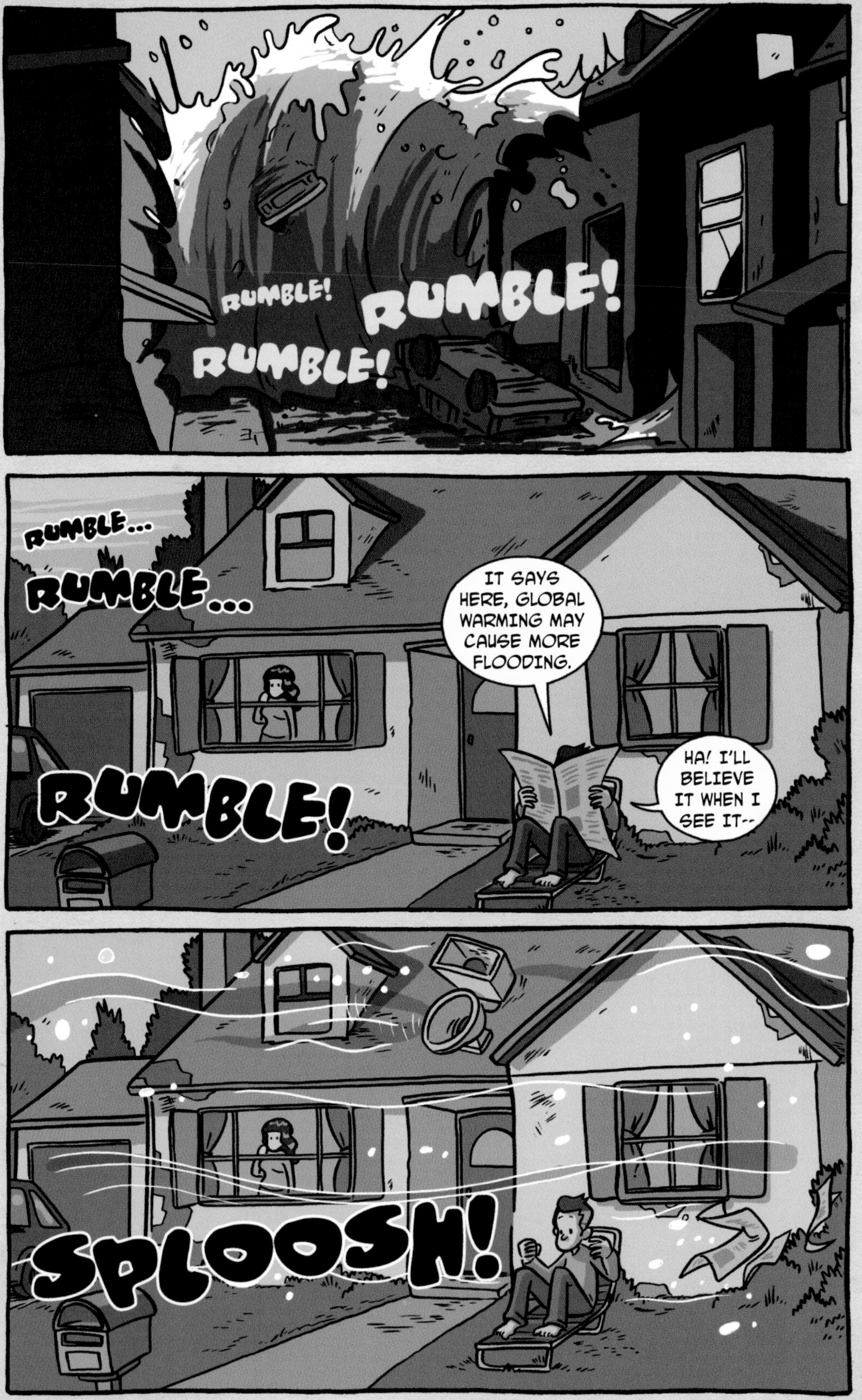
RUMBLE!
RUMBLE!
RUMBLE!
RUMBLE...
RUMBLE...
RUMBLE!
IT SAYS HERE, GLOBAL WARMING MAY CAUSE MORE FLOODING.
HA! I'LL BELIEVE IT WHEN I SEE IT--
SPLOOSH!

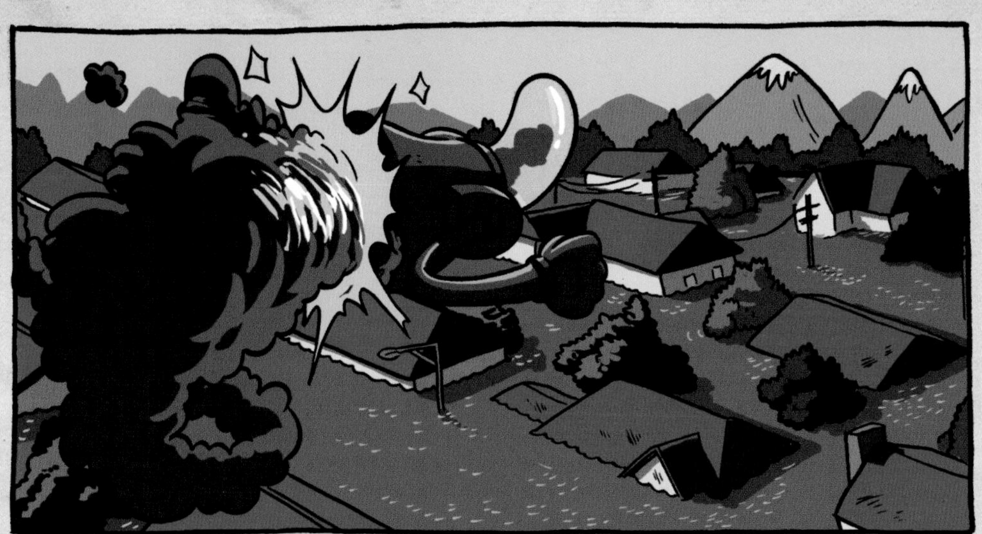

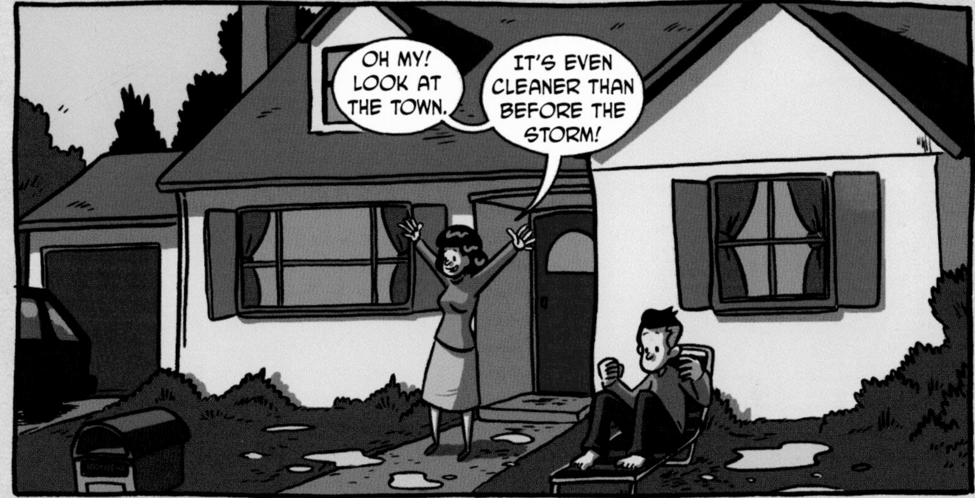
OH MY! LOOK AT THE TOWN.
IT'S EVEN CLEANER THAN BEFORE THE STORM!

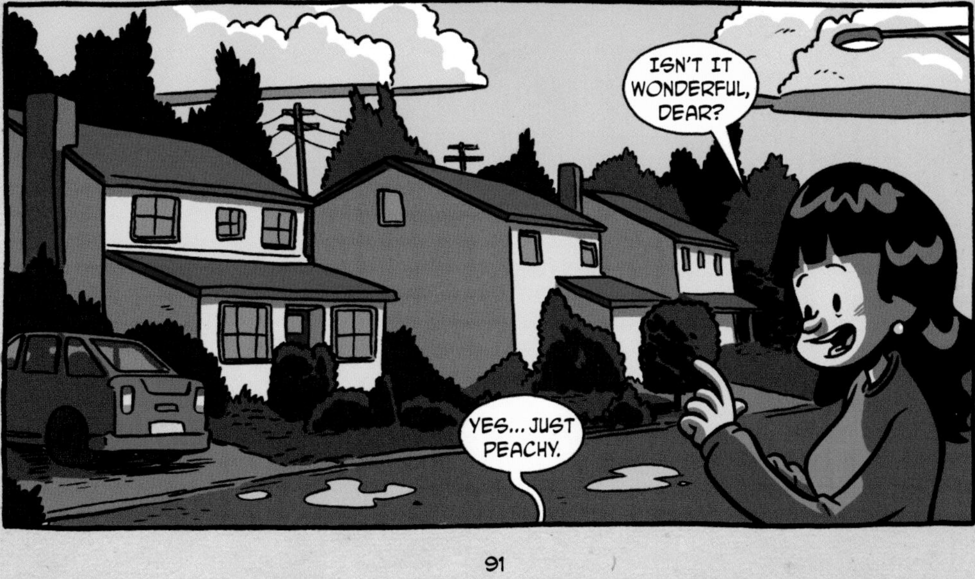
ISN'T IT WONDERFUL, DEAR?
YES... JUST PEACHY.

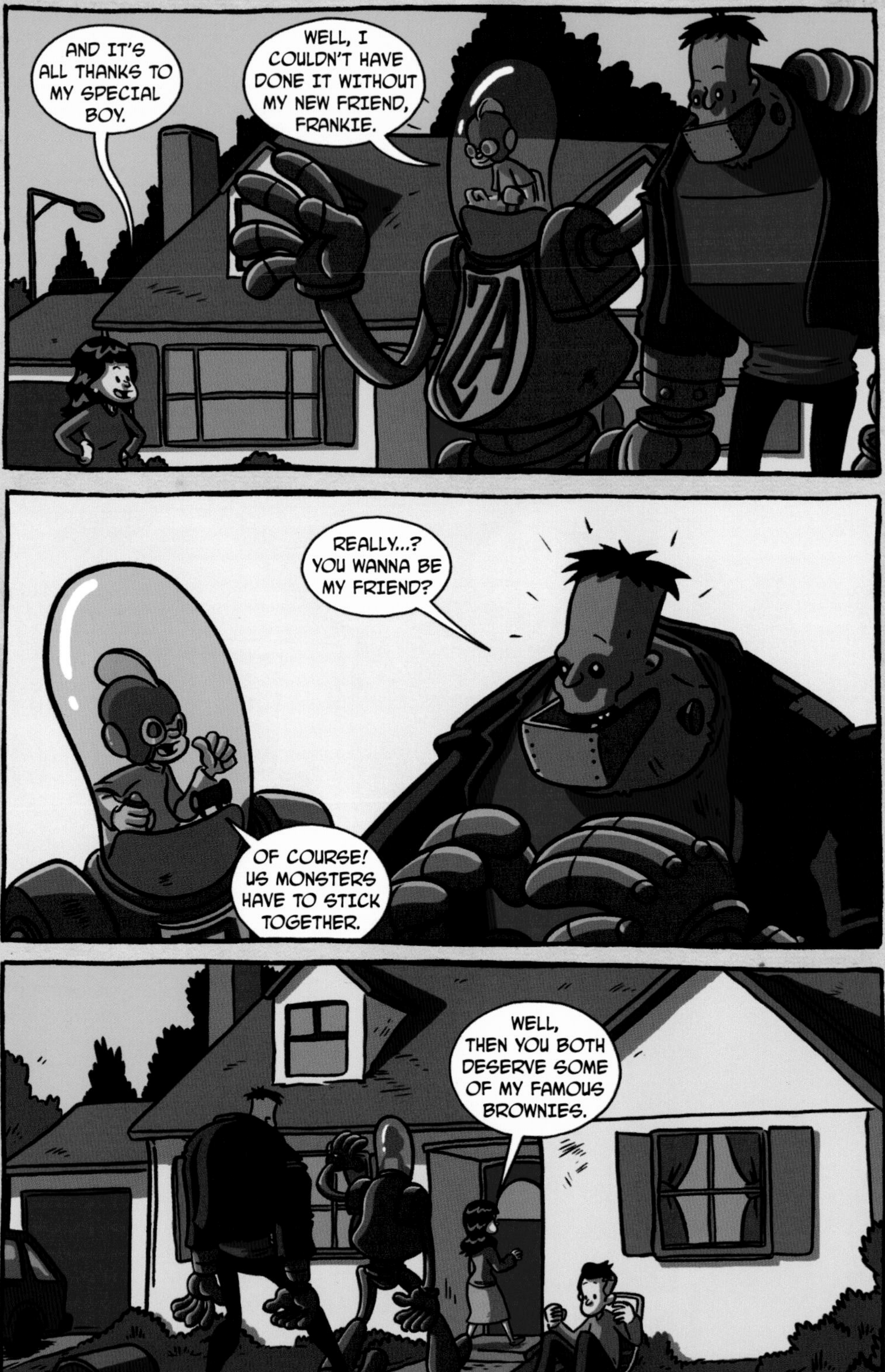
AND IT'S ALL THANKS TO MY SPECIAL BOY.
WELL, I COULDN'T HAVE DONE IT WITHOUT MY NEW FRIEND, FRANKIE.
REALLY...? YOU WANNA BE MY FRIEND?
OF COURSE! US MONSTERS HAVE TO STICK TOGETHER.
WELL, THEN YOU BOTH DESERVE SOME OF MY FAMOUS BROWNIES.

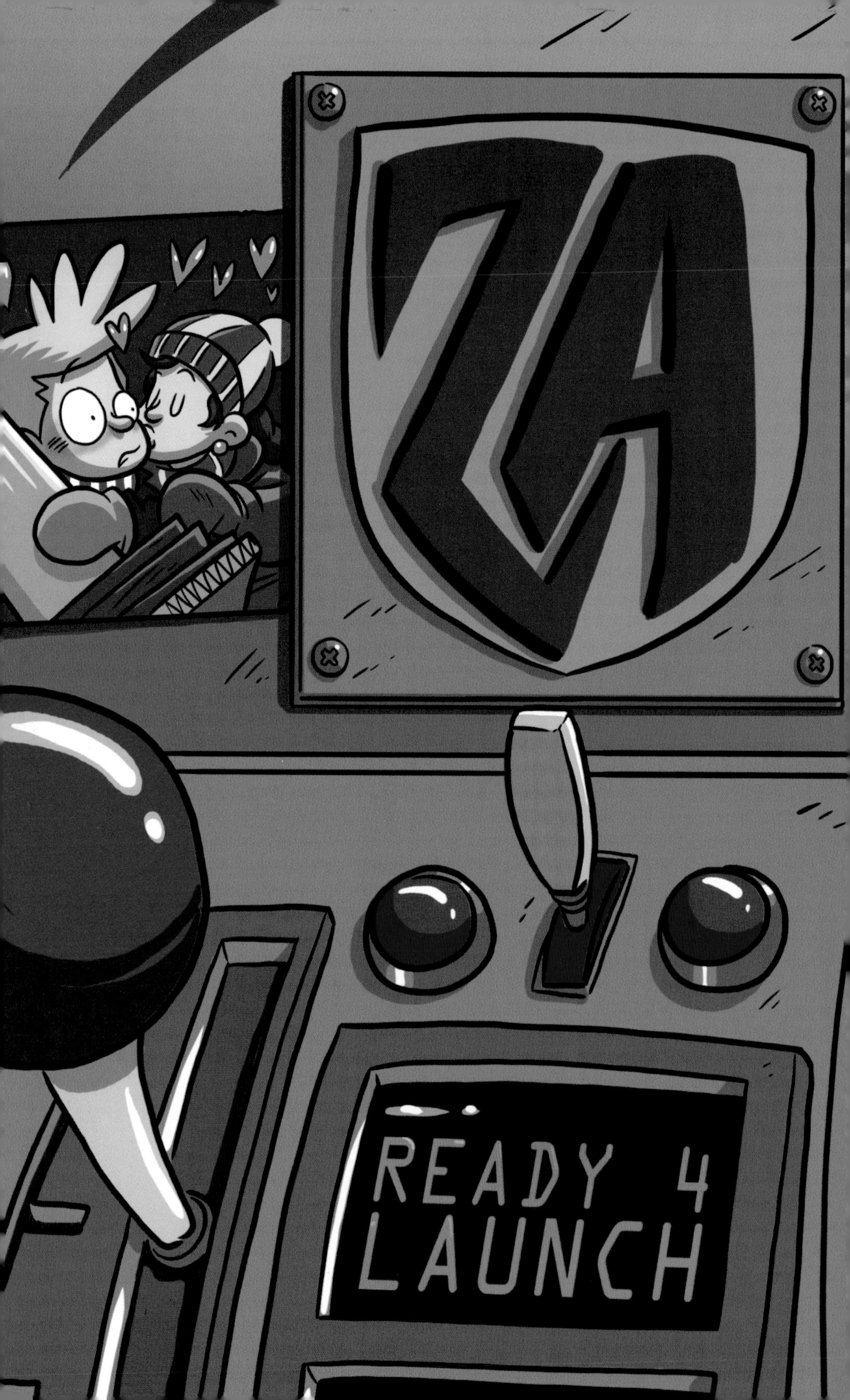
READY 4
LAUNCH

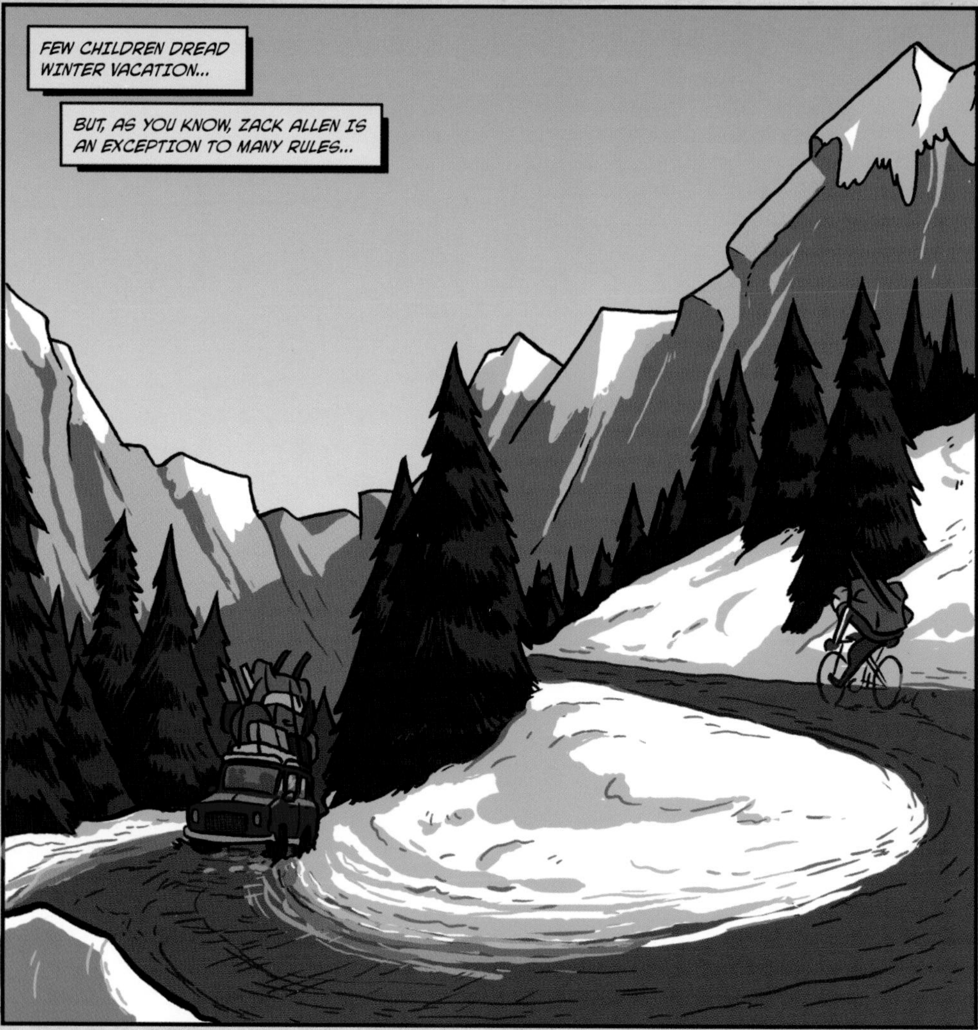
FEW CHILDREN DREAD WINTER VACATION...
BUT, AS YOU KNOW, ZACK ALLEN IS AN EXCEPTION TO MANY RULES...

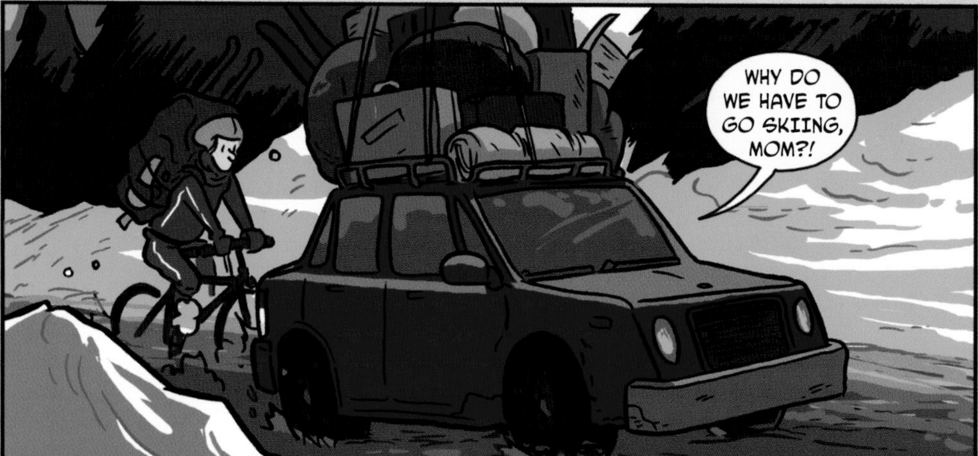
WHY DO WE HAVE TO GO SKIING, MOM?!

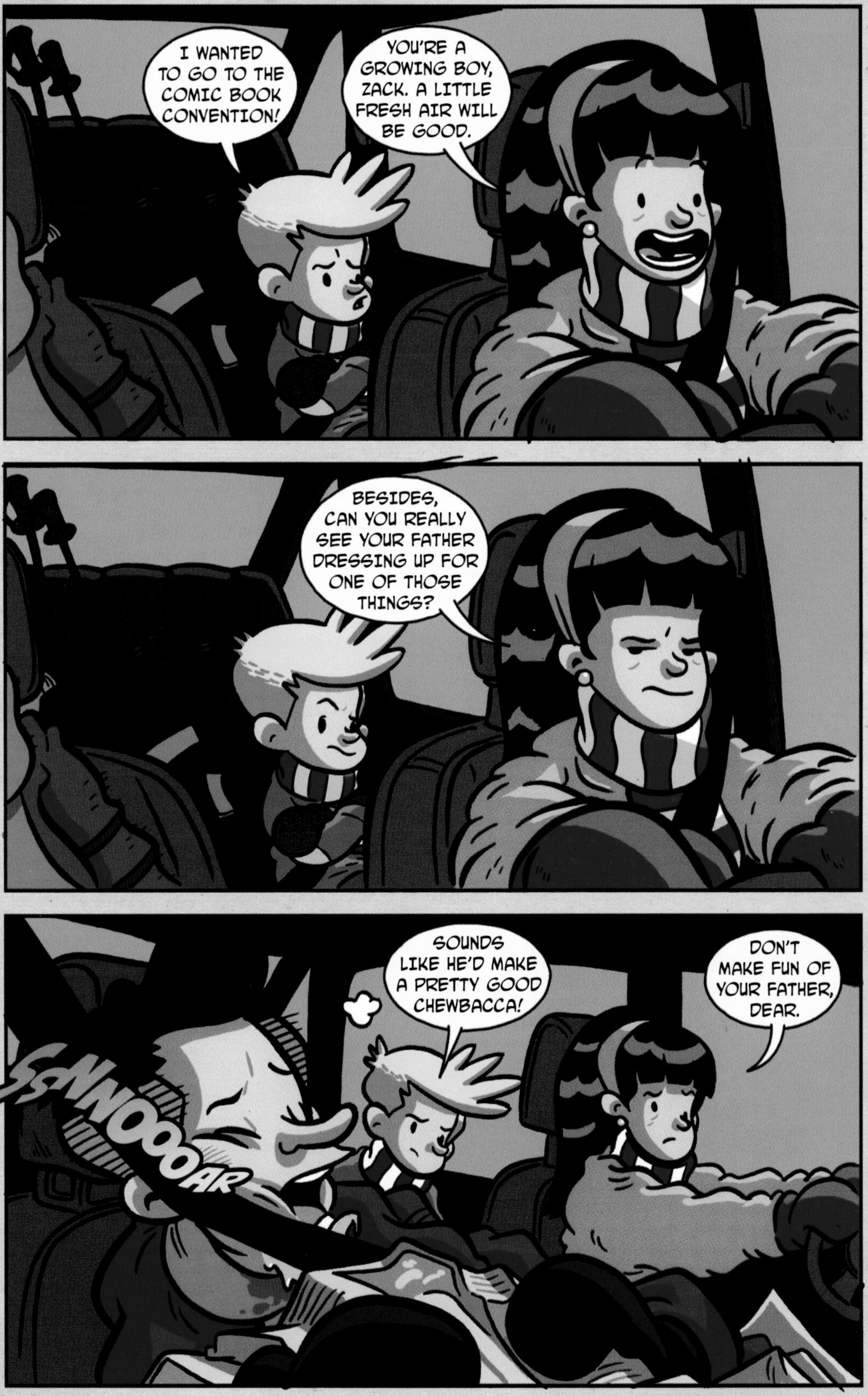
I WANTED TO GO TO THE COMIC BOOK CONVENTION!
YOU'RE A GROWING BOY, ZACK. A LITTLE FRESH AIR WILL BE GOOD.
BESIDES, CAN YOU REALLY SEE YOUR FATHER DRESSING UP FOR ONE OF THOSE THINGS?
SSNNOOOAR
SOUNDS LIKE HE'D MAKE A PRETTY GOOD CHEWBACCA!
DON'T MAKE FUN OF YOUR FATHER, DEAR.

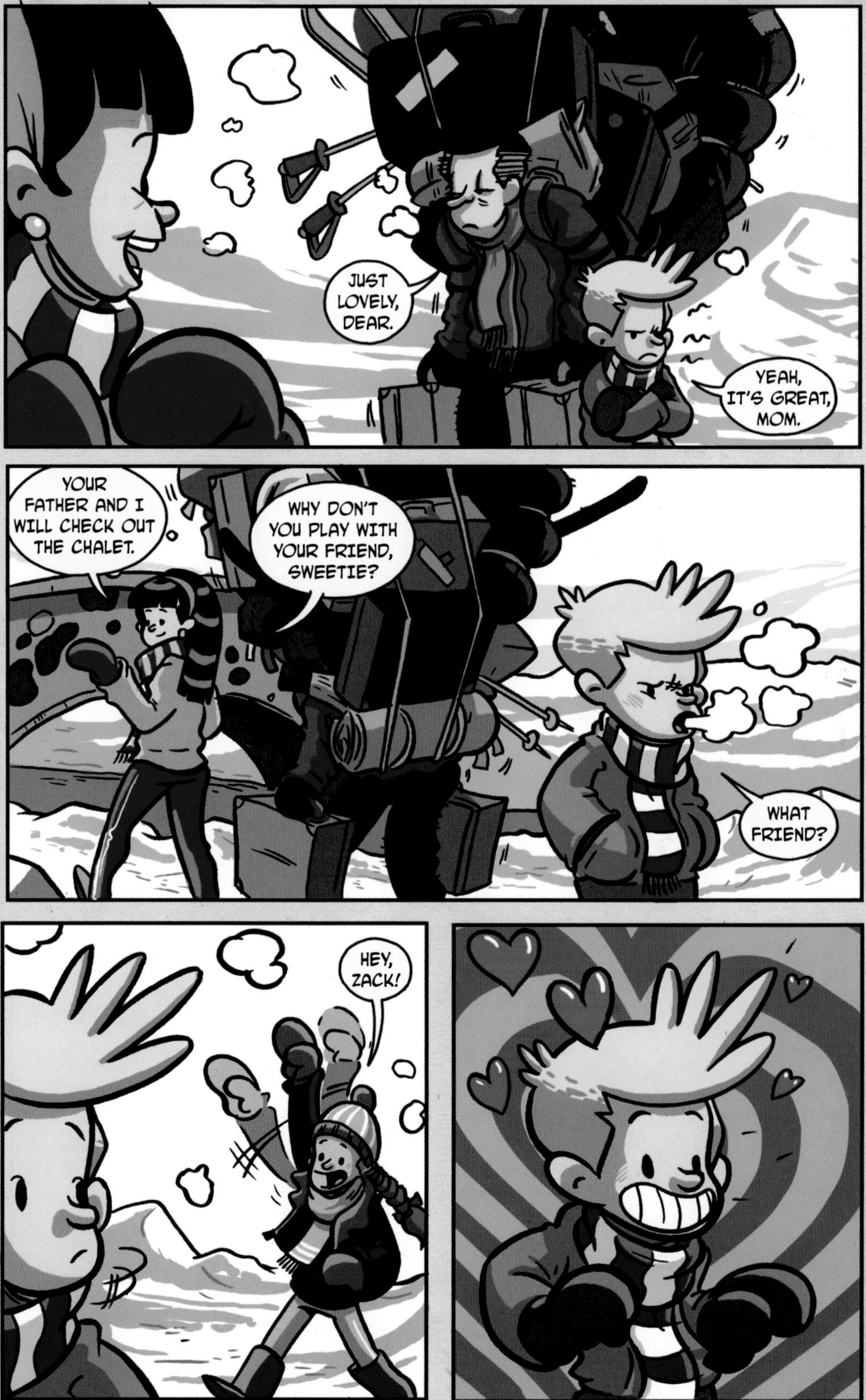
JUST LOVELY, DEAR.
YEAH, IT'S GREAT, MOM.
YOUR FATHER AND I WILL CHECK OUT THE CHALET.
WHY DON'T YOU PLAY WITH YOUR FRIEND, SWEETIE?
WHAT FRIEND?
HEY, ZACK!

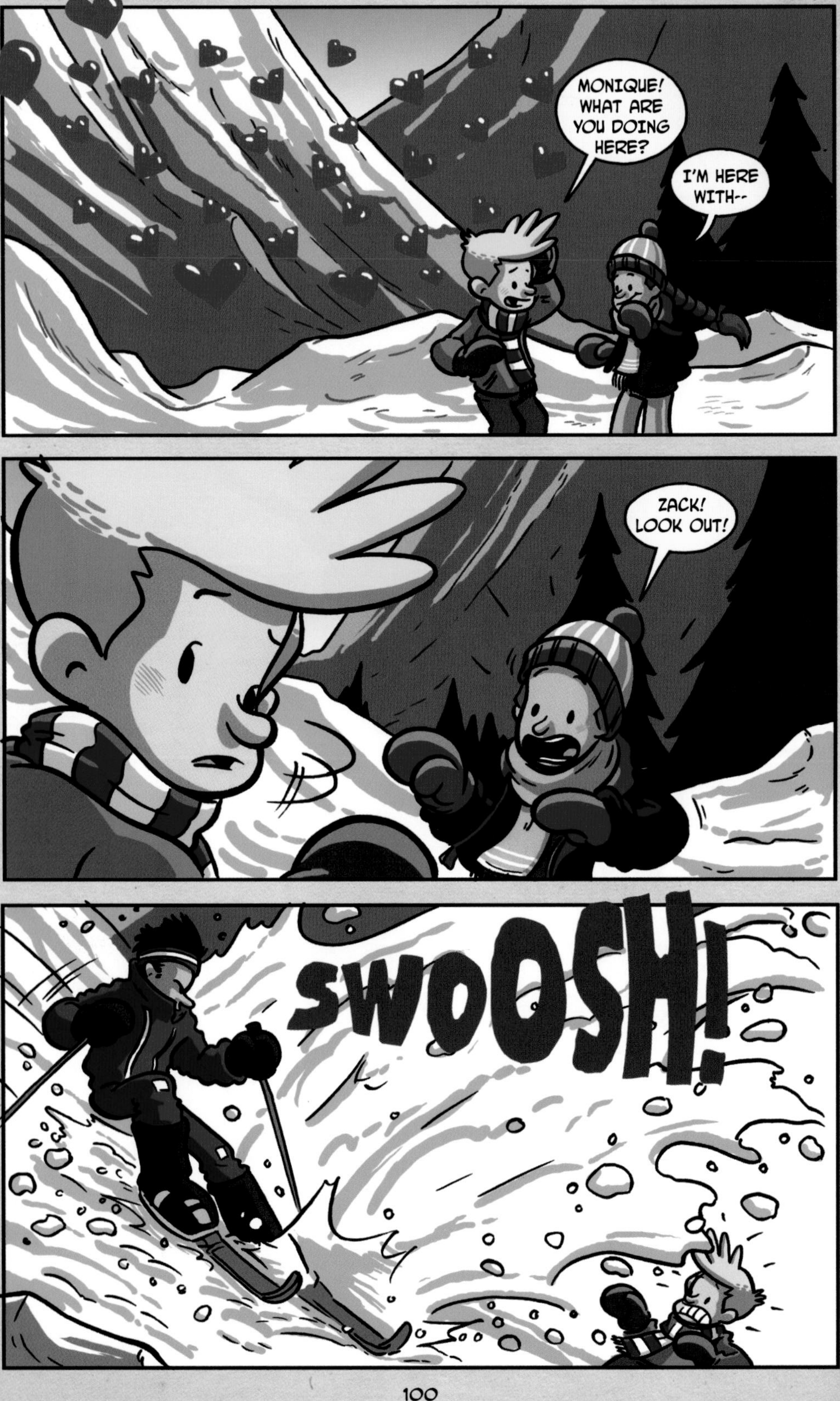
MONIQUE! WHAT ARE YOU DOING HERE?
I'M HERE WITH--
ZACK! LOOK OUT!
SWOOSH!

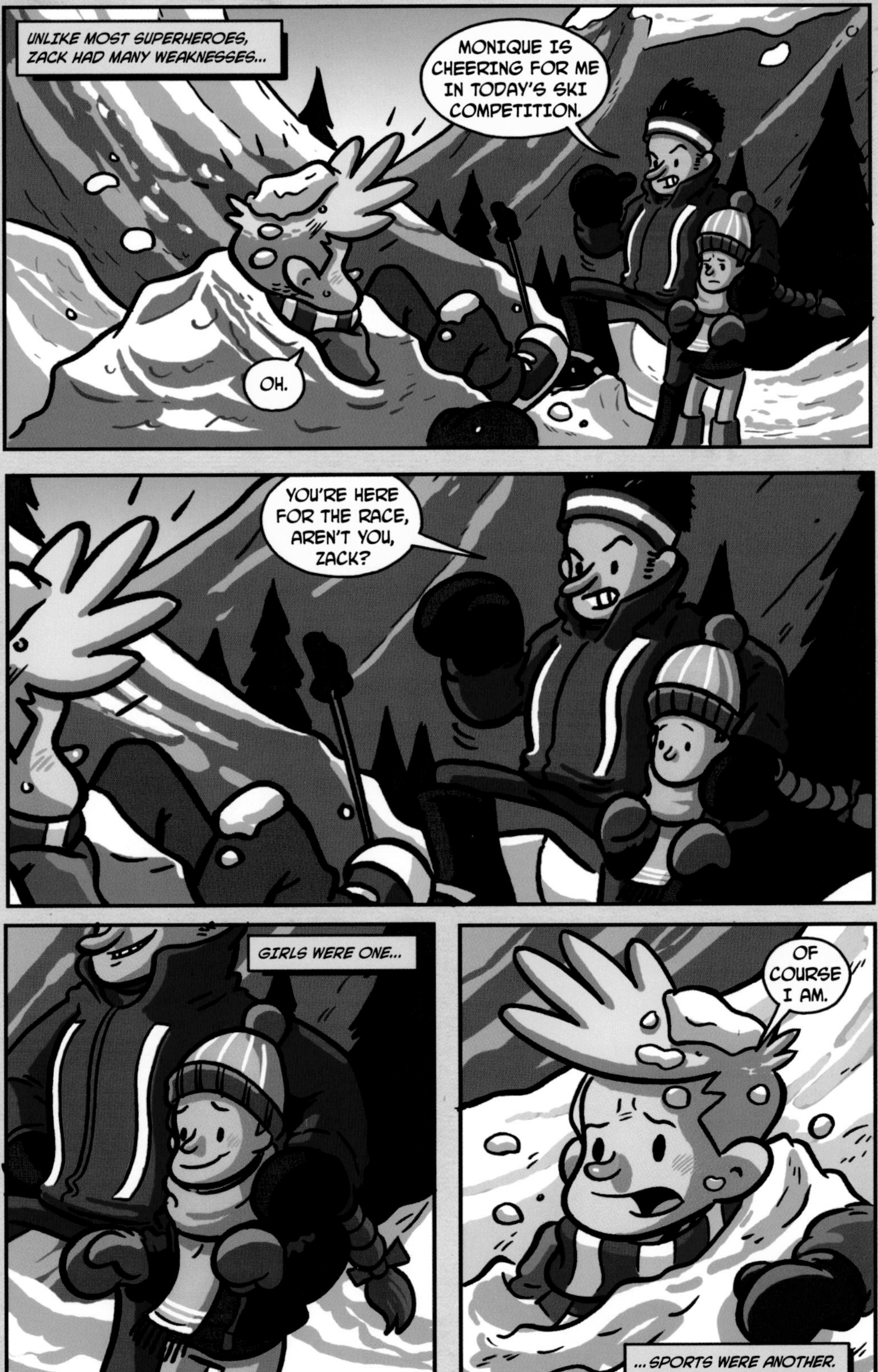
UNLIKE MOST SUPERHEROES, ZACK HAD MANY WEAKNESSES...
MONIQUE IS CHEERING FOR ME IN TODAY'S SKI COMPETITION.
OH.
YOU'RE HERE FOR THE RACE, AREN'T YOU, ZACK?
GIRLS WERE ONE...
OF COURSE I AM.
...SPORTS WERE ANOTHER.

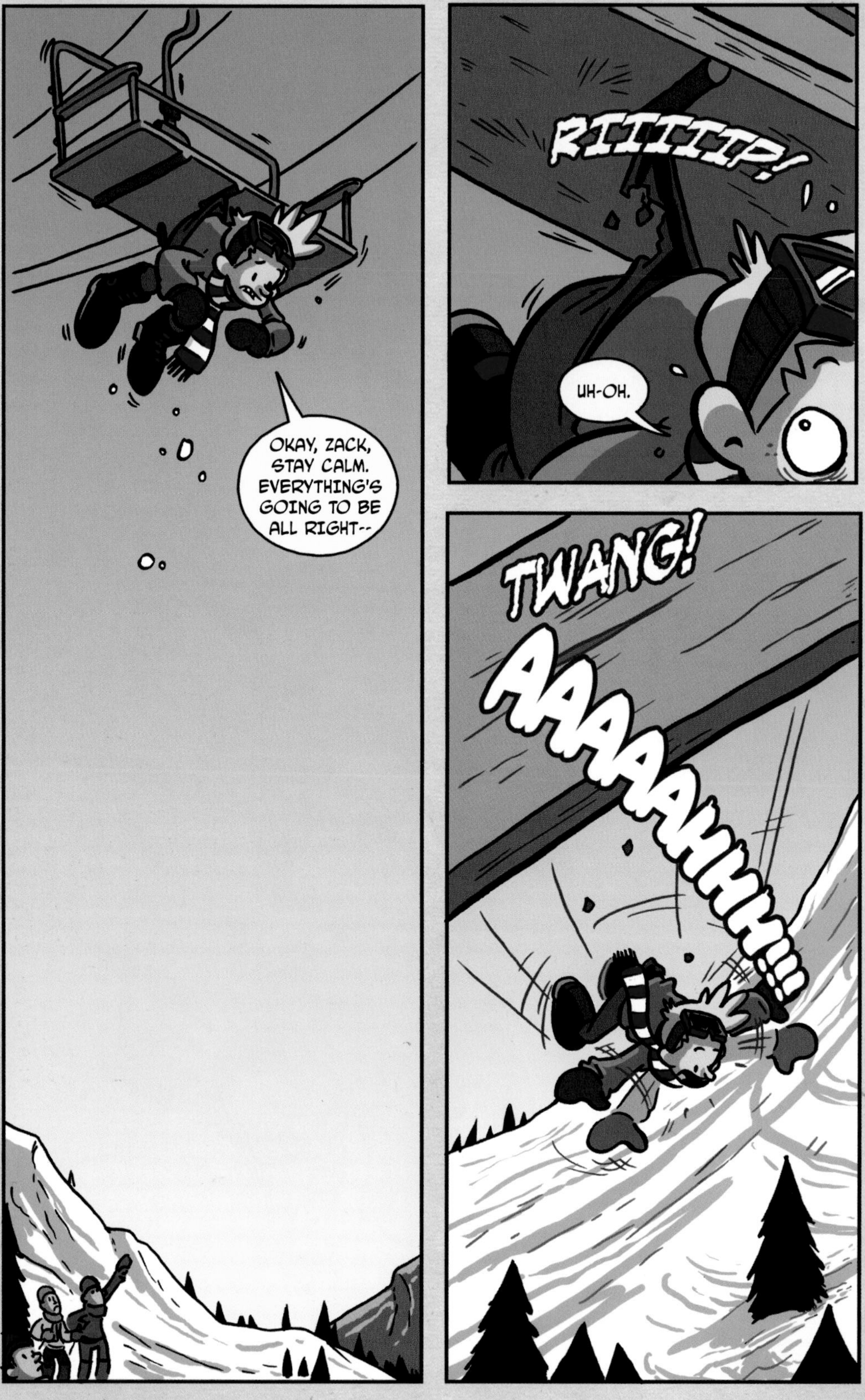
OKAY, ZACK, STAY CALM. EVERYTHING'S GOING TO BE ALL RIGHT--
RIIIIIP!
UH-OH.
TWANG!
AAAAAHHH!!!

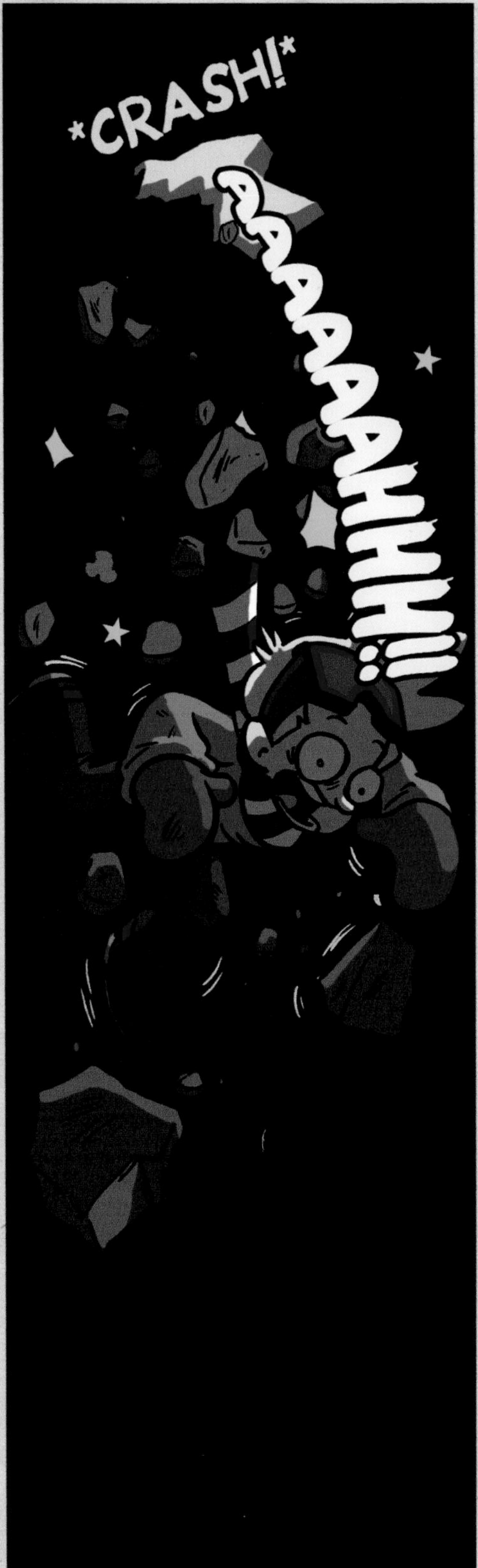
CRASH!
AAAAAAAAHHHH!!!

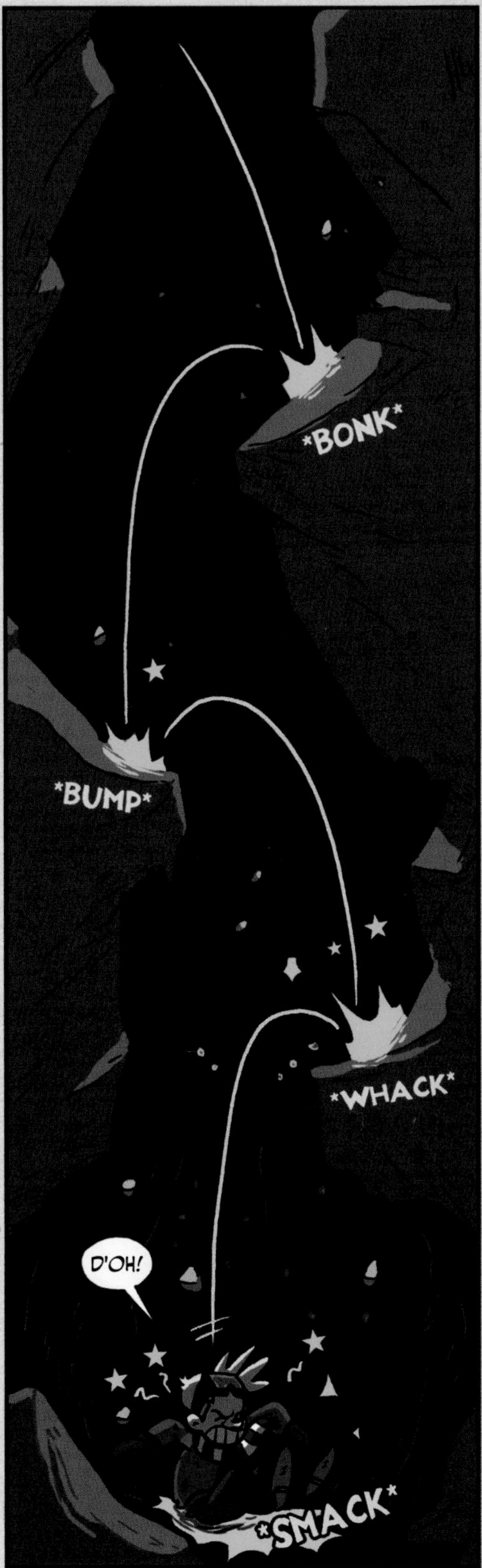
BONK
BUMP
WHACK
D'OH!
SMACK

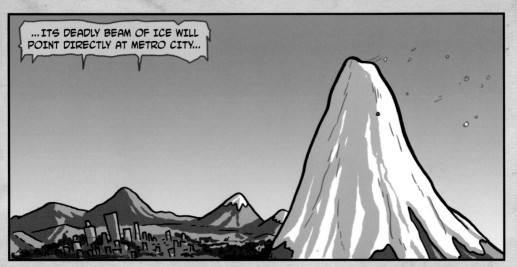

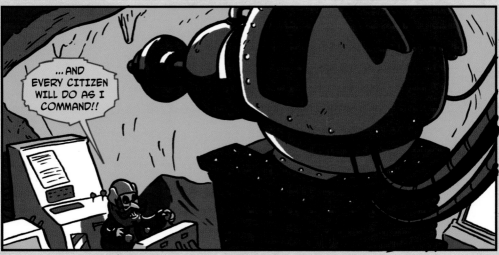

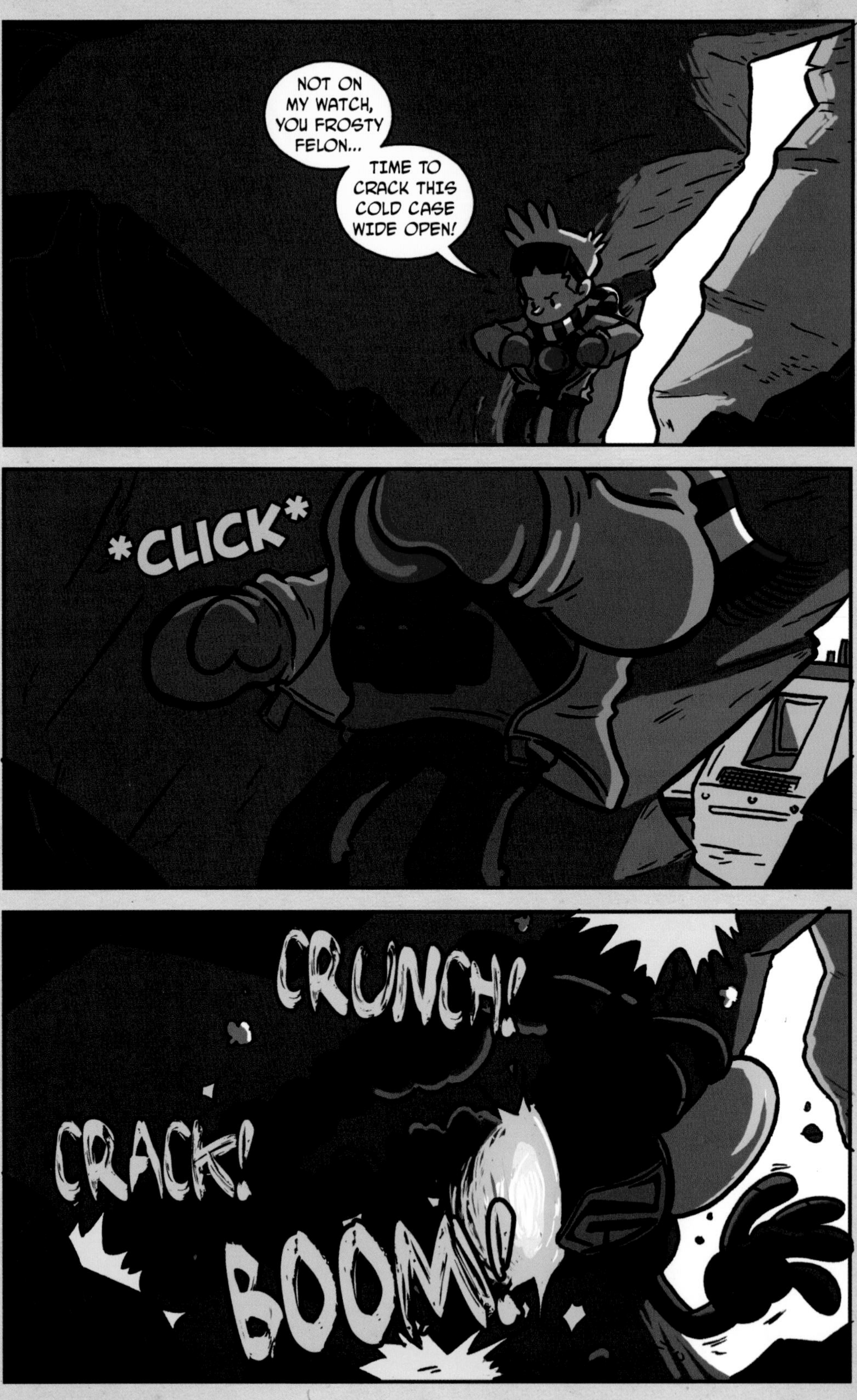
NOT ON MY WATCH, YOU FROSTY FELON...
TIME TO CRACK THIS COLD CASE WIDE OPEN!
CLICK
CRUNCH!
CRACK!
BOOM!!

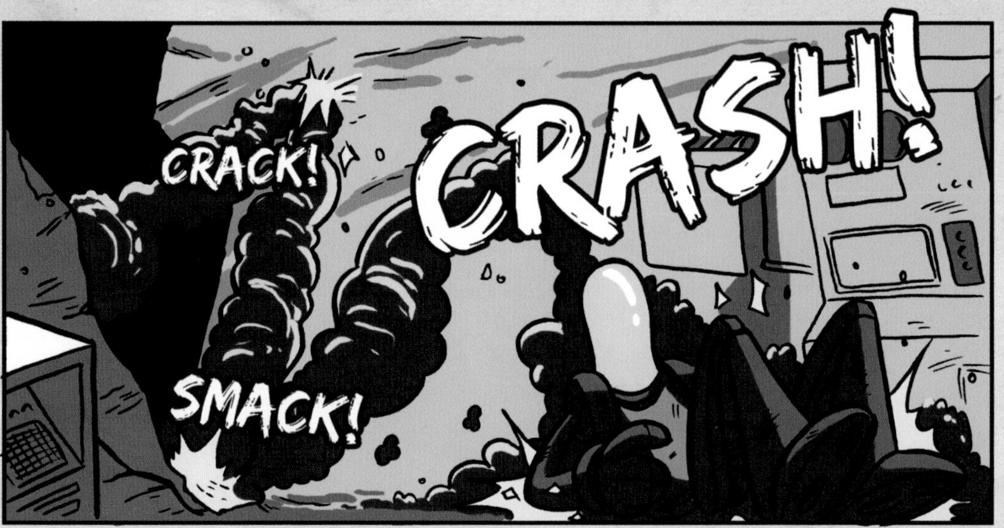
CRACK!
SMACK!
CRASH!

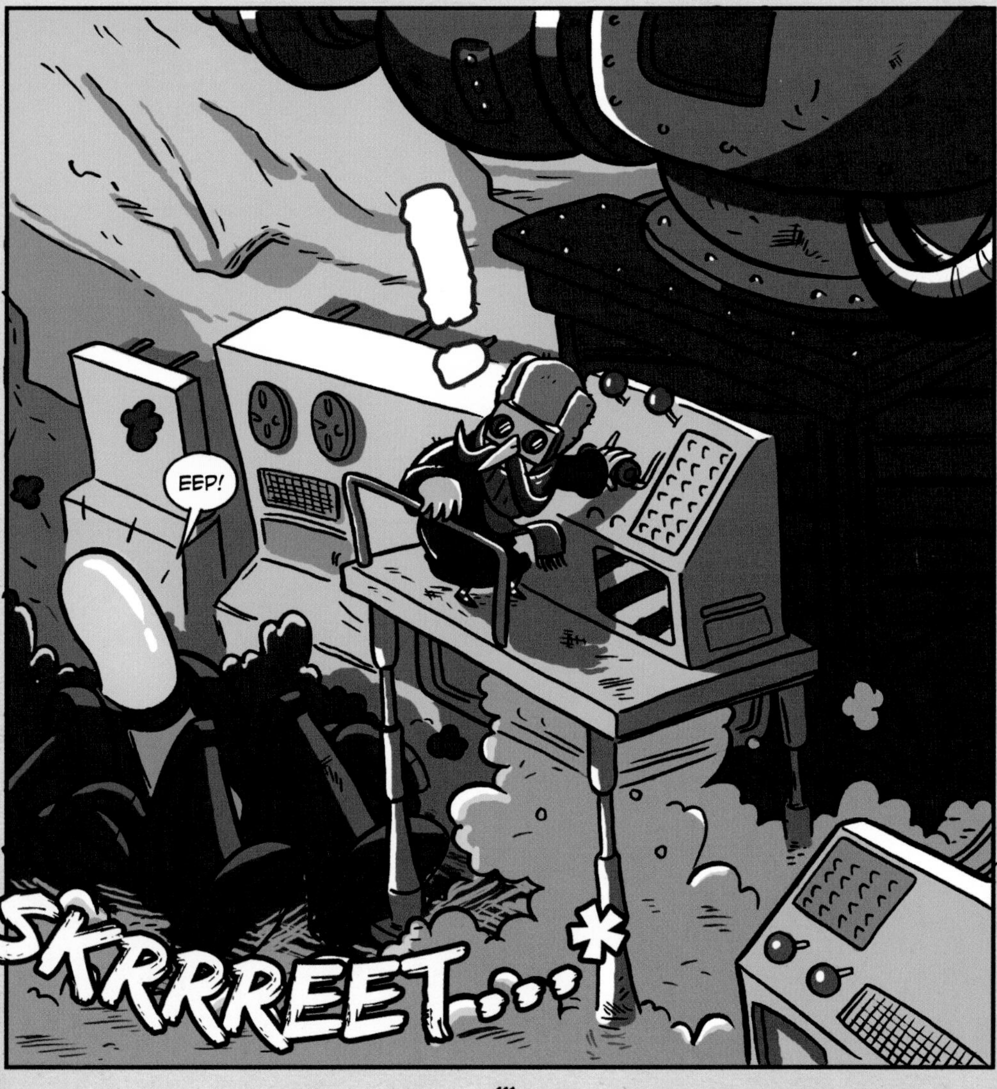
!
EEP!
SKRRREET...*

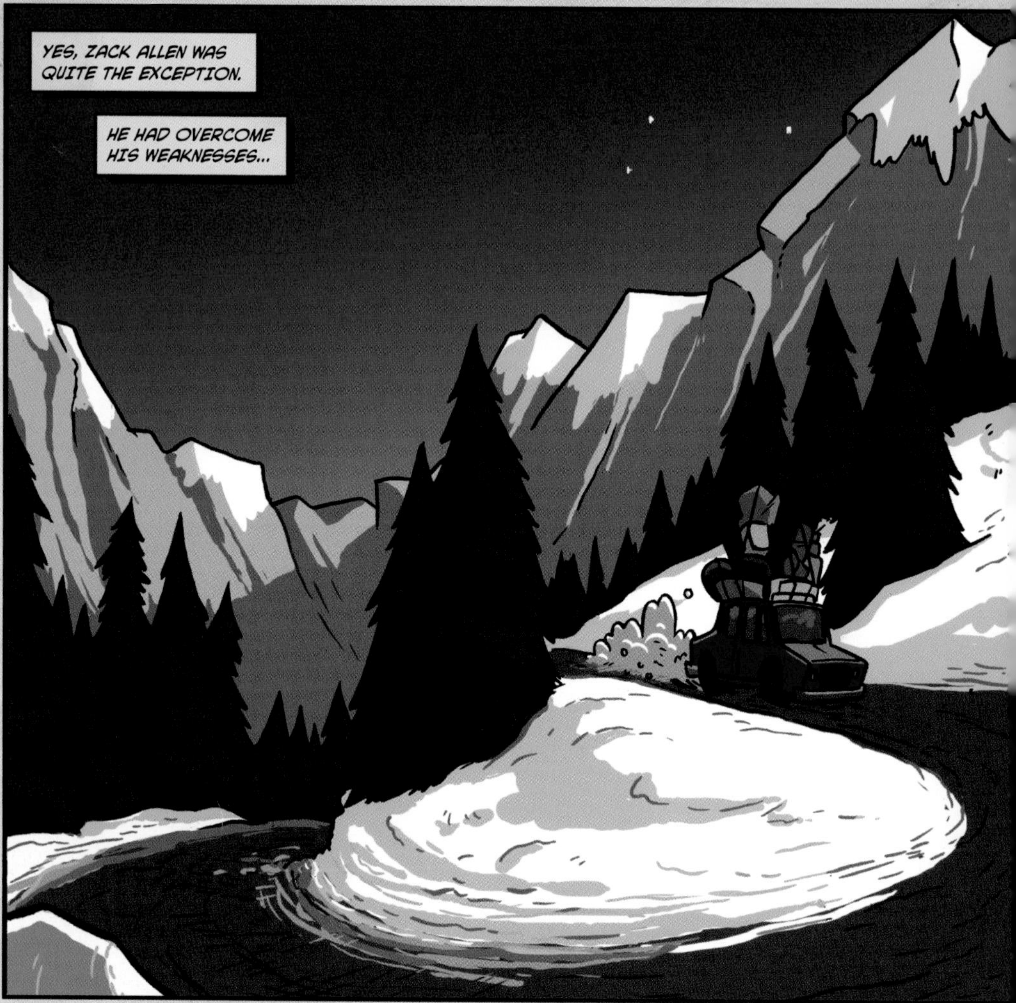
YES, ZACK ALLEN WAS QUITE THE EXCEPTION.
HE HAD OVERCOME HIS WEAKNESSES...

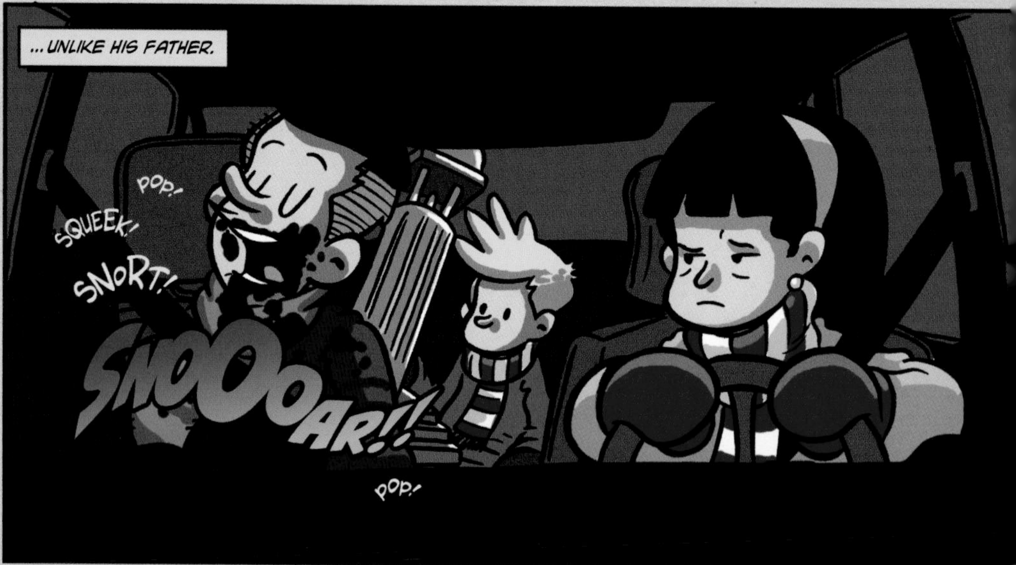
...UNLIKE HIS FATHER.
POP!
SQUEEK!
SNORT!
SNOOOOAR!!
POP!

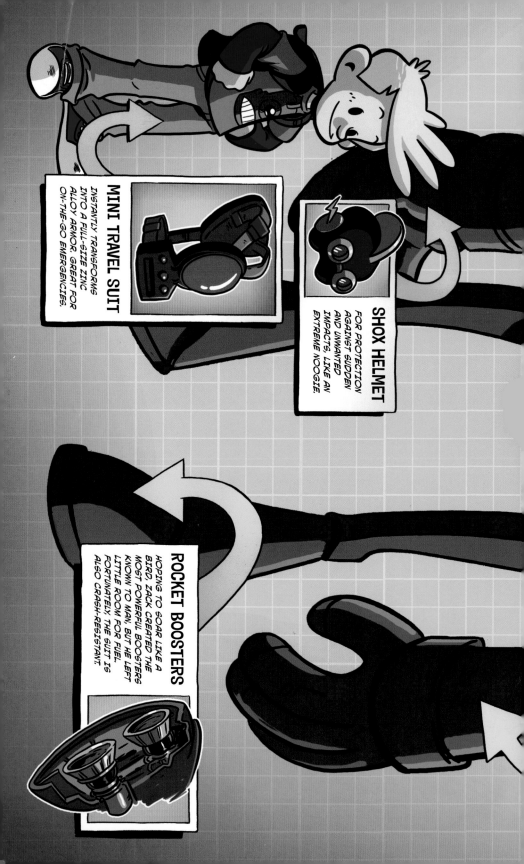

MINI TRAVEL SUIT

INSTANTLY TRANSFORMS INTO A FULL-SIZE ZINC ALLOY ARMOR. GREAT FOR ON-THE-GO EMERGENCIES.

SHOX HELMET

FOR PROTECTION AGAINST SUDDEN AND UNWANTED IMPACTS, LIKE AN EXTREME NOOGIE.

ROCKET BOOSTERS

HOPING TO SOAR LIKE A BIRD, ZACK CREATED THE MOST POWERFUL BOOSTERS KNOWN TO MAN, BUT HE LEFT LITTLE ROOM FOR FUEL. FORTUNATELY, THE SUIT IS ALSO CRASH-RESISTANT.

Zinc Alloy

SUPERHERO SPECS

ZACK ALLEN IS JUST A REGULAR KID. WELL, EXCEPT THAT HE BUILT A TOTALLY INDESTRUCTIBLE ROBO-SUIT IN HIS BEDROOM. BUT EVERY KID NEEDS SOME BULLY PROTECTION, RIGHT? HERE'S A LOOK AT ZACK'S ALL-TIME GREATEST GADGETS--CREATED TO SAVE THE WORLD AND MAKE THE LUNCHROOM A SAFER PLACE.

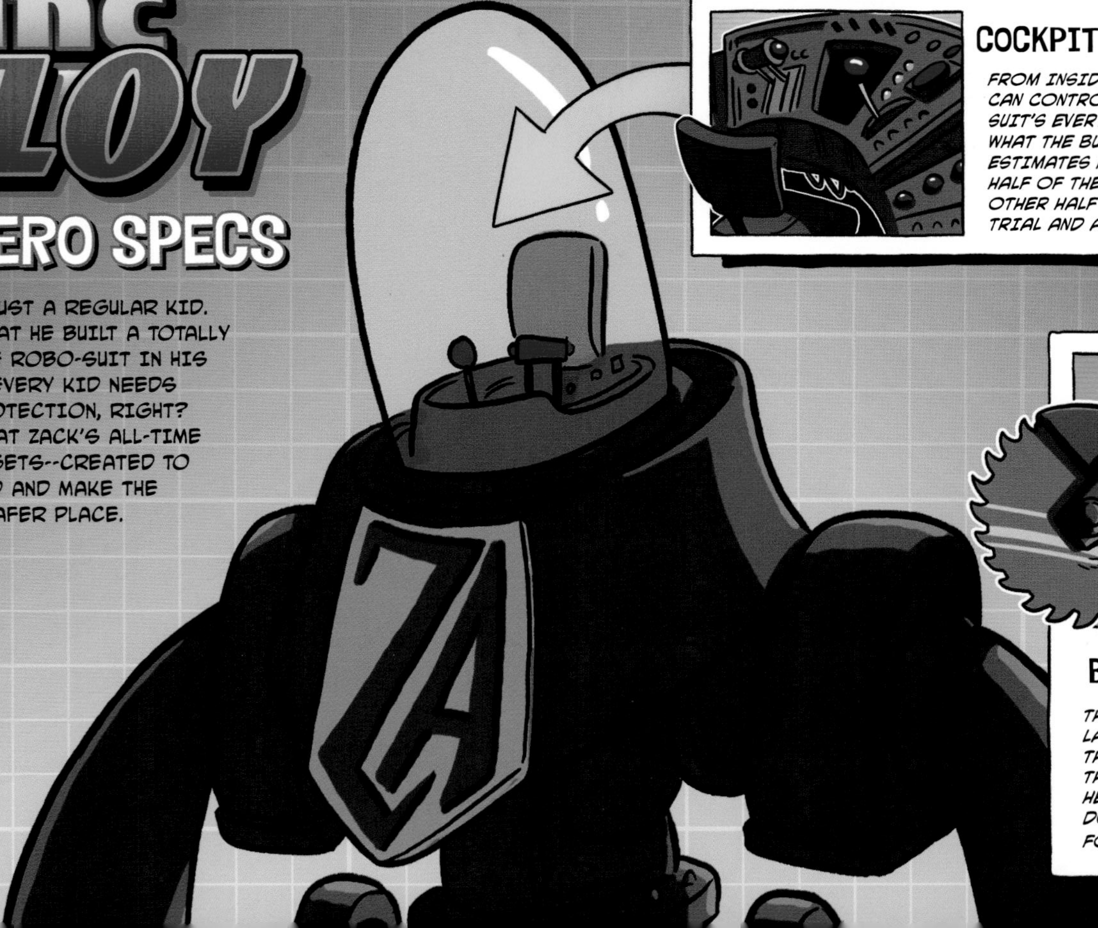

COCKPIT CONTROL PANEL

FROM INSIDE THE COCKPIT, ZACK CAN CONTROL THE ZINC ALLOY SUIT'S EVERY MOVE--IF HE KNEW WHAT THE BUTTONS WERE FOR! ZACK ESTIMATES HE KNOWS WHAT NEARLY HALF OF THE 1,579 BUTTONS DO. THE OTHER HALF HE'S LEARNING THROUGH TRIAL AND A WHOLE LOT OF ERROR.

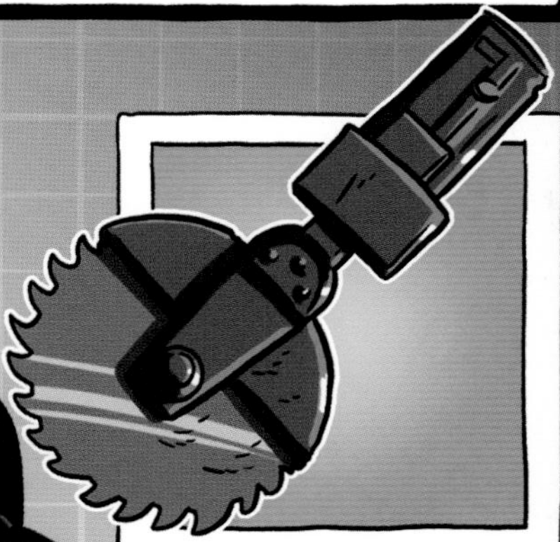

BIONIC BUZZSAW

THE BUZZSAW WAS A LAST-MINUTE ADDITION TO THE ZINC ALLOY SUIT. ZACK THOUGHT A SAW MIGHT HELP GET THROUGH LOCKED DOORS, BUT IT'S NOT BAD FOR SLICING PIZZA, EITHER.

BUILDING
THE INVINCIBLE BOY-BOT

(SKETCHES BY DOUGLAS HOLGATE)

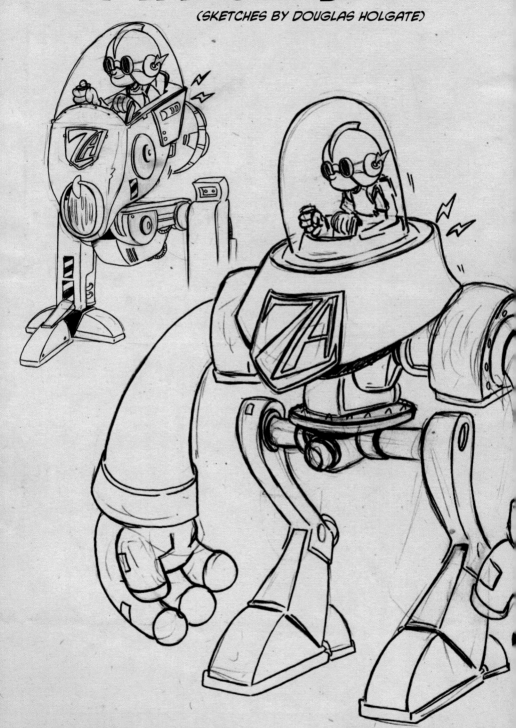

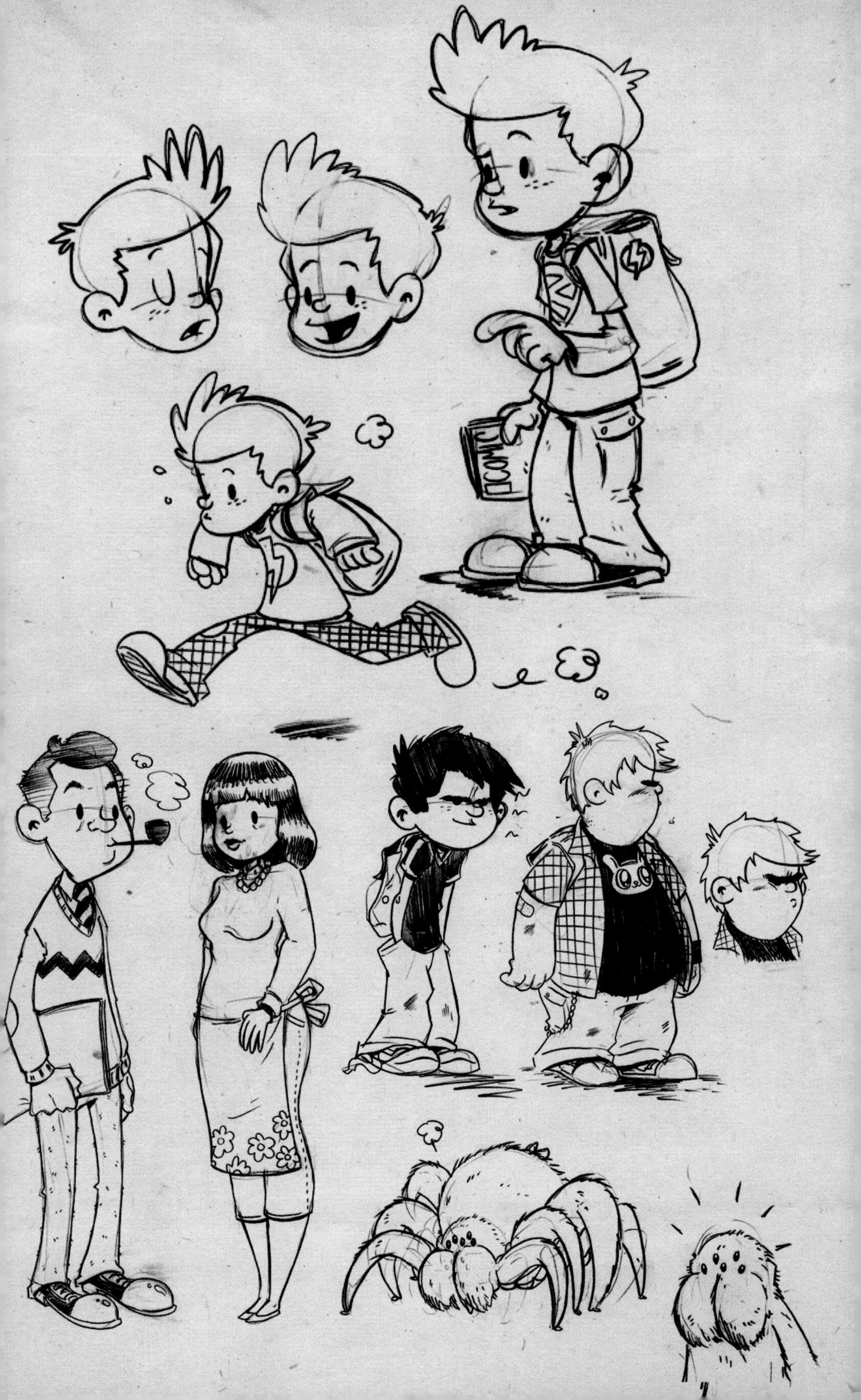
COMIC

CREATORS

ABOUT THE
AUTHOR

DONALD LEMKE *WORKS AS A CHILDREN'S BOOK EDITOR. HE HAS WRITTEN DOZENS OF COMIC BOOKS, INCLUDING THE ZINC ALLOY SERIES AND THE ADVENTURES OF BIKE RIDER, AND MANY CHAPTER BOOKS FOR DC COMICS. DONALD LIVES IN MINNESOTA WITH HIS BEAUTIFUL WIFE, AMY, THEIR NOT-SO-GOLDEN RETRIEVER, PAULIE, AND A BLACK CAT NAMED DYLAN.*

ABOUT THE
ILLUSTRATOR

DOUGLAS HOLGATE *IS A FREELANCE ILLUSTRATOR, COMIC BOOK ARTIST, AND CARTOONIST BASED IN MELBOURNE, AUSTRALIA. HIS WORK HAS BEEN PUBLISHED ALL AROUND THE WORLD BY RANDOM HOUSE, SIMON AND SCHUSTER, THE NEW YORKER MAGAZINE, MAD MAGAZINE, IMAGE COMICS, AND MANY OTHERS. HIS WORKS FOR CHILDREN INCLUDE THE ZINC ALLOY AND BIKE RIDER SERIES (CAPSTONE), SUPER CHICKEN NUGGET BOY (HYPERION), AND A NEW SERIES OF POPULAR SCIENCE BOOKS BY DR. KARL KRUSZELNICKI (PAN MACMILLIAN). DOUGLAS HAS SPORTED A POWERFUL, MANLY BEARD SINCE AGE 12 (PROBABLY NOT TRUE) AND IS ALSO A PRETTY RAD DUDE (PROBABLY TRUE).*